Darkly Dancing

Chloe Hammond

Darkly Dancing

Book 2 in the Darkly Vampire Trilogy

by
Chloe Hammond

Copyright © Chloe Hammond
First edition 2018
Published by Reeves Publishing

Acknowledgements:

I wish to thank all my author friends who keep me inspired and share all the ups and downs of writing. Extra special thanks are owed to Angelika Rust and Claire Evans for their much-appreciated beta reader help. Your input has really helped to polish and shine this novel.

I want to thank artist Alexis Kaelynn Johnson who worked so very hard to help bring my imaginings into reality on this cover.

As always, I could not have published without the exacting and patient work of my editor,
Catherine Lenderi.

And last, but absolutely not least, my love and thanks to my husband, Garry. He puts up with my disappearances, even when I'm still in the room with him, slipping away to create my own world.

Dedication:

This is for you, Dina. My Layla.
I can't believe you'll never find out what happens.
I miss you every second of every day.

A Quick Recap Of Darkly Dreaming, Book 1 of The Darkly Vampire Trilogy

If you haven't read Darkly Dreaming, I strongly recommend that you do, this is designed only as a reminder for those who have read the book.

At forty years of age, Rae's favourite way of escaping her troubles was still slipping away into daydreams. Sickened by her inability to move forward from the wreckage of her marriage; she could not leave her husband easily, but also could not stay. Her best friend Layla's marriage ended because she could not have children, and her husband had an affair. Rae and Layla ended up living together again, but the easy friendship of their youth had been sacrificed to their marriages, and they weren't sure they had forgiven each other. They decided to travel Tours, France, with other university friends, to re-explore the town they stayed in after university, hoping to regain what they had lost.

The trip did not go as planned. Running amok at a festival, a group of vampires rebelling against their Pride infected two of their friends with the ancient vampire virus. After seeing their other friends off at the airport, Rae and Layla returned to the hotel and discovered one friend was dead, and the other terribly transformed. A vicious fight ensued, when Rae and Layla were both infected with the virus themselves, which turned them into New Ones—fledgling vampires.

The enigmatic Pride leader, Guillaume, came to limit the damage the rebellious troublemakers had caused, found Rae and Layla as their metamorphosis started. After the transition, he whisked them away to the farm where the vampires lived, deep in the French countryside. On their way, he explained what being a vampire entailed. They were not the undead, they were alive, but had metamorphosed into something utterly different, with special powers and terrifying strengths. Rae and Layla were Pretty Ones, their Gift is an overpowering sexual allure. At first, they were unable to control this Glamour, with embarrassing consequences.

When they got to the Pride, they discovered the vampire who had turned them was now friends with Patrice and Suzanne, matriarchs of the group who caused such damage in Tours. These vampires revelled in their strength and power and enjoyed the hunt and kill. Other than Rae and Layla, two men, David and Brian, had also survived being infected. The four became friends, and Layla discovered gentle David was the love of her life.

Their little group struggled to retain their humanity in a world of savage drives, and bitter rivalries. Rae fought the new urges which threatened to overwhelm her with forbidden hungers. Especially when she discovered that as a vampire she cannot dream anymore; but blood straight from the victim allowed a narcotic escape into their memories. Still, she was grateful for the excuse not to return to her husband. However, he followed her to France, so she met him, while heavily disguised, and could finally put an end to their relationship, without guilt.

None of the New Ones were very welcome in the Pride, especially not ones that caused as much trouble as these principled New Ones, and their uncontrollable counterparts. Soon loyalties were tested to their limit. A death sentence was passed on all New Ones, and although this was reprieved, the tensions in the Pride quickly escalated again. A deadly battle ensued, during which Rae and Layla, with other members of the Pride, managed to kill Suzannah and Patrice, and their awful group.

From the first moment she saw him, Rae fell head over heels for reserved Guillaume, but although he initially seemed to return her affections, he soon started to ignore her. Rae was heartbroken and tried everything to win his friendship at least. She discovered that Guillaume did not feed on human blood when he was first infected, and he suffered continual pain as human blood was needed to complete the transformation. When they discovered that one of the girls the other vampires turned was a Healer, Rae realised she could save him from this discomfort, creating a plan for the vampires to hunt and feed on the evil within society, not the vulnerable. Guillaume still ignored her, though.

Rae was not aware there was a High Council of the oldest vampires that oversaw all the vampires. They ensured the balance between vampires and humanity was retained, and that the existence of vampires remained a legend. Breaking the Vampire High Council rules, which include not killing another vampire, is punishable by death. The remaining Pride members tried their best to keep the killings secret, but spies soon informed the Council, and the friends were summoned, along with the Pride Leader and his closest allies, to account for their behaviour with their lives.

The sinister Ancients of the High Council decided they could only come to a conclusion on their fates by exploring each vampire's motivations. To do this, they fed on each of them; an unpleasantly intimate experience. While they waited for the Council to pass their death sentence, Guillaume finally approached Rae to explain himself. He did not have the words, so he invited her to feed on him. Rae witnessed the images of his past where brutal Pretty One Patrice controlled him completely with her Glamour, and the two of them ravaged whole villages in a gluttony of destruction. Guillaume hated what he had been under her power and could not bear to risk falling under another Pretty One's spell.

Although Rae knew she would never control him, she understood why he could not expose himself to the risk. She was devastated but accepted he would never love her. Shockingly, the High Council decided to give the Pride one last chance to live peacefully. After Guillaume's revelations, Rae knew she couldn't bear to return to the Farm, and when the Council offered her a place with them, she was tempted, but she did not trust them, so she refused. Rae, Layla, David, and Brian settled in a rural cottage in Brittany. Rae was adopted by a small grey cat, and discovered the joy of hunting with her. They seemed to be settling into a peaceful new existence, but Layla soon felt bored, and one of the Council had said something about being aware of the Chameleon. Trouble was brewing, but as we left Rae at the end of book one, she was exhausted, self-absorbed, and oblivious.

Chapter One

Rae

'If you could eat anything in the world right now, what would it be?' Layla murmurs dreamily. It's a favourite game of ours since we were infected with an ancient blood virus and became vampires. We both feel frustratingly constrained by the limits of our blood diet. Especially since our morals won't allow us to eat the tasty version of that; because it comes from humans. Thin sour cow, bitter sheep, or thick muddy pig's blood is pretty much the range of our choices. I've developed a taste for rat blood, and go hunting with my little grey stray, Babette, but you have to catch a lot of rats to feed an adult vampire. *A lot.*

Lying in the meadow behind our cottage in rural Brittany, France, Layla picks a buttercup and twirls it idly under my chin.

'Salmon fillets, cooked slowly in garlic butter so when you stab your fork in, it separates into buttery chunks that melt in your mouth. Served with French beans, mmmm, and asparagus. No potatoes, I'll have two salmon fillets and a mound of vegetables. Oh, and lots of fresh black pepper grated over the top.'

We lie in a respectful reverie for a moment or two imagining the tastes and textures. Then the kettle starts to whistle from the kitchen and I jump up and trot indoors. I pour the water into the cafetière and take our big pottery mugs from the cupboard above the kettle. I found them online, hand-thrown, hefty receptacles glazed in the most delicious lapis lazuli blue, that fill our hands with their satisfying curves. Online shopping makes life much easier for a vampire. That and a post box at the end of our lane, so the postman never comes near.

'Are you having sugar today or not?' I ask through the open window. I don't need to shout, vampire senses mean Layla can hear me. We can't actually drink the coffee, but we've become attached to the ritual of making good coffee, and holding it in our lovely mugs, inhaling the scent, and warming our fingers. Sometimes we add a vanilla pod, or a sprinkling of cinnamon to change the aroma, and with or without sugar makes a difference to the smell too. After a suitable brewing time, I pour the coffee and carry both mugs over to our long oak refectory table. I might be a vampire, but that much balancing still involves clamping my tongue between my teeth in concentration. Luckily, the accelerated healing deals with the cuts my pointy teeth crimp into my tongue.

As I put our drinks down, Layla sways in to join me, and Babette hops up onto my knee. I pop her little feather cushion onto my lap so she can get comfortable. My firm and rubbery vampire flesh does not make a good cat bed.

'What about you?' I ask Layla as she breathes in the swirl of steam rising from her cup, and Babette starts busily kneading and purring.

'Roast chicken, with the skin, and mashed potatoes, with loads of butter and pepper.' I nod excitedly, eager for her to continue. 'And roast potatoes, and roast parsnips, and carrots cooked in orange juice and cinnamon, and cauliflower cheese, made with reeaaallllly mature cheddar, lashings of thick meaty gravy, and sprouts and broccoli.'

'Oh yes, I want broccoli with my salmon too, with the garlic butter poured all over it so the butter soaks into all the little buds. Every mouthful's a blissful buttery garlicy bite.'

'Mmmmm.' We go back to clutching our mugs, eyes gazing into the past where those meals were a possibility. We did try cooking food once, to see if we could enjoy the smell of that as much as the aroma of coffee, but we were horrified to discover that bacon just smelt like singed hair to our vampire noses. We've had to settle for our imaginings.

Fruit and spices can send us into raptures, but only in the same way the perfume of lilies or freesias did when we were human; not something you'd want to eat. In summer, we place bowls of strawberries on the window sill for the sun to warm so the kitchen fills with the scent of summer. In winter, we wrap curls of lemon and orange peel around cinnamon sticks and put them on top of the log burner so the tangy sweetness mixes with the wood smoke for a scent that is pure winter. I still hate cloves though, and sage, they are like a punch in the face when I catch an unanticipated waft.

'Or a bacon buttie.' I put my mug down. We always come back to a bacon sandwich, and our descriptions get better every time. 'Really good organic bacon, the sort that doesn't leak water when you cook it, so you can get it properly crispy.' Layla is watching my mouth with ravenous eyes, gobbling up every word. 'Big, corn fed organic eggs, fried so the edges go crispy and brown, but the yolks are still running, and dribble down your chin. Then some sliced beefeater tomatoes, fried with salt and pepper, and a huge field mushroom, fried in butter, all slapped between wedges of fresh bloomer.'

'No, no, Tiger bread,' Layla begs.

'Yeah,' I agree, completely lost in my description. 'Cut really thick, and slavered... Oh shit.' I've become overexcited and waved my hands around describing my creation, and now I've knocked my coffee all over a laptop someone has left on the table.

'Fuuuuuck,' I shout, leaping up and grabbing it out of the pool of liquid and trying to shake it dry. Babette shoots for the door, disgusted at the disturbance to her siesta and startled by the shouting.

'Shit, it's Brian's. He's going to kill me.' Brian and I really don't get on, ever since my new vampire Need caused us to do the unmentionable the first time we met post transformation. Managing my Pretty One attributes was a steep learning curve, but that was a lesson I could have done without. Layla has snapped out of her trance and grabs me a cloth and the towels. She starts mopping the table and floor while I open the laptop to try to dry off the keyboard.

It flickers into life as I madly rub it, using my long purple talons to get the cloth right between the buttons on the keyboard. His last programme opens. I'm surprised at Brian, he's Mr Perfect, and I would have expected him to close his laptop down properly every time he used it. I wipe up the stream of coffee that has pooled at the back hinges, and then start to close his programmes down—Google maps. Idly, I wonder why on earth he was on there, but most of my mind is taken up with hoping I haven't permanently damaged his laptop. I know he has all his photos of his fiancée on here, and he will hate me even more if he loses them thanks to my clumsiness.

I click on the power button, but it won't turn off because there are still programmes open. I sit down higher up the table, away from the spill to concentrate on what I'm doing and see the minimised tab at the bottom of the screen. I click it, and Facebook pops up. God, he's been haunting his Megan's profile again, watching her rebuild her life without him. Only there's a Private Messaging box open in the corner of the screen. With her name at the top of it.

'FUUUUUCK!' Layla drops my empty mug back onto the table, startled by my exclamation. 'He's been messaging her.' Layla doesn't need telling who's messaged who. We've worried about this since infection. Brian promised us he only looked, but didn't make any contact. 'Oh God. He's meeting her.' Layla drops the towels and cloths, and slides next to me on the bench, reading the messages with me.

We read it from the bottom of the screen, too impatient to scroll to the top first, so we recreate Brian's initial tentative contact through to their plans to meet in a nearby hotel backwards. That's why he was on Google Maps; finding somewhere.

'Where is he? I'm going to punch his fucking lights out.' Layla jumps up and runs out of the kitchen. I'm not an advocate for violence normally, but he has put everything at risk. If the High Council finds out, they'll kill us all. Chloris's warning 'Beware of the Chameleon' springs to mind. He must have been at it back then, and they uncovered his plans when they drank his blood to raid his memories over the death of Patrice and her New Ones. God, I discounted it, thought I'd misheard and she'd said be aware of, because we didn't know he was a Chameleon then. We were oblivious to the way he's able to fade into the background so he's unnoticeable when he's threatened or scared. It takes a while to notice someone's not where they should be. Fucking High Councillors and their fucking riddles. Why didn't she just tell me properly?

My mind is spinning out of control, I'm panicking. I look up at Layla as she runs back into the kitchen, closely followed by her lover, David.

'He's gone.'

'What?'

'He's gone, he's taken the car.'

I stare at her in utter horror for a moment, and then slam the brakes on my speeding mind. I have to be calm, and untangle this nightmare one strand at a time. It's all too easy to leap to a worst case scenario immediately, but I need information.

I sit back down, pull his laptop back towards me and read through the messages slowly, collecting as much information as I can.

'He's meeting her tonight, at 8 p.m., so it'll be dark. At a hotel...' David has grabbed his laptop and logged in. 'Find me the quickest way to run there,' I ask him. He raises his eyebrows, but doesn't argue.

'He's booked her a room, has told her she's in room 107. Told her to leave her window open, he's told her some bollocks about the scents from the rose garden, but I think that's how he plans to get in without being seen. He said that room is recommended on Trip Advisor because of the views over the garden, and the way you can smell the roses on the evening breeze. Quick, Layla, look for the hotel on Trip Advisor.' Layla dashes off to get her laptop while David and I explore the quickest cross-country route, avoiding buildings of any kind. It's a long way, and I don't have much time to get there.

I really wish I had a mobile phone and could use its Sat Nav, or Google Maps to get there, but I haven't charged mine since hunting the child-murderer in Brittany. I don't want to speak to anyone I used to know, my voice is too different now. Even when I turn the Glamour right down, it is slinky and provocative. I have told everyone who cares that I do not have mobile reception where I live, and told them to email or Facebook me. I have two Facebook profiles, human me, and vampire me, so I can control what the humans know.

There was a landline into our cottage in Brittany when we

moved in, and we kept it, so we could have Broadband. The only ones with that number are Guillaume's Pride at the Farm; Elaine phones from time to time to check we are okay in her brusque and abrupt way. The girls, Georgette and Annie, occasionally ring for a chatter but they prefer Facebook now they have the profiles David created for them.

I'm going to have to memorise the route to the hotel across the fields. Thank God for my vampire brain; as long as I concentrate, and no one has cut down any woodland or built any houses since this satellite photo was taken, I should be okay.

'That idiot thinks she will still be able to love him despite his changes.' I shake my head sadly, I'm furious with Brian for threatening all of our lives, but I can't help but pity the man and his delusions. We are monsters now, no human could love us, but he seems incapable of realising this.

'Here,' Layla calls. There aren't many reviews of the hotel, it's just a little family-run place a couple of towns over, and the third review down reveals why Brian has booked that room in that hotel. A woman who stayed in room 107 last summer has raved about the peace—the room is down a corridor by itself, and above the breakfast room. She has also waxed lyrical about the rose garden, and the woodland out at the back of the hotel. She has even helpfully taken a photograph of the rear of the hotel, and circled her room, with 'I was here' scrawled across the photo.

This information floods me with relief; I know where I'm going, and what I'm looking for. I just need to get there in an unfeasibly short amount of time.

'Do you want us to come?' Layla asks as I do up the hood on my anorak, covering enough of my face to avoid alarm if anyone catches a brief glimpse of me.

'No, I'm less likely to be seen if I go alone. Three of us would be more likely to be seen. I'm still hoping to god he'll see sense and come home without seeing her.' I give Layla a last look, of despair and hope, and set off at a sprint, terrified at what I'm going to find, and with no idea what I'm going to do if he goes ahead and meets her.

* * * *

I run and run in as straight a line as I can manage towards the hotel, leaping fences, wading through rivers, slipping in cow shit. I've come barefoot, I don't really wear shoes any more. I find even the softest, lightest ballet pumps chafe and constrict my vampire toes; they like to spread and grip so I'm as sure-footed as a cat on any terrain. It seems to get darker with every step, the April twilight settling fast. My imagination throws up awful images of what I am going to find when I get to the hotel. I imagine Brian walking over to his fiancée, and her running screaming into the main body of the hotel, with Brian running after her, so everyone sees him, and then I would be forced to kill them all.

I am loath to kill innocents, but the danger to vampires and humans alike would be too great if our existence was discovered. If scientists found out about the Gifts our virus bestows, invulnerable Super Soldiers would soon be developed, and ever more brutal wars would rip humanity even further apart. I can't risk turning them all though, the outcomes are too unreliable. Look what happen with Suzannah, and the other New Ones Patrice turned. That rebellion almost destroyed Guillaume's whole Pride.

I plough on, my mind running as fast as my feet. I imagine arriving just in time to see him tell her, so I can catch her as she runs screaming from the monstrosity her beloved has become. But then I would have to kill her, and Brian wouldn't let me do that, so I'll have to kill him too. I try to picture any sort of positive outcome to the situation I'm sprinting towards, but I can't.

I crest a wooded hill and the hotel is finally below me in the valley, on the edge of a small town. I'm heaving for breath; the run has pushed even my vampire speed and strength to its limits. I pause for a moment, hands on knees dragging cool air into my burning lungs. To my left, something catches in the moon's light, I creep a couple of steps closer, and realise that it's our car. Brian has driven it up a farmer's track and left it there, screened by the trees, then walked down to the hotel. I scowl at his audacity. I signed Guillaume's paperwork, the house is in my name, and the car came with the house. Technically, that's my car, he should have had to run, and be stood here now with warm cowpat between his toes, and I should have had the comfortable drive. Dick. I scrub my slimy toes in the dew-dampened grass.

My breathing has calmed so I can creep up to the open window at the back of room 107. I crouch and leap, and easily catch the roof of the single floor extension at the back of the hotel that houses the breakfast room, and then tiptoe the couple of steps to the open window. I stand beside it flattened to the wall, listening. The light is on, and I can hear someone in there huffing and shuffling. I can hear the frictioned scratch of cheap fabric rubbing together, it sounds like they are sitting down, but wriggling.

'Come on, Bri,' a female voice mutters, followed by an elaborate sigh. I peek around the edge of the window, glad that the darkness makes me almost invisible to the human in the brightly lit room. No sign of Brian. I glance at my watch and it's five past eight. He's late. He's kept her waiting, it's almost a year since he vanished out of her life, and now he's late. No wonder she's huffing.

She's sitting on the bed, blonde hair in a high ponytail, which flicks out at the bottom, level with her shoulders; she wears a perky floral dress and Mary Janes, with ankle socks. Her handbag is small and embroidered with flowers and dotted with beads and sequins so it twinkles in the ceiling light. She's pouting. I'm surprised. She is so determinedly girly, not the sort I would have imagined for Brian at all. I had imagined someone as wholesome and sporty as him. Just as Megan checks her watch, the en suite door behind her swings softly open.

In motion, I see her sense the disturbance, and swivel to look over her shoulder as Brian steps into the light. I watch her eyes bulge, and her mouth drop open as she hauls in air to scream. I bound through the window and clap my hand over her mouth, while I send a tidal wave of Compelling to turn her to mush in my hands.

'What the fuck, Brian, you total tosser. You scum bucket fuckbrain, you complete and utter... idiot.' I'm so angry I've run out of swear words.

He disappears.

'Oh no, you fucking fucking fucking don't.' I'm spitting with fury now. I let go of Megan's face before I accidentally crush her skull, like an empty coke can. She sags sideways into a heap on the bed. 'You show yourself, and you explain yourself, and you tell me why I shouldn't kill you both right now, and give us a way out of this mess, which doesn't leave us all dead at the hands of the High Council.' He slowly re-emerges from the beige wallpaper, but remains a wishy-washy biscuit colour only one shade more vampire than the wall behind him.

'Erm...'

'No. No erm. Solutions, now.'

'I just thought, once she saw me, and she knew it was me, we could talk, and then I could turn her, and we could set up our own Pride.'

'Does she want children, Bri?'

14

'Yes.'

'Does she love her Mum, Bri?'

'Yes.'

'Has she got sisters, friends, a job she enjoys?'

'Yes.' His muttering gets quieter with each syllable.

'How could you do this to her, Brian? I mean, really? You know what this means for her.' He doesn't answer me.

'Or didn't you actually think any of this through at all, Bri?' My hands are on my hips and my chin is jutting aggressively at him, while I stare so intensely he knows he can't keep getting away without answering.

'Well, I just knew that once she knew it was me...'

'You thought that you, on your own, could outweigh all the things she will have to lose? We didn't have a choice, Bri, and we hate those who changed us. You've taken hers away. Our only option is to turn her into her worst nightmare. How do you think she's going to feel then, Bri?' He's silent, looking at the floor.

'What if she turns out like Mel, and you don't fancy her anymore?'

'Oh, I'd still love her,' he assures me earnestly.

'Oh, well, that's reassuring,' I sneer. 'So, what if she dies during transition?' He just gazes at me beseechingly.

'You are a cock, Brian. A total, utter, cock,' I snarl. He nods glumly.

'I was just so alone.'

I shake my head at him in disgust, and lift Meg up, flopping and compliant.

'Get down into the bushes behind the breakfast room, and be ready to catch her when I drop her down to you. Then take her to the car. You can Compel, can't you?'

He shrugs. 'Never tried.'

'You're a...'

'Dick, yeah, yeah, I know. I've listened to the lessons; I've just never tried it. You stop, let me try now.' I stop controlling Megan's fear, and a few seconds later she springs upright and opens her mouth to yell. Brian lifts a hand, and she slumps back down. Brian looks at me happily, as if he expects praise, I scowl at him and he droops again.

'Trust you to have a girlfriend who actually unpacks her bags on her first night.' I huff as I whizz around her room flinging her belongings into her case at full vampire speed. I chuck Meg back over one shoulder and grab her case in my other hand. 'Get out of the window so I can pass them through.'

God, he's infuriating, no brains at all. I never have to tell Layla the obvious stuff like that, she reads the situation, and is already doing what I need her to do as it needs doing. I pass the case through first, then Megan and finally give the room a last quick check to make sure there's nothing incriminating left lying around. Whatever the outcome, we need it to look like she left of her own free will. I climb out through myself and pull the window shut behind me. I can't lock it, but at least it won't be gaping wide open, causing suspicion. Vampires don't have fingerprints, so I don't need to worry about anything incriminating giving our presence away.

Once Brian is back on the ground, I throw the case down to him. He misses it. I stare at him open-mouthed, and then shrug, pick Megan up and chuck her down too. He catches her at least. I leap down beside them, grab the case and sprint for the trees. Once we reach the car, I stop and take her phone out of her handbag, I remove the sim and destroy it. Brian starts to speak, and I just give him the look. We get into the car and I drive us home silently.

* * * *

'Come on, genius, what's your plan?' I ask Brian as I settle his droopy and compliant girlfriend onto the sofa in the cottage. He gawps at me blankly. 'Once you've infected her, then what?' He still gawps, and it takes everything I have not to punch his gormless face. He looks hopefully at Layla and David who have crowded into the lounge behind us as we came in. They ignore his looks, and lounge in the armchairs opposite the sofa. Although they are simmering over with repressed excitement at something out of the ordinary occurring, they can feel my bubbling fury and are wise enough to keep themselves out of it.

'Once you've infected her, then what?' I demand again. 'Assuming she survives,' I add. He shrugs. He actually shrugs.

'What about blood? Human blood? She has to have human blood for her first feed, or would you subject her to an eternity of pain, so you aren't alone?' I'm reaching fever pitch, I can feel the distortions of the Rage starting to lengthen my fingers and distend my jaw. The temptation to rip out his and his stupid girlfriend's hearts, and deal with the problems that way tears through me; I have the right, indeed the obligation, to do exactly that. Brian disappears again.

'Fucking man up, Brian.' David has had enough of his friend's snivelling.

'And her friends and family, what are you telling them?' Brian has turned his back on me, huddled beside the fireplace, behind the armchairs, a soft golden lump to match our pretty walls. He hasn't considered anything, just acted on his desire to see his love again. I ignore the little voice that asks me if I wouldn't have done something similar if there was the tiniest chance Guillaume could love me back.

The Rage is twisting me, lengthening my bones and sharpening my voice to a vicious screech. As always even while the change is agony, the rush of pure fury that floods me is oddly delicious, washing away social niceties as it does. I have forgotten, though, that while I am in the Rage state, I cannot Compel Meg. David and Layla are transfixed by me, unsure what I am going to do next. Brian has turned his face into the corner cowering away from me as I stride across the room and tower over him, screaming my outrage. He correctly interprets my temptation to deal with this problem in a neat vampire fashion.

No one notices Meg come to from her daze. This time she does not scream, or draw attention to herself, instead she leaps up and races to the door, slipping past David and Layla while they are distracted. I only realise she is fleeing when movement catches my eye and I see her frantic shape streaking up the front garden towards the gate through the lounge window. I spin and follow her. With my vampire speed I am much, much faster than she is even while she is filled with the adrenaline of terror.

I grab the back of her cardigan as she flings herself over the top bar of the gate, and yank her backwards, which is how come she is up high enough to punch me in the mouth, as hard as she can. It doesn't hurt me, but my Rage extended, meshing, dagger point teeth gouge and slash her fingers, and my mouth is bloody with saliva and the torn gums of transformation. I drop her onto the ground, where she rolls onto her back, hands raised to hit out again. The silly girl thinks that hitting me has made me drop her. Suddenly, I am washed through with a sense of futility, and deadening calm. I turn to where the others are crowding the cottage doorway watching us in appalled fascination.

'Well, it's done,' I tell them quietly as my limbs and jaw retract, with the grinding ache that is not soothed by the flames of anger, and instead fuels my disgust with myself.

'What?' Brian pushes forward past the other two.

'She hit me in the mouth,' I tell him, but he still looks confused. 'My mouth was bleeding from the Rage change, and she cut her hand on my teeth.' My mouth has already healed, her hand hasn't.

'What the fuck?' Meg splutters from the ground. Brian runs to her and crouches beside her. She recoils, repulsed. She is beetroot with terror and exertions, but even as I watch her, the colour fades from her face until she is pale green and shaking. 'Wha...' she starts, but as she struggles to rise, her eyes roll back into her head and she collapses into a heap, unconscious.

'We've got, what, twenty-four hours before she comes round? And then another twenty-four hours to get her fed. Brian, I should be making you do the hunt, but I will need you here when she wakes up. Take her to your room and sit with her,' I command. 'Layla, David, I need you to go and find me a piece of human scum to feed her. There's no time to set up a hunt, so you'll need to pick a large city, and find someone nasty. Try to make it someone who won't be missed, and make sure you aren't seen. You've got forty-eight hours.'

Chapter Two

Layla

You might expect me to object to being spoken to so imperiously. This regal tone is what has made so many people dislike Rae over the years, both as human and vampire. But I know her, when her brain is working fast to come up with a solution to a problem, one that allows for the least negative outcomes, she doesn't waste time being nice to people. Which is why even people who profess to hate her will follow her in an emergency; she will be coming up with a solution before other people have truly recognised there's a problem. David's like me, he doesn't care as long as she can fix this. He knew Megan when they were human, but he's never said much about her, which leads me to suspect he doesn't like her very much. He's a sweet man and his silence speaks volumes, because he normally has something positive to say about most people. But he doesn't like to gossip, which is a bit disappointing, to be honest.

'What's she like?' I ask to break the silence. David is driving, face set like stone in the light from the oncoming cars. We've been driving for a few hours now; we bypassed Rennes, and Nantes agreeing they were too close to home, and agreed to head as far down France as Bordeaux.

'Good at getting what she wants,' David indicates, and passes another car. I wait a few moments, and he doesn't enlarge on this statement. This is as damning a statement as I've ever heard David make about anyone since the battle that killed off Patrice's New Ones. I watch the scenery become more built-up through the windscreen and try to ignore the fizz of excitement that sparkles in my blood. I must have wriggled despite myself, because David looks at me out of the side of his eye, and his mouth tightens. He knows how bored I've become by life in our tiny Pride, but he shares Rae's belief that we need to stay safe.

Eventually, we reach Bordeaux, and drive towards the station. I climb into the back of the car and cover myself with a blanket while David cruises slowly up and down the back streets of the area around the train station looking for an area where girls loiter in the spotlights cast by lamp posts. Once we find a suitable area we crawl up the nearest side street and park. Slipping silently through the shadows we seek our prey. We see plenty of working girls and their johns, but these are not our targets.

We keep searching, until we spot a heartbreakingly young girl climb out of the front seat of a BMW, which slides silently off into the night. The girl wipes her mouth unhappily, and digs into her bra to get her bundle of notes. She smells of hairspray, overpoweringly sweet perfume, and spermicide. A shadow detaches itself from a nearby doorway, and a slender polecat of a man approaches her, holding his hand out for her cash. The tang of sweat, tobacco and briny semen reaches us on the other side of the road. A pimp who likes to test his wares.

He takes the whole roll of notes from her and slides it into his back pocket. The girl squeaks in protest, cowering like a kicked puppy, but she needs the money enough to protest anyway. She is expecting the blow when it catches her around her head, but it still sends her staggering. He avoids bruising her valuable face. Inside I boil for her, she is like so many of the lost girls I met while working in a rape crisis centre, lured to the UK by the promise of bar work, kept there by threats of violence to their families. Kept obedient by the need for the Alice in Wonderland Forget Everything pills their pimps hooked them on with free samples. He pushes her once more, roughly enough to make her stumble to her knees, where he kicks her so hard she retches, and then he stalks off, flicking a larger fold of money open and sliding the new notes into the centre as he goes.

David and I glance at each other, no discussion's needed; this is our quarry. We stalk and glide along behind him, keeping to the darker patches. Silent chortles of glee shake my shoulders—so this is what Rae meant about the thrill of the hunt—the hunger coils and roils in me, heightening the pimp's scent into a delicious perfume of blood. Finally, he lets himself into a detached house, but before he can shut the door behind him, we have descended like soundless, swooping hawks, and David effortlessly holds the door against his shoves, while I sinuously slip inside.

For a moment, I gaze at him, head on one side, overwhelmed with the lust to kill, to feed. I pant with the need, breasts heaving in the V-necked T-shirt I'm wearing. I let him see me and recoil, I let him open his mouth to scream, while David shuts the door and stands behind me, then I Compel him, just a little, holding him to silence but keeping him aware while I turn to grin widely at David over my shoulder. His eyes are dark and excited too, and they drop to my heaving tits. This is living; excitement thrums through me, making me reckless and exhibitionist. I stand on tiptoes, and push my arse into his crotch. He's already rigid and ready.

He hesitates for a moment, but then he's fumbling his flies

down, yanking my jeans until the button flies off, and dragging my knickers to one side so he can plunge himself, burning and colossal into my molten cunt. He fucks me, frantically and furiously while the pimp watches, unable to move to even look away. I like him watching, I like the bulge that tents his trousers, and I like his damp patch that spreads as David arches and staggers behind me, tipping me into my own climax.

* * * *

In the car, David is silent as he concentrates on the road back home. I am fizzing with hunger, I long to rip into the pimp, slumped and Compelled in the back seat.

'So,' David starts, still staring out of the window screen. 'That. What was that? I mean, when you say you're bored, and you want to go out more, did you mean for sex like that? With people watching?'

'No!' I laugh. 'When I say I want to go out dancing, I mean, I want to go dancing.' I close my eyes and wriggle in my seat, waving my arms to an imaginary rhythm. 'That just happened, I was taken over with hunger, and since I can't feed on him, you had to do.' I giggle and writhe some more, shooting him a look out of the corner of my eye. 'Anyway, I didn't hear you complaining. You were rock hard.'

'It was incredible, wild and filthy, but I wouldn't want to do it with an audience again. I feel strange now, grubby.'

I pat his leg reassuringly, already lost in my own music in my mind, dancing madly in my seat.

Rae

'There you go.' I shove the semi-comatose man towards Brian. Meg woke up a few hours ago, and he has been sitting in his room with her, explaining her new reality. She seems to have transitioned well, she has the usual vampire features of luminously pale skin, tight and taunt as a dolphin's, massive eyes, and elongated limbs. Her Gift is not immediately apparent, as mine and Layla's Pretty One traits were. From the raised voices I've heard from the room all afternoon, she is not pleased by the transformation.

'What?' Brian gawps at me.

'This man is for you to feed to Meg. He's a pimp, so he's no loss to the world.'

'But she'll see his memories, won't she? As she feeds?'

'Yes.'

'You can't inflict those memories on my Meg.'

'Keep him deeply Compelled and his memories won't be as vivid.'

'This man is a criminal, she doesn't need to know what he's seen and done.'

'Oh, you'd rather her first action as a vampire was to murder an innocent then?'

'Can't you get the blood bags, like we had?'

'Where from? Click my fingers and they will appear? You tell me where I can get them without putting us more in danger than we are, and I'll get them.' My already frazzled fuse is close to burning out completely, but Brian seems oblivious.

'I just don't want my Megan having to witness what this man has done.'

'Listen, this is your mess, Brian. You sort it out. If you would rather go out yourself, and find a nice vicar with wholly uncorrupted thoughts for your Princess, you do that. Alternatively, you can bleed him out yourself, and give her the blood by the glass full.' While Brian stands immobilised by indecision in his bedroom doorway, I notice, over his shoulder, that Meg has scented the prey. She sniffs loudly, and then slips over to the doorway with vampiric speed. She sniffs again, and then ducks under Brian's arm. With a shriek of delight, she launches herself onto the man, ripping his throat out effortlessly.

* * * *

I know Brian isn't going to be any good at helping Megan come to terms with being a vampire. He hasn't brought her out since her transition and I worry that she's anxious about what's happened to her. I remember the terrifying hours after my own transition, once we were at the Farm, when Guillaume and the others tried to manage the crisis Suzannah and Patrice had caused. I'd had so many questions in my head, so much I needed to know. I might be furious with Brian, but none of this is Megan's fault. I go to their room and tap on the door.

'What?' a girly voice responds.

'Ah, I just wanted to see how you are? Can I come in?'

'Okay,' she answers. I might be wrong, but I'm sure there's petulance in her reply. I push the door open to be greeted by the sight of Brian in bed, fading miserably into the striped sheets, while Megan settles herself into the armchair besides the bed, leaving me nowhere to sit so I am forced to lean in the door frame. I am uncomfortably aware I've interrupted them having sex.

'Well?' she demands pertly. 'What do you want to know? Am I delighted you turned me, you vicious beast? No, I'm not. Do I want to speak to you? No, even if you've got the decency to put your fangs away this time.'

'Hold on a minute. This was Brian's stupid plan, not mine. I would never have done this to you. He set this whole thing up.' My voice rises in frustration, and she flinches theatrically. 'And it was you who punched me in the mouth, I never bit you. You infected yourself.'

'Poor Bribri missed me. I know exactly what happened. You can fuck off now,' she says sweetly.

* * * *

I try again the next day, less conciliatory, and more Pride leader who is explaining the rules. It doesn't go much better.

'Has Brian explained the rules to you?'

'Rules? Whose rules?' she sneers.

'The High Council's rules? This Pride's rules?'

'The High Council?' She is perching on the end of the bed, looking at herself in the mirror on the dressing table, French braiding a section at the front of her hair, shoulder turned towards me. She is ostentatiously refusing to give me the attention I need from her for this conversation. I glower at the patch of wall where Brian had stood when this conversation began. I haven't even attempted to sit down today. Instead, I stand in the centre of their room, legs shoulder width apart, hands firmly on hips, chin up, demanding respect.

'Right. Megan stop faffing with your hair and look at me. Now,' I command. She huffs, but turns towards me, pouting sullenly. 'The High Council are the oldest existing vampires. They have a very simple set of rules; One. You do not let humans know, or even suspect, we do actually exist, ever, or they'll kill you. Two. You do not kill another vampire without their permission, ever, or they'll kill you. Three. You do not turn another vampire without taking full responsibility for them, and registering them with the High Council, or...'

'They'll kill you,' she finishes for me. 'Yadder, yadder. Have you registered me?'

'Nope, Brian will do that this afternoon. I am not taking responsibility for you, he is.' The wall swallows uncomfortably.

'The main thing to be aware of is that the High Council's rules mean you need to cut all contact with your old life. You need to send emails this afternoon telling everyone you have come to France to join Brian, and you are both going to live off grid, and can only email occasionally when you get into town to buy what you can't grow.'

'Okay. Whatever. Off you go.'

'Our rules, enforced by me, as I am the Pride Leader,' I start strongly, but she interrupts again.

'What's all this Pride bollocks? Is it a gay thing?' She tilts her chin at me.

'No. Idiot. It's a lion thing, you stupid cow,' I snarl. 'Now shut your mouth and listen to me while I explain the rules to you. I will keep them simple. Once I'm sure you understand them all, I shall leave you alone. Feel free not to speak to me again.' She sniffs but holds her tongue.

'In our Pride, in addition to all the High Council's rules, we do not kill humans. We do not turn new vampires. We all contribute to the household, either financially or practically. We do not keep secrets, but we do respect privacy.' I glare at Brian, who's just started to emerge from the wall. He fades back in. 'We put things back after we use them, and finish jobs we start.'

'On pain of death?' she sneers. 'You're doing really well at enforcing those rules, aren't you?' I ignore her jibes, as I have to concede she is correct. I shot a venomous glance at the patch of wall which is Brian.

'Oh, and we don't do anything that puts the rest of the Pride at risk from the High Council.' I'm still scowling at Brian.

'Whatever,' says Meg.

'Brian,' I speak to the armchair, he's moved to sit with his head in his hands. 'Make sure both of you learn those rules. Properly this time. If you don't want to live by them, you can leave any time you wish.'

'Hey! Hold on,' Meg calls as I'm about to leave the room. 'If I can't kill humans, what am I supposed to eat?'

'Cows. Sheep. Pigs. I'll let Brian explain to you.' I smirk at her look of disgust. 'Then, Brian, I expect you downstairs in half an hour to ring the High Council.'

After Brian's uncomfortable conversation with the bureaucrats in Germany, he skulks outside to fetch Megan some blood. I gesture to Layla to join me at the bottom of the stairs as he returns, closing their bedroom door behind him. We crouch together, hands over mouths to stifle our sniggers until the silence is broken by her shriek of rage and glass smashing. Then we scuttle off chuckling. We know we're being mean, but we don't get much entertainment nowadays, and, well, the silly little bitch deserves it.

* * * *

It's another two days before she finally leaves the bedroom and stalks amongst us like a cross hen. Tempting as it is to continue to poke at her and watch her flutter and squawk, I resist.

'Have you got any idea what your Gift is yet?'

'Gift?' She eyes me as if I'm a slug she's stepped on with bare feet. I roll my eyes. Brian hasn't even told her the basics.

'We all have a special skill or strength, a gift. Something

that the virus has selected from the evolutionary development of our DNA, and then enhanced to fantastical levels. Surely, you've noticed that Brian changes colour to merge with his background as a defence mechanism?'

'I thought that just happened because he hates you. I didn't realise it was a *Gift*.' Her voice drips with sarcasm.

'Listen, Megan.' David is leaning forward to catch her gaze with his stern stare. 'You can continue to be a silly little bitch, or you can choose to make everyone's life, including your own, a lot simpler by closing this'—he claps his own lips closed for a second with his fingers, then grabs his ears—'and opening these. None of us are in this for kicks. None of us have any obligation to look after you, or explain this to you, or even accommodate you.'

'Are you going to let him speak to me like that?' she squawks at Brian.

'Now, mate...' Brian blusters, but David cuts straight across him, still looking only at Megan.

'Brian has broken all of the rules of this Pride. He has completely betrayed us, and put us all at risk. He has abused the kindness we've shown him, when we have no obligation to support him like we have.'

'Oh, I see. It's all because I can't earn any money. I knew you'd throw that back in my face,' Brian whines.

'Well, to be blunt, what would you do without us?' David's gaze is hard and challenging, and Brian shrivels further beneath it. David holds the silence for several uncomfortable seconds, then he stands up and claps Brian on the shoulder. 'She's your responsibility, Bri, you did this, and you need to explain what's what, teach her the ropes. We shouldn't have to put up with this attitude problem in our home. Now, Rae, Layla, and I are going for a nice swim while you two have a proper chat about what you are and what that means. Then you can come and join us, if you still want to be part of this Pride.'

'Oh, my God! I knew you never liked me,' Megan shrieks. 'I should tell your wife where you are...' Brian catches her arm, and pulls her towards him, muttering at her to calm down. I grin happily at David, and Layla and I link arms with him and merrily march down to our river bank to splash and play in the rippling light and glittering water.

Layla

'Ah, that's Rae's mug,' I warn Meg, as she grabs it out of the cupboard.

'Oh, is it?' she asks innocently, pouring half the cafetière of Lavazza I've just made for Rae and me into the mug. 'Well, I'm sure she won't mind if I borrow it. Shall I pour yours now too? Sugar today?' Before I can answer, she's poured, then she plonks it in front of me and curls herself into Rae's seat opposite me. 'God,' she says, sniffing up the coffee vapour. 'Don't you get bored?'

And this is how come Rae walks in and finds me and Meg having a heart to heart over her coffee, in her mug, in her seat. She stands in the doorway, bewildered for a moment. Meg sees her, smirks and stands up. 'Here's your coffee,' she says. 'I didn't think you'd mind. It's not like you can actually drink it.' Rae stares after her, open-mouthed as Megan swishes past her in her cute polka dot dress. She didn't grow much with the transition, so she still fits into the clothes she brought with her, all of which are very pretty and girly. Not something I'd be seen dead in, especially not the ankle socks, but she wears it all with a certain panache, cherry hair clips and all.

'What the fuck?' Rae is looking at me now, obviously feeling betrayed by my friendliness with Meg.

'Ah, come on,' I say. 'She's not so bad once you get to know her. Just try talking to her. I know all that little girl lost shit gets on your tits, but push through that and she's a laugh.' Rae looks as sour as a Pretty One can as she tips her coffee away and washes up her cup. Instead of putting it away, she keeps hold of it and starts to leave the kitchen.

'Rae, sit down. I'll make you a fresh cup. We all have to live together in this Pride, which means we all need to get along. You need to try a little.' She pauses at the door and turns back to me.

'I did. It's no good, she hates me. She blames me for turning her, even though she hit me. And to be totally blunt, I can't stand her either, all those frills and faff, it's just a distraction. She is as cold as ice and as manipulative as hell underneath. Watch your back.'

'Where are you going?'

'To my room.' She doesn't look at me as she speaks; her face has gone pinched and haughty. When you know Rae well, you know this means she's cut to the quick.

'Why are you taking an empty mug?'

'I'm going to keep it safe in there. I don't like her using it.' She rubs her thumb over the curved lapis lazuli side as she speaks.

'Oh Rae, you bought those mugs for us, for our morning coffees.' I'm about to add that they belong together, but she just nods and turns away.

'Yes,' she says softly as she leaves the room.

Chapter Three

Rae

Despite my protests, I have listened to Layla. I do recognise that we all need to get along if this Pride is going to work, and as the leader it's my job to set a good example. I'd expected us to be more of a co-operative, but apparently, that isn't going to be the case. I've ordered Meg her own mug in an attempt to heal the rift; a similar shape and size to ours, but in cream with baby pink polka dots. It arrives on a miserable drizzly morning, and I go to fetch it from the post box at the end of the road when the text from the delivery company informs me it has been delivered. Since the incident with Brian, I keep my phone fully charged at all times. I'm not risking anything like that again.

Walking down the lane in the soft rain, my senses are filled with the mushroom scent of moist earth and the vibrant green zing of fresh growth in the hedgerows. I find myself coming to, after being lost for long seconds in bedazzled contemplation of a perfect spider's web, strung with tiny raindrops that have been transformed into tiny globes of aurora borealis. I might not be able to dream now that I'm a vampire, but I often find myself getting caught by something beautiful I wouldn't even have noticed as a human, something that tantalises my senses and then I lose great swathes of time enthralled.

When I get back to the cottage, I go upstairs and change before giving Megan the package. I won't get ill or stiff from wearing wet clothes, but I don't want them to end up smelling damp like Brian's sometimes did before Megan's arrival. It's an excuse to try the new extra sensitive washing powder I've found. The high street highly perfumed stuff is unbearably chemically, and I'm hoping the gentle chamomile scent will mean I don't have to hang my clothes outside for two days before I can wear them after every wash.

Megan makes a big fuss about the mug when I finally give it to her, after I've loaded the washing machine and replaced the flowers on the kitchen with the fresh poesy I've just picked. She keeps thanking me and showing the others, and then puts it into the cupboard next to Layla's. I am gracious, and we are officially friends. My mug will continue to live in my room.

Later that afternoon, Brian comes to the kitchen when I'm doing some admin work for my boss. I'm a virtual P.A. for the Probation Service now, a big demotion and pay cut from my old role, but one I can do without having to see my old colleagues face-to-face. You don't need much money as a vampire, but you do need some. As well as grocery orders we can collect at our local supermarket's 'Drive' facility to avoid raising suspicion, which we drop off at our local homeless charity, I need to pay Guillaume for this cottage.

'Um, ah, I just wanted to, ah, thank you for the, ah, mug you bought Meggie,' Brian is mumbling in the doorway, wringing his hands. 'That was really special for her, really made her feel like one of the Pride. Like she belongs.'

I want to punch him, but I smile nicely, instead. 'So, have you two worked out what Megan's Gift is yet?' I ask to change the subject. Being gracious is starting to make me feel like a cat with a hairball.

'Hmm, no, not er, as yet.' Brian looks uncomfortable, this is a subject he prefers to avoid. He doesn't really like to acknowledge that he or Megan are vampires, living a strange betwixt and between existence, no longer human, but refusing to accept himself as he is now. Meg seems hardly affected by the transition, she's still small and slender, and shows only the most basic vampire characteristics.

We've seen no sign of the Gifts we're aware of. I've tried thinking very spiteful thoughts concerning her remarkably knobbly knees, which she keeps carefully hidden with her skirts and frilled petticoats, but she hasn't responded, so she's not Psychic. Or she can resist my bait.

'Come on then.' I jump up from the table, full of false cheer. Brian flinches. 'There's no time like the present, is there?'

In the garden, I find Megan and Layla chattering away on a picnic blanket in the orchard. Megan has Babette on her lap and is stroking her, lifting her back every time the little cat tries to walk away. I make a mental note to cut back on Babette's food; she's looking a bit plump.

'Let her go please, Megan.' I try for breezy and relaxed, like it doesn't really bother me that she is forcing my obviously reluctant cat to sit on her lap. I suspect it may have come out as more of a snarl. Megan smirks, and then draws breath to answer me, still holding Babette, who has now started to struggle in earnest.

'Now, please.' It's no longer a request.

'Ah, Rae...' Layla interjects, but I shoot her a quick glare and she shuts up, annoyance pinching her lips, and her eyebrow flicking archly at me.

'Let her go now!' I shout at Megan. Babette is clawing at Megan's arms while Megan laughs and laughs. I crouch down next to them and reach out to snatch back my cat. And Babette takes one look at me and hisses in my face. I'm so shocked that for a second I don't absorb what Layla is telling me.

'That's not Babette,' she says. Megan looks into my face, laughs again, and lets the little cat go. It streaks across the garden, a furious flash of ruffled grey fur. I should have known better, Babette never goes near Megan, and even Layla sitting there would not tempt her over. I've allowed Megan to make an utter fool of me. And shut Layla up when she tried to warn me, I could kick myself. I smile grimly, instead.

'She's from the next village,' Layla explains. 'We saw her on our way back from dropping off the groceries to the hostel. She's probably Babette's sister. We just thought you'd laugh; it was just a joke. We didn't expect the cat to get so upset. Or you.'

'Well, catch it, and take it back home,' I tell Layla. She opens her mouth to complain, but I am not in the mood for a discussion, and turn my back.

'Megan, we're going to find out what your Gift is,' I announce chummily.

We spend the next couple of hours trying everything we can think of to see if we can discover her Gift. We time her running across the garden, encourage her to guess which card we are holding, do things and tell her to make us forget, all to no avail. Or at least, she isn't sharing any new traits with us. By mid-afternoon we are all thoroughly bored of trying to identify every Gift any of us have heard of. As we give up, and gather our belongings together before walking up from the river meadow barn, I slip away and surreptitiously hide in the barn, so when they stroll through, chattering idly, I can push a bale of hay off the top of the stack down onto her. All in the name of science I tell myself.

She shows no sign of any greater strength than an ordinary vampire as she pushes it back off. In fact, she seems weaker than most, because it actually floors her. I hurry on ahead and hide in the kitchen making coffee for everyone to make sure she doesn't realise it didn't just fall. When Layla tells me what happened, I make a point of reminding Brian he was in the middle of restacking the bales yesterday. I allude to his habit of not finishing a job he starts and suggest he must have left them unstable. He looks stricken, and I almost feel guilty, but I'm still too cross with all of them.

* * * *

After a brittle but quiet few days of everyone doing their best to be polite to each other, Megan has asked for a house meeting this evening. I'm apprehensive. She's being delightful, fussing around everyone as we sit in the lounge, checking if anyone would like some blood, offering glasses round to everyone from her tray. Trust Megan to provide snacks, I didn't even know we had a tray. I refuse her offering, and she smirks, and then takes her seat on a taller stool she has brought through from the kitchen, ostensibly because there aren't enough seats, but really so she can sit higher than the rest of us. She's usually perfectly happy to squeeze into the armchair with Brian, so we can all see how dainty and tiny she is.

'So, I've asked for us all to meet together tonight because I have a point of principle I wish to raise on behalf of everyone.' I just look at her blandly. I refuse to rise to the bait of being told the others need to use her as a mouthpiece as they don't feel they can talk to me themselves. But I don't look at the others; I don't want to see if they are nodding.

'Rae,' she says as sweetly as saccharine, clasping her hands in her lap and tilting her head as she speaks to me. 'You told me you have a no human blood rule in this Pride, however it appears that this isn't a rule that everyone agrees with completely.' I feel my heart rate speed up slightly, I do not like the way this conversation is going. I do not like this alignment of Megan with the rest of my Pride, and me, in the wrong, on the outside. I remain silent though, waiting to see where this progresses.

'I do feel, Rae, that we should live in a democracy. I feel that deciding what we eat is, well, a bit dictatorial, really. Cow blood is bloody disgusting, isn't it?' She titters at her own use of a swear word, and the poor pun it produces. 'It's so nasty, even you won't drink it.' She gestures to my untouched glass on the tray, and I curse myself for my petty refusal of her hospitality, I played right into her hands.

'Layla told me about the system you came up with, to hunt bad people, to do good while still being able to actually be a vampire. To feel the thrill of the chase, feed on the blood that tastes so delicious and then lose yourself in that amazing thing that happens when you get to watch their memories, the thing that's like being drunk, or stoned, but better.' I switch my gaze to Layla, gutted by her betrayal.

'Meggie wanted to know about how different Prides function,' Layla explains uncomfortably, smiling winningly at me. *Meggie?*

'Rae—' Megan is tooth-achingly sincere. 'I do feel this is an issue that needs to be decided democratically, rather you getting to decide how the rest of us live. Don't you agree, guys?' My eyes haven't left Layla while she wriggles uncomfortably. I never forced her and David not to eat human, they just never wanted to join in when other Pride members at the Farm hunted, so the no hunting humans rule had never been discussed, it was just a way of life that followed us from the Farm. I had only decided it was a rule while speaking to Megan, because I wanted to enforce some order, at least until I had the measure of her.

'I just think it's something we could be allowed to decide for ourselves?' Layla asked. 'I'm not saying I want to eat human, just, well, it's something that should be down to individual choice like at the Farm.'

'Fine. Megan, if you wish to hunt, you can, as can everyone else who wants to. But there will be some rules to protect the Pride. We must hunt together, we must select our prey carefully, following the procedure I created, we must always test to ensure we have the right person, and we must hunt in different places each time we hunt. It goes without saying that we must destroy all evidence, so the kills always look like suicide.' Everyone nodded, while Megan tried to smother her smug smirk at her victory.

'Megan, come with me, we'll bait the trap.' Despite myself, I feel the flutter of excitement the hunt always arouses in me, the snake coils of hunger swirling in my gut.

* * * *

I should hate setting the trap with Megan. We barely speak, just the bare minimum as I take her photo, and then Photoshop it to make her look like a human teenager. I stick snap chat filters over it, and edit them to moody themes. It doesn't take long to create the Facebook profile of a fourteen-year-old, furious with the world. I should hate watching the sharks circle in for the kill, men from their twenties to their sixties messaging her within minutes wanting photos, to chat on facetime or skype, offering to buy her gifts for photographs. It sickens me, but my own predator senses are triggered, and I am like a cat with a mouse, playing with it as I lure it to its death.

I find an online site that sells cheap clip-in veneers and order us all a set to wear over our spikey vampire teeth. When they arrive a week later, they are ridiculously white, and Layla and David entertain themselves taking silly Selfies with their 'TOWIE' teeth. I let them have their fun, then take them back and soak them in cold tea for two days. Once I wipe the worse of the tannin staining off, they look more flawed and good enough to pass as human to a quick glance, even if they are uncomfortable to wear.

I show Megan how to choose a spot to lure our prey to. I'm engrossed as I search Google maps for a suitable spot, one that's remote, but where a stranger's car won't be obvious; somewhere where a teenager might go to sulk, but also where a predator might choose to commit suicide in a fit of remorse, or fear of being caught. Megan doesn't chat with me while we work, indeed she seems far more interested in the profiles of the men we may kill, than the precautions I preach to avoid arousing suspicion. Her nails strum her frustration and her eyes flicker past me to the faces on the screen behind me, while I try to explain things to her, and I see the joy of the hunt too starkly in her face.

I find a place on the map, close to Calais, between Sangatte and Escalles where there is a stretch of coastline with no houses, and steep fierce cliffs a man in despair could jump off late at night, or be pushed from, without being disturbed. There's a large lake and a patch of forest nearby. Plenty of places for an unhappy teen to escape to for peace from her parents nagging. I post pictures I collect from Trip Advisor and Google Images, descriptions of solitary bike rides away from everyone. Finally, I find the perfect place, a barren slab of concrete labelled as Blanc Nez, behind a flimsy fence, and reached by a twisting gravel track. It offers the perfect lookout spot to watch the sullen sea from, a place for a local teenager to hide from the world. I share this picture with the heading 'My Favourite Place, My Sanctuary'.

Then I post several vague but unhappy posts, escalating in anger and teenage sense of hard-done-byness, until we are ready to hunt. I've checked the tide times, and I pick a day when the tides are going to reach an early summer high, and the forecast is fine. I pile the whole Pride into the car, I want everyone to be involved. I'm hoping the grumblings of boredom will stop if we go hunting together once a month. I fill the boot with the tools we'll need to rid the world of one more predator, then let Layla drive, while I am on Facebook laying the breadcrumb trail for our monster to follow to his fate.

Layla

Despite myself I get caught up in the thrill of anticipation. I haven't seen Rae like this before, silent, calculating, deadly. She completely ignores Megan's excitable babbling. I wish she would shut up. I really hoped Rae and Megan could bond over this hunt together, in the same way I saw Rae bond with Elaine and Simon after their hunt to get the blood to save Guillaume. There's no way they'll get closer with Megan squealing excitably, though. I check the rear-view mirror and see Brian looking drawn and anxious, squeezed between David and Megan, shooting occasional worried looks to the back of Rae's head while he pretends to be listening to Megan. I realise he is sharing my concerns and crushed hopes.

It's twilight as we arrive at the car park about a mile from the plateau Rae chose for our hunt. We all wear dark grey tracksuit bottoms, black trainers, and hooded anoraks that zip up over the lower halves of our faces, and come low over our foreheads. Rae has deliberately ordered us larger coats than we need so the sleeves hang low over our hands. The colours will allow us to fade into the shadows while we await our prey, but to the innocent passer-by we look like a hiking group. Apart from Megan, she wears black skinny jeans and a grubby T-shirt. Even she is silent now, as we file away from the car and jog to our destination.

By the time we reach the concrete slab, the light has faded to the strange in between that confuses the human eye, not yet dark, yet no longer light, rinsing the colour out of the landscape and distorting shadows. Vampire eyes can still see perfectly though, and I watch as Megan settles herself in a hunched huddle, gazing mournfully out to sea. Rae, David, Layla and I lie flat in dips and behind tussocks of grass, in a loose circle around her, fading into nothing as the night darkens.

The first sign that things might not go as planned comes when a middle-aged couple strolls past us heading towards the car park that's closer to the cliffs than the one we parked in. Their damp little dog tags along behind them, nose busily to the grass as she weaves along rabbit trails. The couple are already almost level with Megan when the dog sees her and freezes before setting up a frenzied barking, stiff-legged and bouncing with fear and fury.

'Oh dear, we are sorry, this isn't like her at all,' the woman apologises, as she steps closer to Megan. 'Trixie, Trixie, come on, silly girl.' I expect Megan to compel the dog until it passes her calmly, and nod at the woman, or at worst ignore her. Instead, she looks up into the woman's face and hisses like an angry cat so the woman shrieks and stumbles back a step, and her husband jumps up from where he was kneeling to fix the little dog's lead to her collar and hurries back towards his wife.

Rae rises silently from her hiding place behind the husband and dog and instantly the dog stops barking, and the husband's steps slow to a stroll, while his wife watches them move towards her with a beatific smile.

'Oh, please do ignore her,' Rae croons softly. 'She's such a naughty girl; she takes those awful drugs, and runs away. Don't you worry, I'll get her home safely now.' With that she stands between Megan and the couple, back turned as if speaking earnestly to a troubled girl, as they saunter back to their car. She waits while they leisurely climb into their car, and then raises a hand in farewell as they drive away.

'Don't you ever do a thing like that again,' she snarls at Megan. Megan does not reply, but I see her chin jut out as Rae walks back to her hiding place.

I don't notice him approach initially, I've grown bored with the waiting and I'm busy making lascivious gestures at David, carefully out of Rae's eye line, to let him know what I fancy doing when we get home. Some change in Rae's stance, a tiny rustle of her jacket draws my eyes back to her. She is as poised as a panther, quivering with anticipation as the man saunters over the brow of the slope towards Megan. I see her lift one cautionary finger to Brian who has started to move towards his fiancée.

'Emilie? Is that you?' His heavily accented French gives him away; he's travelled a long way for this treat. Everyone waits in frozen fascination as Megan turns her face up to him. He is supposed to be so heavily Compelled now that he will follow her complacently to the car. There, we can cut him to test and confirm he is the predator we hoped to attract, then slice his wrists with the razor blades that wait there. His blood can be collected and saved, and he can be left on the beach, an apparent suicide, a man who regrets the atrocities he has committed.

Instead, Megan turns her face up to him, and grins widely, exposing both sets of razor sharp teeth. For an instant, the hunt hangs in the balance, the man's face is a frozen mask of terror and repulsion; mouth slowly opening to scream. Even as his bladder empties, she could still Compel him and lead him, docile, to the car.

Instead, like a striking snake Megan uncoils and tears his throat out in one fluid motion. Aghast, no one moves towards her as hot blood, rich and pungent, pumps over her mouth and throat. She casts the briefest glance of triumph towards Rae before a shriek of pure terror rises from the scrub bushes between David and Brian. A male figure scurries off, stumbling desperately, his now flaccid penis flapping through his open fly in such a grotesquely comic way that a whoop of laughter burbles from me unbidden.

Within a second, Megan has dropped her meal, and is upon the second man. It seems for a moment she will just play with him, but as soon as Rae moves towards her she is upon him, feeding greedily. The first man is still spluttering and gasping, drowning in his own blood. Rae walks over, takes one gulp of blood, and then snaps his neck unceremoniously.

'Oh, what a waste,' Megan admonishes, before returning to feeding, her prey's struggles weak and futile. Rae strides over, grabs the struggling man with one hand and yanks him out of Megan's grip. Megan hisses furiously, but Rae just narrows her eyes slightly, then takes a small taste. She crumples her nose in distaste, snaps his neck, and throws him back to Megan. Megan starts to protest, but Rae doesn't even look at her. She returns to the first body and crouches beside the corpse, shoulders drooped, and rubs her face. Several minutes pass, silent apart from Megan's slurping.

'I fucking hate bad table manners,' Rae mutters, and then turns away from her resolutely. She digs into the man's jeans pocket and pulls out his car keys, then goes and checks the pockets of the man Megan still feeds on, ignoring Megan's territorial growl as she ferrets through his jeans and jacket.

'No keys. He's a local.' Rae mutters to me. I sidle alongside her now, fascinated and repulsed.

'Want some?' Megan asks me. We both ignore her. Rae thinks a moment longer.

'Right, Brian, go and get that one's car.' She gestures to Megan's first kill. 'It's a small white Citroen 1, a hire car, so it's got a Sixt sticker in the window. Bring it to the closest car park.' Now I understand why she fed, it wasn't that the blood scent overcame her; she needed to raid their memories to plan how to deal with this god awful mess. Brian opens his mouth to object, but Rae just looks at him until he takes the keys and trudges off. He only pauses to cast a forlorn look towards Megan, who merrily ignores him while she sucks the final

45

mouthfuls of blood from her dinner.

'Layla, David, I need vodka, cigarettes and a lighter, fast.'

'Where...?'

'I don't care, just get some, quickly.'

I know better than to expect a twenty-four-hour garage or supermarket in rural France. I know our only hope of finding what she needs is to steal them. A local Tabac might well be open, but even with our jackets done up, we still look too strange, too memorable, to the locals. As it turns out, luck is on our side, the third house we try is empty and unlocked. The owner is messy, so it takes us a few minutes to find his vodka under the sink, but his spare cigarettes are easy for our vampire noses to sniff out, even with the overbearing smell of ashtray and feet to contend with. There is a large box of matches by the greasy cooker which I grab as well, then shoot David a triumphant grin.

Rae

'What are these?' I hold up the big economy box of matches that no man would ever take out with him. 'I said a lighter.'

'You also said to be fast, and that was all we could find,' Layla snaps back.

While they've been gone, Brian has found the first victim's car, and driven it as close to us as he could. I got him to keep watch while I carried first one body, then the second and sat them in the front seats of the car. Megan sprawled nearby and watched our endeavours like a sated lion, fuzzy with the blood high, and disinclined to help. Once we had the two corpses sitting in the front seats as I wanted them, chairs reclined, flies open, hands reaching, I slipped the car into neutral and Brian had just started to push it across the tufty grasslands towards the cliffs when Layla and David returned. I decide to go with what they've brought. I tip the vodka over the two bodies, especially around their faces and necks, and slip cigarettes into each man's hand.

There are so many flaws and improbabilities with this set-up that it makes my head spin, but this is the best I can come up with in the circumstances. The most important thing is to get rid of the evidence. Once the bodies are staged, I send Brian to dig up the two areas the bodies lay on, as deeply as he needs to, to remove every trace of blood and bag up the earth in the bin liners I brought with us to cover the car seats with, if the hunt had gone to plan. Then pick every blade of grass that was dripped on as I carried the corpses to the car. He starts to object that he does not have a shovel, but I growl at him that he needs to make it look as much like a dog has dug playful holes as possible, so he needs to use his claws.

'Every single drop, Brian. Do not make me come over there and clean up after you,' I caution grimly.

With David's help, we push the car to the most sheltered cove, around a point from the nearest town, but with a cliff high enough to offer a significant drop. Then I open the front windows, light their cigarettes, coughing and gagging at the foul flavour, and start the engine.

'Let's hope to fuck this works,' I mutter, and latch onto the side of the car, leaning through the window to shove the driver's foot onto the accelerator. The car veers off towards the cliff tops and I fling myself backwards out of the vehicle just before it soars out and across, to land in a crushed heap on the rocks below. I peer over the edge, breath held, until the vodka catches from the cigarette, and the car bursts into flames.

'Were they both...' Layla asks. I nod in reply, arms crossed, mouth set. All we can do now is hope it is too late in the night for anyone in the vicinity to notice the distant glow of flames; hear the boom of the petrol tank catching fire; or worse yet, smell the sickening porky smell of the roasting bodies. I can only hope that the high tide rises to wash the crumpled car out to sea before anyone notices the wreckage, but not too soon that the flames haven't scorched the flesh enough to disguise the vampire feeding injuries. And pray that the fish will swim through the open windows and continue the work the fire has started, and the salt water will continue, to destroy all the evidence of foul play.

Most of all, though, I have to get us all away from here. If anything suspicious is found, we need to make sure that nobody remembers the five darkly dressed figures that stole through the night. On the long, silent, drive home I stop at a river and get Brian to shake in the clods of earth and handfuls of blood clotted grass that he collected from the site. While we watch them wash away, I turn to him.

'I wash my hands of her, Brian. I will not take responsibility for that vampire. You need to ensure she complies with Pride rules, or she will have to go. This is the final warning,' I say, and we both glance at where she lolls against the rear window, stupefied with two people's death memories. 'I will not protect her from the High Council. I will not shelter someone who endangers us all.'

'If she goes, I go,' he replies.

I don't know what he expects me to say, so I just nod. 'So be it.'

Layla

'No, that's not fair! I can't believe you would even ask me,' I yell.

'What option do I have? Do you have any better ideas?' Rae shouts back. She's brought me out for a drive in the late evening two days after the disastrous hunt. I can't quite believe there's been nothing on the news, but Rae advises us not to relax too soon, they could be found any day. Not enough time has passed yet for all the evidence to be eroded.

We usually people-watch when we come out together, a pastime that still entrances her, but I find it a bit boring now that I no longer share the concerns of those we watch. Instead, we have come to a quiet car park overlooking a pretty river with a gloriously romantic weeping willow sweeping down its banks to tickle its waters. When we got here, I made a mental note to bring David here for some alfresco fun, but then Rae asked me to supervise the hunts from now on, and all thoughts of fun are wiped from my brain.

'Stop her hunting,' I exclaim, the solution seems simple to me.

'I thought of that. She wouldn't comply. It is better to authorise it and monitor her than to have her do it secretly and mess it up again, with no one to clean up the mess this time. The High Council won't care whose fault it is; the whole Pride would be held accountable.'

'What on earth makes you think she'll behave any differently for me? You monitored every stage and look what happened anyway,' I protest hotly.

'I really think she wanted to show me up, to make me look like a fool in front of you all. I don't think she would do that with you, she likes you more.'

'Not really,' I sulk. 'She only pretends to because it pisses you off.'

'Well, she can stick to the hunting rules for you to piss me off too,' Rae snaps. 'Look, Layla, I wish I didn't have to ask you, I really do, but there really is no choice. I've thought of every option. She does not understand how dangerous the Council are, or she doesn't care. Whatever I say to her is just a challenge to do the opposite. This is my last chance at keeping the Pride together. If this doesn't work, I'll have to send her away.'

'Do that now! What are you waiting for?' My voice goes shrill.

'If she goes, Brian will go. I thought that might upset David? And where would they go? I don't trust her at the Farm; we still have enemies there just looking for a chance to make trouble for us.'

I know she's right. David seems to feel a responsibility for his friend, even while I can't see the attraction. I know what it feels like to be with someone who doesn't respect your friendships though, so I try not to be dismissive. Well, not too often anyway, the guy is a total dork.

'It was you who supported her to demand hunting in the first place, all that everyone should have the right to choose bollocks.'

It's a low blow, and I can tell she knows it, but she keeps her face blank and looks straight ahead, and I know I've lost.

'Fucking Hell, Rae, I can't believe I've got to do this.' We are silent a few moments longer. She's good at this, letting silence do the work. 'Well, I want my objections minuted.'

'Let the record show you really didn't want to do this.' Rae grins at me, her shoulders dropping back down from her ears.

We sit for a while then, chatting about unimportant things, laughing about how henpecked Brian is. He would never admit it, but I'm sure he must be regretting ever making contact with Megan.

'Rae, if I have to do this, I want to do it my way,' I say just as she takes hold of the keys in the ignition ready to head home. She drops her hand back into her lap and turns to look at me, her leonine eyes roving my face.

'What do you mean?' Her shoulders are creeping back up towards her ears again.

'I'm going to need to get Megan on my side.' Rae nods. 'I'm going to tell her that you were going to forbid hunting. I'll say I persuaded you to give it another go, with me in charge this time. I'm going to tell her I want to use it as a chance to get out and about with David on our own while she hunts. She knows I've been getting bored. I am going to put the onus back on her; I'll do her a favour, if she'll do me one.' Rae thinks for a few minutes; I can see her inner control freak warring with her recognition that beggars can't be choosers. Finally, she nods slowly.

'Okay, that might just work,' she says.

I'm glad, because I really don't think there would be another way to do this successfully. And, actually, the idea of time alone with David, out and about at night, is one that's growing on me, it could be fun. And there's been such a lack of fun recently.

Chapter Four

Rae

Over the next months the only way I cope with Megan's infringement into my life is by escaping with Layla for a while in the soft hours of dusk when she isn't wrapped up with David or supervising a hunt. We take the car and drive to towns to watch people eating and laughing together in groups outside restaurants. The car's blacked-out windows mean there is no chance we will be seen, and we can slip back into our old games from university, creating whole fictitious backstories for the eateries patrons.

Old men sitting with young girls are long-lost fathers, newly reunited with the grandchildren of their wartime love child. Handsome boys lounging in groups heckling the pretty girls are smouldering poets, and the willow slim girls waitressing the tables are actresses, just awaiting their big break. Each time they tuck their hair behind tiny shell ears, they might be exposing their candle-kissed profile to the movie mogul who will discover them, and whisk them away to stardom.

Tonight it's raining though, so there is no point going out, there won't be anyone about to watch. We are all gathered in the lounge to watch a film, but tempers are already fraying. I'm about to suggest we have another go at finding out what Meg's special traits are together, when there's a knock at the door. We all freeze. No one knows we're here, apart from Guillaume's Pride, and they would telephone in advance if they were coming to visit. I sniff deeply, searching for any trace of human. I frown. I can smell human blood, but not living human. I lift my finger to my lips to silence the others, and gesture for them to stay where they are. I start to sidle towards the front door, but a merry strumming of nails on the lounge window makes me jump out of my skin. I'm sure I catch a glimpse of the telltale vampire claws before the hand withdraws, and there's more rhythmic tapping on the door.

'Helloooooooo,' tinkles a melodious voice, and I hear giggles and whisperings. The hackles stand up on the back of my neck. Definitely vampires and not a voice I recognise. Nothing good has ever come from meeting other vampires, and I have no idea why this group are here.

'Cooeee,' she continues, 'We've come to visit. Do open the door, Darlings, we've brought blood.' I look back at my Pride sitting together in the lounge, Brian has faded into his armchair in terror, so it looks like Meg, perched on his lap, is floating; but her face sparkles with excitement and anticipation, and I feel my stomach curdle with trepidation. I just know this is not going to go well, and she is such an unknown quantity, I have no way of predicting her behaviour. I look at David and Layla for reassurance; David is standing, chest puffed for confrontation, and I feel better. Until I see Layla and my heart freezes, she is also leaning forward, and although she is trying to hide it, her face echoes Meg's excitement.

'Hurry up,' the vampire calls again, 'it's pissing down out here, lovlies.'

I pause for a moment longer, anxiety thrumming through me, but then I shake back my hair and straighten my shoulders. The door handle jiggles, and I know there is nothing I can do to avoid this confrontation; I can only try to wrench back some control. So I move silently to the door, and then just as the vampire on the other side sets up another tattoo of knocking, I whip the door open so she staggers a step forward.

She quickly recovers herself, and seems totally unfazed by her stumble or my silent disproval.

'Oh hello, there you are,' she burbles effervescently. 'Hope we aren't disturbing you? I know it's awfully rude to just turn up without an invite, but, well, the moon is high, and I was in a partying mood, so I just grabbed the boys, and some blood and headed on over to introduce ourselves to the new kids on the block.' She waves a wine bottle at me, but the contents are darker and more gluttonous than the burgundy the label advertises.

I blink and stare at her; she's huddled under a huge lurid golfing umbrella, wearing a silk gown, tattered and grubby, and damp at the hem. A tiara sits wonkily on her untidily piled platinum hair. She looks like a student at the end of a raucous summer ball. Even the blood stains down the front of her dress could pass for wine in the twilight, to a human. I instinctively distrust her posh tones and overly chummy manner, her eyes are glazed with the narcotic effects of a fresh feed, and she is glowing with the excitement of a hunt. She has killed recently, and near our home.

'Oh, do excuse me, I'm being insufferably rude, aren't I? I'm Abigail, Lady Abigail Paddington-Smythe.' She beams extending a dainty white hand towards me. I look at it, and then I look at her. She is exceptionally beautiful, and not just from the blood and the hunt. She has turquoise blue eyes that tilt at the corners like a cat's, English roses flush the immaculate marble of her oval face and long neck. Her long straight pale hair might be artfully messed up, but her whole scruffiness has a contrivance I don't believe. She is delightful.

And dangerous.

At the mention of partying, Layla and Meg have pushed in beside me to get a better view of the excitement. The male holding the umbrella handle steps forward from behind Abigail to introduce himself, but I'm still staring into Abigail's cerulean eyes trying to decide whether to shake her hand or not, when I hear Layla gasp.

'Hi Layla, Rae.' I look up, straight into Sebastian's smiling face. I can't believe it's him. I stare and stare, and everything else fades away so all I can see is his smile. He hasn't changed since he broke my heart at university. Strawberry blonde curls frame the face of a Pre-Raphaelite angel, and his smile still looks just as beguiling to me, despite his sharp white teeth. He opens his arms to me, and I throw myself into them.

'Where... This... How...' I don't know where to start, and he cups the back of my head with his big hand, and shushes me, crooning.

'Later, later, we'll talk later. Let me look at you.' He pushes me back and ranges his eyes hungrily over my face, and for the first time I'm glad I'm a Pretty One, and I'm sorry about my scar. I feel the Glamour start to thrum, like a blush from his attention, and for once I don't force it back down. I let myself sparkle at him. I see his eyes widen in appreciation, feel the burn of the Need ignite in us both, but I quickly subdue the intensity of my Glamour as Abigail whoops beside me.

'Oh steady on, Mrs! Get a room for God's sakes. Ooof.' She fans herself exaggeratedly with her long pale hand. 'Well, I can see you two don't need any introductions. This, however, is Mattie.' She beckons the other vampire from behind her for introductions and I gasp. I have seen vampires who are creamy, even golden, like Jerusalem marble, their ethnicity as humans affecting their shade as a vampire, but always paler than they were as humans. This male is jet black though, and although not tall, he is massive, slabs of muscle hewn from obsidian. I can see his face is like Mel's, and the bodyguards at the High Council, crags and planes of smooth dark flesh. For a second, I find him terrifying, but then he turns his eyes from Abigail to look at me, and I see they are the orange of sunstone, with vibrant gold flecks, and they are kind and gentle as he looks back to her ladyship, besotted.

Later, while the others chatter excitedly in the lounge, Seb and I sit opposite each other at the kitchen table, pale fingers entwined, gazes locked. He tells me about being Turned in a quiet lane when he got lost on the way to his parents' new house for the first time that Easter holidays. He'd met interesting people on the train, stopped for a drink at Chepstow where he changed trains, and missed his Dad's lift. In the days before mobiles this had meant walking home, as he'd spent all his money in the expensive station bar.

Still gently buzzed he'd wandered into the balmy spring evening as twilight fell, taken a wrong turning and ended up in quiet country lanes. Abigail had approached him, and the next thing he knew he was waking up in her car, changed.

'Abigail infected you?' I'm surprised. I still harbour such fury towards Mel for infecting me and she was newly transitioned herself, and out of control, although I'm pretty convinced she would have anyway, new or not. I can't imagine choosing to stay with my infector.

'She is the best thing that ever happened to me.' Seb has a slightly fanatical glimmer in his eyes.

'You like being a vampire?' I can't hide my surprise. I mentally reassess the sympathy I had been feeling towards the young Seb, bumbling drunkenly home.

'Oh my God, yes. I love it. I love the smells, the colours, how strong I am, how fast I am. I'm not accountable to anyone now. I'm free, really free.'

'But what about your family, and your friends, and food,

and booze?' *And me?* I add silently.

'I have a new, better family now, and who needs alcohol when there's blood? The hunt, the chase, the kill?' His eyes were blurred by the lingering effects of his last kill, he was still flying from adrenaline. I know that high, and he is right, nothing that humans can take comes close.

'How did you handle your family, though? No one knew what had happened to you, but no one was worried.'

'I rang them and told them I'd met some cool people, and was off to travel Europe with them. They were fine, it wasn't the first time I'd bumped into adventure. Or at least they were for the first few years, but then I found out they had reported me missing to the police. I suppose I should have phoned them more often, but you know how it is, I had nothing to say to them anymore. It's easier now for you new vampires, with texts and Facebook.'

'What did you do?'

'I arranged to meet them, and then well, you know.' He shrugs. I stare at him.

'No, what?'

'Well, I had to, you know, end it. I made it quick, made it look like suicide, like they couldn't get over me moving away.' I stare at him still; he clears his throat and shuffles in his seat. 'I had to, they weren't going to leave it alone, and if the High Council found out, they wouldn't have been so careful, wouldn't have made them happy first. Abigail and I and the rest of our Pride were in danger, there was no choice.' He looks up at me through his eyelashes, the appeal I could never resist.

'There was only one regret I ever had,' he whispers, taking back my hand that I'd jerked from his grasp in surprise at his confession. 'I missed you so badly. I felt so awful I couldn't tell you. I knew you'd worry.' He rubs his thumb over my knuckles, soothing me, bewitching and beguiling, returning me to my besotted teenage self. 'I wanted to find you, change you too,' he confides. 'But Abigail was jealous, wouldn't let me. I was her favourite toy for years. When I heard though, that someone with your name had been changed, I just knew. Especially when I heard about Layla too, only you could manage to get infected with your friend. You two were always a double act.' He chuckles huskily, leaning closer, so close our foreheads touch, our eyelashes flutter and touch. 'I had to come,' he breathes. 'I had to see if it was you.'

Finally, he closes the gap and kisses me. Softly, then firmer, sucking my bottom lip, and we are lost, mouths swollen centres of our worlds as he slips his tongue into my mouth, sucks my top lip, tasting me, rediscovering me, eating my soul.

* * * *

In my room, I recline naked on my bed, arm flung over my head, confident in my new, vampire desirability in a way I never felt as a human, even while I keep my Glamour simmering low. I am soft and fuzzy with lust as I watch Sebastian undress. He looks even more like a Greek statue now, marble smoothed by centuries of dallying fingers. He leans his forearm on the ceiling beam above the end of my bed, rests his forehead, and studies me where I lounge. Filled with desire and daring I languidly raise one knee and tilt it, opening my secret centre to his view, knowing it blooms hotly red for him, broadcasting my wanting.

'So Rae, how about some of that Glamour I've heard so much about? You might be a Pretty One, but you're still quite a lump.' He growls his request, so it takes a millisecond to register, but when it does, my desire is doused as thoroughly as if he has thrown icy water over me. My knees clamp closed, and I almost spring upright dragging my sheet round me, but somehow I resist. A flood of fury protects my dignity, so instead I cross my legs neatly at the ankle, and I level my gaze at his flaccid member.

'Still have trouble getting it up?' I simper. 'Oh, poor Seb, can't blame alcohol now, can you, sweetie? Never mind, dear. Go and watch the film with the others. Don't worry about me, I'll sort myself out. You were never that good, even when you could rise to the occasion.' I wave him off with my little finger.

'We only came because your Pride kept hunting on our patch,' he hisses at me, before grabbing his clothes and stalking out of my room while pulling his top on. I manage to keep my catlike smirk in place as he leaves. Then I expect to dissolve, but I don't, the rose-tinted glasses are finally shattered, and after all these years I see him as Layla always has, an utterly contemptible dick. And a floppy one at that. His leaving shot niggles at me, though.

Layla

When Seb skulks back into the lounge, there is something missing from his demeanour, and I'm not the only one who notices. Abigail looks up as he comes in, and if I hadn't been scrutinising him from habitual distrust, I might have missed the almost imperceptible head shake. Abigail's nostrils flare for a second, but then she starts chatting innocuously again while she hops up for her seat next to Mattie and drapes herself across Seb where he has flung himself in the armchair. She is so sanguine I start to doubt I actually saw the tiny interaction between them and relax and enjoy Abigail's raucous tales again.

When Rae stalks into the room a few minutes later, silent fury hums around her. If you didn't know her, you might not see it. She was good at this haughty blank face as a human, and as a vampire her stone smooth expression is impenetrable. I know her though, and I see her fury in her rigid shoulders and tilted chin as clearly as if she was a cat metronoming her bad humour with the tip of her tail. However, there's also a slight flare of her nostril, a swish of her hair, and a certain extravagance in how she crosses one angry leg over the other as she takes the only vacant seat, which declares triumph as well. Whatever happened, she gave as good as she got. Someone's ego has been annihilated, and from the look on Seb's face, it was his.

I watch the politics play out as Meg keeps prattling on with Abigail obliviously; Brian is quiet, watching. David's hand is heavier on my leg, tensing as the mood shifts. Mattie leans forward and says something to Rae, quietly so I can't hear, but it makes her laugh out loud, and she relaxes back into her seat to chat. David's hand softens, and Brian rejoins the conversation with Abigail, Meg and Seb. It's been fun for a while tonight, having guests, hearing news, speaking to others outside our tiny Pride, but I know Rae well enough to know this party is over.

* * * *

I keep my ears open and as dawn breaks, I hear Rae slip out of her room and glide soundlessly downstairs. Only my vampire senses allow me to detect her soft movement, and only then because I've been primed for her. Equally quietly I slide out of David's sleeping embrace and follow her into the kitchen. Rae's standing over the boiling kettle, lost in thought, and jumps, squeaking with fear when I softly pull back a seat.

'What the fuck! Layla?' she gasps.

'Gossip. Now!' I demand. Rae nods towards the door, and I click it closed, while she takes my mug from the cupboard and makes us both an Earl Grey. I raise my brows at the deviation from our usual coffee, and Rae responds with her sphinx face, so I know I'm still not completely forgiven for the coffee with Meg incident. I swallow my irritation and wait for her to begin. She takes a huge sniff of the bergamot-infused steam, and then opens her big, peridot eyes and sighs.

'What a twat,' she exclaims, and I can't help a strangled squawk of mirth that I quickly smother with my hands. I've waited two decades to hear that. I grin and lean in over the table for her tale.

'Oh, my God. What a twat,' I echo her earlier exclamation after I hear what he said. Then I hoot when I hear her pinkie putdown. I don't care if he hears. I hope he does, and guesses what we are talking about.

'Was he always that bad?' Rae asks once we've gathered

ourselves.

'Often worse,' I tell her bluntly. If she's finally ready to hear, I'm more than happy to tell her. 'Nobody liked him. You idealised him, sat him on this unreachable pedestal that anyone else would have tumbled off, but him, he just climbed higher, until he singed his wings, like Icarus. Can you imagine anyone else we know just disappearing, and nobody caring enough to find out where they were?'

'I thought his friends did?'

'No, they tried his old number, got unobtainable, and didn't bother. I went to the office and was told they'd had a letter from his parents that he'd gone travelling, and that was it, no one liked him enough to look harder, no one else missed him, no one else thought he was reliable enough to even be concerned.' Rae looks at me levelly, nodding faintly.

'He killed his own parents,' she tells me softly, shame flooding her eyes. 'When they started asking to many questions.' She stares at me, beseeching me to judge her gently. I know my eyes are round with shock, I open my mouth and draw breath to ask how she could have still taken him to her bed, after she heard that, but I know her addiction to him was strong and destructive. My questions would not achieve anything other than a redrawing of her drawer bridge. Instead, I shrug and shake my head, and ask her a wide, less exacting question.

'Why the fuck were you ever with him?'

'I think I fell for his traits I envied. I was so desperate to please, and he did not give two hoots who he annoyed. I was so insecure, I hated how I looked, I wasn't like any of the girls on TV.'

'But that was a good thing,' I interject, surprised. 'That was your mystery and enigmatic air.'

'Nope, that was my crippling shyness, and deep sense of

worthlessness. He was utterly sure. Of himself, his beliefs, and his own self-worth. I put him on the pedestal, and demanded 'higher', I longed for a tiny fraction of that confidence. I didn't realise it then, but my family felt so unreachable, always busy, and always closer to each other than me. I think I felt that if I could get him to love me, maybe, I might feel I was good enough.'

I wipe a cranberry tear from her cheek, and sniff back my own. Ah, my beautiful friend, this is why I have wanted to scalp him of his copper curls, and gouge out his denim blue eyes for twenty years.

'Would you have?' I ask. Could he have been the one who held the key to Rae liking herself?

'No, probably not. If he'd decided he loved me back, I would have discovered his feet of clay. I would have realised he was only human, and transferred my impossible target to some unobtainable other.'

'But the way you let him speak to you,' I say sadly.

'He was just giving voice to what was in my head anyway. He saved me the effort from telling myself.'

'God, hon, I had no idea things were that bad. Why didn't you tell me?'

'I didn't recognise it for what it was myself, fully, until last night. Now it's like a switch flicked in my head, and I hold him in utter contempt.'

'Does this mean you've finished mooning over Guillaume too? Are you giving up inappropriate men at last?' I can hope, can't I? But her face closes up again, like a flower in the evening.

Rae

As the shadows lengthen into late afternoon, I take a mug of coffee out to the garden and sit on the bench with my knees folded up to my chin and the mug resting on them so I'm leaning forward, my nose level with the aromatic steam. I close my eyes and relax into the scent as the last rays of sunshine kiss my limbs. With a chirrup Babette hops up beside me, and I fondle her silky ears while she fills the air with her sing-songy joyous purr. Lost in this happy little world, I almost jump out of my skin when a male voice calls me through the kitchen window.

I turn and see Matthieu waving at me, I wave back reluctantly. I don't want my peaceful reverie broken, especially not by one of the visitors. He grins and turns from the window, and my heart sinks as two seconds later the front door opens and he appears in the doorway. With two bounds he's sitting on the other end bench, with Babette, big-eyed and flat-eared between us. He holds his massive hand out to her, and she sniffs at it suspiciously. To my amazement, instead of stalking off with a tail flick, like she does with most of the other vampires, she rubs her face against him and sets up purring again as his huge index finger finds the sweet spot under her chin, so her eyes glaze, then close, and her paws set up blissful kneading.

I sniff my cooling coffee to hide my irritation.

'What on earth are you doing?' asks Matthieu.

'Smelling my coffee,' I reply shortly.

'I can see that. Why?'

'Well, I can't drink it, can I?' I look at him, expecting derision, but see only genuine curiosity. I soften. 'I missed it; I missed the comfort and the ritual almost as much as actually drinking it, and then I realised that I could still have the ritual, and feeling the warmth while I smell it with my new senses is almost as good as drinking it used to be. Isn't there anything you really miss?'

'Oh yes, red wine. One glass, with dinner, savoured slowly.'

'Red wine would be a good one to smell, again so much of the pleasure is in ritual,' I start. His heavy brow drops over his eyes, and it takes me a moment to realise that it's his confusion that makes him look so ferocious. It still takes a few seconds for my heart to slow back to its usual rhythm. He's just so... big. I continue. 'You know, opening the bottle, letting the wine breathe, then the pouring, the swirling around the glass and smelling. All before you would taste, you can still do all these things, and your vampire nose would smell so many new levels of perfume within the wine.'

'You're right.' He grins. 'I never thought of it like that. I want to try it now. Where can I get some wine?'

'There's a good Merlot in the cupboard in the kitchen. The sellers left it for us—' Before I've finished my sentence, he's up and in the house. I can hear him clattering around. I consider calling to let him know where the bottle opener is, but it's in the utensils drawer, which is logical, and I can hear him opening drawers and cupboards without hesitation, so I'm confident he'll find it.

Within moments he's back outside with the bottle, the corkscrew and two stumpy glasses. I raise my eyebrows at the presumption.

'It's your idea, you'll join me, yes?' His grin falters slightly, and I find myself unable to disappoint him. I nod, and his face relights with happiness.

He settles himself on the bench; gives Babette an ear scratch to soothe her back into sublime sleep; and then reads the bottle's label. I'm about to get snotty and point out that he doesn't have much choice, and he'll have to make do with what we have, when I realise that this is part of the ritual for him.

Sighing happily, he squeaks the cork out, and then sets the bottle into the pebbles between his feet.

'You only drink animal blood, don't you?' he asks. I nod, again I expect derision, but he is already continuing his train of thought. 'I've heard that it's horrible, really bitter.'

'Actually, only herbivore blood is bitter. Pig blood is thick and muddy. Rat blood isn't too bad, though,' I explain.

'Rat blood?' He's startled.

'Yes, Babette and I hunt together.' I'm haughty.

'Doesn't it take ages to catch enough? There's not much blood in a rat, surely?'

'Oh yes, and my life is brimming over with other things I should be doing instead?'

'Hmmm,' he concedes my point. 'You could try mixing coffee with cow blood? See if it tastes better?' I shake my head.

'Nope. Our taste buds are transformed. I tried just holding coffee in my mouth, just a sip, to taste it and it tastes of mud, and ammonia and something else, I can't name that is plain awful. It might smell lovely but it tastes hideous.'

'Oh,' he deflates, and I'm touched that he thought he'd come up with something I'd enjoy, if slightly scornful that he thought I wouldn't have already tried it. He's quiet for a moment, and then perks back up as he remembers his wine and picks the bottle up. It's had time to breathe now, so he pours a glass, swirls it, sniffs it, nods and hands it to me. Then he pours himself some, and I know he won't be able to resist as soon as he buries his nose in his glass and his eyes close in bliss. As I watch, he tilts the glass, and dips just the tip of his tongue in, and then his head jolts back as if he's been scolded and he spits and blows raspberries and wipes his tongue on his sleeve, and I'm laughing and laughing, and then the rich warm peals of his mirth mix with mine.

'Well?' I ask when I can talk again.

'Urgh, I don't know, I never tasted anything that nasty as a human. Let me see, imagine petrol, and um, burnt rubber, and you know that high nasty smell when you burn curry powder. Gahch, that's nasty.'

We giggle some more and sit together on the bench in companionable silence, purring cat between us, swirling and smelling our wine. As it warms, the layers of fragrance unfurl, taking me down through berries, velvet, copper and rust, to earth and moss. It's easy to lose myself in the complex perfume, and many minutes pass before I glance up and see Matthieu's orange eyes sparkling as they gaze at me.

'Thank you,' he says, and his straightforward sincerity makes my stomach scrunch. I drop his gaze.

* * * *

As the twilight gentles into night, I collect a portion of blood from the nearest field of cows, rewarding my donor with baguette spread thickly with butter and salt. It's not just the hostel that benefit from the food orders Layla 'click and collects' from the nearest big supermarche. I remembered giving cows salt sandwiches on my childhood caravan holidays with my grandparents, and French cows have turned out to be just as partial.

When I walk into the kitchen with my jug of blood, Matthieu is waiting for me, bouncing with excitement.

'Look what I made,' he exclaims, holding up a mangled stainless steel tea-strainer. 'No, watch.' He laughs at my bemused expression. He slips the stem of a tall wine glass into the warped handle of the strainer, which leaves the basket section to sit on top of the bowl of the glass, but it's folded in half, so it not only doesn't cover the whole bowl, but it can hold coffee beans too. I realise what he's done, he's created a pomander so I can smell coffee while I sip blood, without it polluting it and making the blood undrinkable. I feel excitement quicken.

'Ooo,' I squeal. 'That might work, that just might work.' I'm already biting my tongue as I carefully pour my blood into the glass, making sure I don't allow any to touch the strainer and ruin the whole experiment. Being a vampire hasn't completely cured my clumsiness, and this needs concentration. I take a cautious sip. It doesn't taste like coffee, as such, but it's a lot better than plain cow blood.

Excitedly, the two of us settle to an evening of experimenting. We collect a variety of bloods and herbs, so we can try each with different aromas to see which works best. Personally, I don't feel red wine soaked into a cotton wool ball to keep it in the strainer goes too well with any of the bloods, but Matthieu likes it with sheep. Surprisingly, coriander, my favourite herb as a human doesn't really work with any of the bloods, and sage, my most hated herb, after cloves, is remarkably good with pig blood. Cloves are still awful. We can only keep the jar open for a moment before the caustic smell strips our nostrils.

Eventually, we get really creative and mix one crushed sage leaf, with a spiral of lemon peel and a small sprig of rosemary into the pomander, and microwaved some of the pig's blood, so it's piping hot, and then take a sip with the pomander of herbs on the side of the glass. It's actually delicious, not delicious like human blood, but really very drinkable. It's my turn to bounce with excitement as I hold the glass out to Matthieu. He takes a connoisseur's sip, smacks his lips and then grins in triumph, nodding.

'Thank you, Matthieu,' I whisper.

'Call me, Mattie,' he responds huskily, and I feel my tummy do that strange flippy thing again.

Layla

Rae and I are clearing up the mess she and Matthieu made playing with the blood and herb combinations when Abigail saunters into the kitchen and leans against the table, sniffing at the strange combination of scents still filling the air.

'What on earth were you lot up to in here?' she asks. 'You were making such a racket we could hardly hear our film.' Rae turns away and starts busily washing up the array of glasses we've used, and I don't know what comes over me, but I can't resist.

'We've been trying different things to make animal blood taste better,' I explain cheerfully. I know she sneers at us for only feeding on animals, I heard her speaking to Seb about it when she didn't know I was there. Before that I thought Rae's distrust of her was an overreaction. She's always so lovely face to face, so much fun to be around, but hearing what she really thought of our eating preferences voiced so dismissively has chilled my feelings towards her. I can guess that the way she has embraced being a monster, she is unlikely to have ever attempted to get anything other than blood past her lips since she turned.

'And tasting some of the food we miss most, we can't swallow it obviously, but there's still things we can suck or chew which taste phenomenal to vampires.' Rae's head swivels towards me, but Rae is behind Abigail, so she misses Rae's expression.

'Oh?' Abigail asks. 'Like what?' I can hardly contain my grin. Rae's still ogling me over her ladyship's shoulder; I choose to misinterpret her glare.

'Pickled onions are the best, ignore the smell, munch it all up, and then hold the pulp in your mouth, it's like exquisite little fireworks going off on your tongue,' I simper, still refusing to actually look into Abigail's face, instead I peer into the jar and select a big one, stabbing it with a talon. I don't know where these pickles came from, they aren't small, shop-bought silverskins. These are hefty, homemade whoppers, doused in pungent malt vinegar. I think they were here when we moved in, left by the previous owners after being assessed as too vicious for human taste buds. I confess when we first got here, before I knew better, the reason why I know better, I dipped a finger in the jar and licked it. It was as corrosive to my vampire mouth as battery acid.

Rae opens her mouth to interrupt, but then her sense of mischief gets the better to her, and she turns back to the dishes, watching our reflections in the darkened window, while her hands salvage several dregs of blood into one glass.

'Close your eyes, hold your nose, and open your mouth as wide as you can,' I instruct and Abigail sweetly obeys. I swallow my chortles.

Only a flying visit to a neighbouring cow got rid of the taste when I tried one, while also confirming that animals are not susceptible to the vampire virus even when you feed from them directly. I slip the onion into her mouth with vampire speed, before she can recoil from the smell. She bites down, and her eyes fly open, and instantly she turns into a ferocious leopard, spitting, and hissing, eyes blazing, hands clawing, she distorts, jaw distending and shoulders rising lopsidedly as the horror of the battery acid flavour brings on her Rage.

Having seen Rae's transformation, I don't find Abigail's very impressive. I can't help it; I howl and stamp with glee. I shouldn't gloat, but life is so boring here that all entertainment is gratefully appreciated. While I may think Rae is a bit paranoid about our visitors and I appreciate the break from the norm, I do not like Abigail anymore; she is a smug, sanctimonious cow, and her loss of face adds greatly to my delight.

Rae steps back from the sink, a glass of water in one hand, and a glass of thick cold blood in the other. She allows Abigail to hawk and spit into her washing up water, and then hands her the water to gargle with, the dank, chemical taste of tap water will be undetectable to a mouth scorched with vinegar and onion. After Abigail has made an unnecessary to do about rinsing, Rae silently passes her the blood, which she swigs and grimaces over. Wiping the corners of her mouth daintily, with thumb and pinky, Abigail forces an unconvincing bark of artificial laughter.

'Oh la,' she trills. 'How frightfully amusing.' Her ice blue gaze belies her words and she wiggles out of the kitchen, holding my gaze as she goes.

I look towards Rae, who has her back to me again as she empties the washing-up bowl and refills it. It takes me a moment to realise her shoulders are shaking, and once she is sure Abigail has gone, she peeks at me over her shoulder, eyes rimmed with scarlet mirth.

'That's just about the funniest thing I've ever seen,' she gasps between silent heaves of laughter.

Rae

I find myself spending a lot of time with Mattie over the next few days. After we showed our invention to the others, everyone wanted one. So I've ordered several extra stainless steel tea strainers, and Mattie has deftly twirled them into pomanders; but I have jealously guarded that first version he made just for me. We walk by the river together, and talk about our human lives, and ultimately our broken hearts. Mattie was also changed quite recently in vampire terms, turned by Abigail on his way home from his computer course at Poitiers University only ten years ago.

'I don't understand why you don't hate her?' I ask as we kick through the meadow grass, startling grasshoppers and ladybirds.

'I can't, she enthrals me,' he replies glumly. 'I know in my head I should disdain everything about her, her cruelty, her games, but I need to please her. When I do something that amuses her, she looks at me, and her eyes... it's like the sun shines just for me. In those moments, time slows and as she smiles, and that dimple, and I know if I could please her so she always saw me like that, everything would be... Everything would have... I can't find the words. There would be a reason to continue. That's the closest I can come to explaining.' Hearing my own feelings, so clumsily put, makes me cringe inside.

'What about you, though? All I know is that you love this Guillaume, and he does not love you in return,' he probes.

My heart sinks and soars, trying to find the words to

describe why I love him will be like trying to describe colours to someone who does not see. And yet, like the lovelorn everywhere and always, the chance to talk about him is too delicious to resist.

'He's different. He has this command. He can Command, that's his Gift, but he chooses not to use it, but aside from that, his bearing is noble, his shoulders... his eyes,' I pause, aware I'm gabbling and not really making sense. We've stopped in a small coppice of young silver birch, and Mattie sits, patting the mossy ground, his face dappled with golden light and dusty shadow.

'Ugh! Finding the words is so hard,' I grumble as I seat myself next to him. I take a deep breath, close my eyes and picture Guillaume, in his office, weary with pain and worry, beautiful in his concern. I try again. 'It's not just the way he looks, Layla tells me he's not that handsome, but to me he is. He has massive shoulders, and hands like boat hulls, but rather it is him I love. His essence, which is so strong, but so gentle, so tough, but so kind. The way he tries to balance out what is fair and right, and then carries the cost of it on himself,' I pause and sigh, aware I'm still not making much sense.

'Okay, here's an example. There's this little vampire, Annie, she was this tiny scrap of a thing, scared of everyone and everything when we met her, apart from him. I'd watch him seek her out in the gardens, so she could show him what she was doing, and he'd stand and listen, really paying attention to what she said. She bloomed under that attention, and the other vampires would snarl and hiss with jealousy, and pester for his attention, but he'd just hold up his hand for them to wait for Annie to finish. Even if she rushed through what she was saying because of their glares, he would ask her questions, get her to show him again, so she got her time with him before he'd turn to the demands of the rest of the Pride. He had no need to do that. She did not offer anything to the Pride that someone else couldn't do just as well, she was not popular, and befriending her did not win him political alliances or strength. He just saw a small girl who needed his care, so he gave it to her, even when his life was in turmoil.'

I am careful in my tale, even though I like Mattie a great deal; I remember Elaine's caution not to tell anyone that Georgette is a Healer. I know that she is always at risk of being stolen by others for her healing, and the well-being her blood offers. Even those of us who know what she is within the Pride do not share the knowledge with the other Pride members who are not so trusted. Any further explanation of why Annie was so weak, and why she's better now would lead to dangerous explanations.

'At least,' says Mattie, 'your love is someone you can admire. I still don't understand fully why you can't be together, you sound well matched?'

'He was changed by a Pretty One, and she made him do such dreadful things. He does not kill humans now, but she led him on orgies of blood and death, ripping entire families apart as they slept, and dancing around their houses as she burnt them to destroy the evidence. He was powerless against her lusts, and it took years and the help of other vampires for him to regain control of his own being.'

'But I thought you said he could Command?' Matthieu asks.

'He didn't discover that until later, and because he did not feed on human blood when he first changed, only on cows. She abandoned him when he first changed, she only returned for him when she knew he would be grateful for her company and explanations. By then the damage was done, so his Gifts were weak, so he could not Command her. She was ancient, and powerful, and without scruple.'

'Was?'

'I killed her.' Mattie's mouth forms an 'oh' of surprise, and I can't help grinning.

'No, it wasn't a jealous rage. They hadn't been lovers for decades. I think by the end he didn't even hate her anymore, just forbore her because he couldn't get rid of her while she complied with the Pride rules. She had powerful alliances both within and outside the Pride. She was the one who created all the New Ones, who were created at the same time as we were. The ones who infected us. Or rather she created a disobedient bitch, Suzannah, and she spread the virus to others, who spread it to others, who got us. It split the Pride, and one night there was a big battle, and well, I suffer from The Rage really badly, and so does Layla, so we won. I killed Patrice, and Suzannah. And I enjoyed it.'

'Is that why he won't love you back?'

Hearing him say it hurts, like it does every time anyone tells me Guillaume does not love me.

'No. He fought alongside us.' I nearly slip up and tell how he was almost fatally injured, but I remember in time and shut up quickly. 'He fears the control a Pretty One excerpts, he swore to himself that he would never be in another vampire's thrall again.'

'But you would never do that,' Mattie exclaims, and I beam at him.

'Thank you. I'm glad you can see that, but the fact is, I could. He would have to trust me never to choose to. He can't do that. And if I'm honest, if the situation was reversed, I don't think I could either.'

'Yes, you could. If it was him, you could.' I'm startled by how sure Mattie is, he hardly knows me. But, I realise, he's right.

Rae

It's evening on the sixth day of their visit. I'm torn; I don't like Abigail or Seb mixing with my Pride. Abigail is beguiling and fun, but I can feel the mischief in the sudden silences as I walk into rooms. Megan is especially concerning; her cloaked subversion is becoming more blatant and hostile. Whispers and giggles in earshot, replaced by smirks when I look her way, and tinkles of chiming laughter as I leave. Once the visitors depart, we will have to have it out, even Layla will not be able to make excuses for her anymore.

Brian, at least, has the decency to fade into the background in fear every time Megan riles me. She hangs onto Abigail's every word as she tells elaborate tales of hunting and partying while Brian worries at the edges of their group, torn between his loyalty to Meg, and his fears over what Abigail is enticing. David and Layla mingle, making the most of company, asking about other Prides, and other ways of being a Vampire. Seb avoids me indiscreetly, which saves me the trouble of snubbing him. Mattie does not like Seb either, and revels in his discomfort almost as much as I do.

Matthieu is warm and funny. He is the only reason I don't push harder to get rid of them. I hadn't realised how lonely I was, until I have his company. One evening he finds me out in the barn with Babette, and joins in our hunt. We laugh and play, and feed together, and afterwards he looks at me with his strange orange eyes sparkling with excitement.

'I didn't know it could be like this,' he murmurs. 'I didn't know we could live without killing humans.' He holds my gaze for long moments, and I feel unburdened with him, relieved by my opportunity to be completely honest. I don't need to protect Mattie's feelings; he's as in love with Abigail as I am with Guillaume. I don't need to pretend I'm feeling better than I am. I don't need to put a brave face on like I do with Layla to avoid the worried gazing and patting. There's none of her overly cheerful attempts to 'spend more time with me'. He is as refreshing and uncomplicated as a glass of cool water on a hot summer's day. And I miss water terribly, animal blood fills but doesn't refresh.

I lie on my bed wearing a pretty white cotton nightie I discovered on a village washing line late in the night, when Layla and I were prowling and poking around. I couldn't resist, it's so soft and beautifully embroidered, reminding me of the Victorian nighties my Granny showed me, the ones her mother had stitched by hand. Layla was startled by my theft, but I took it. I returned the next day and left a gift of wine and our garden produce on their doorstep, so I feel it was bartered rather than stolen. I still get a small fizz of naughty excitement whenever I slip it on, though.

I'm contemplating how to get Abigail to leave without creating an eternal enemy, while I play internet solitaire repetitively, not really paying enough attention to avoid silly mistakes but refusing to cheat with the undo move button. Holding out until I win fair and square. There's a gentle tapping on my door, and Mattie sticks his head around and grins at me, his face lighting up like the sun.

'Can I come in?'

'Of course.' I pat the bed next to me. He hasn't been into my room before, and I try to ignore the small firework display that starts in the pit of my stomach.

'Abigail has decided it's time to go tomorrow.' He sucks his lower lip and glances at me through his lashes. I feel like someone has chucked a bucket of icy water over me, and the fireworks *pffft* out in the deluge. 'I don't want to go,' he whispers so softly, even my vampire ears strain to hear him. My hand is curled in my lap like a wilted flower, and he covers it with his massive paw, gazing at me intently. 'Can I stay?'

'Have you spoken to Abigail about it?' I ask cautiously.

'Yes.' Matt sighs sadly. 'She looked surprised and asked why I was asking her, you were the one I need to ask. So, er, this is me asking.'

'Of course! Of course you can.' I bound onto my knees and fling my arms around his neck. 'Welcome to the Reeves Pride.' He squeezes me so tightly I think my ribs may snap, but I hug him back just as hard.

'We need to be honest with each other, though,' he says seriously, looking into my face intently. 'We both know that we love others, we mustn't expect too much of each other, mustn't feel like we have to lie to protect the other's feelings.'

'Absolutely,' I agree. 'Friends.'

'With benefits?' he asks softly, sliding his hands up to cup my jaw, thumb tracing my lower lip.

'Fuck, yeah,' I growl, and then he's kissing me, mouth covering mine, soft lips sucking, tongue snaking, as I melt, open, soften. He kisses and nips, licks and caresses. It's a very long time since I've been kissed properly, and I haven't really kissed as a vampire. I don't really count Seb. It is like my mouth is connected directly to those other lips, and I feel lost in his loving, eaten by his lust, soothed by his passion, fired by his wanting me.

Layla

She is as replete as a well fed kitten when she strolls into the lounge in the pink glow of dawn. I'm not tired, and rather than disturb David, I've come to sprawl on the sofa and watch Judge Rinder online. I love watching him slicing greedy people to the quick with icy one-liners.

'Well?' I ask. I saw Matt slip silently into her room last night, and although they might have been silent, her bed told tales on them. I'm surprised to see her up and about, and watch her carefully. This is the first time she's fucked properly as a vampire, and beneath the pearlescent glow of satisfaction, she is glittery with agitation and the need to talk. 'Isn't vampire sex the best thing ever?'

'Yeah.' She smiles, as she pushes my feet over, and folds herself up at the other end of the sofa, resting her chin on her knees and tucking her feet into her stolen nightie. 'Only...'

'What?' I'm incredulous. Surely even Rae can't find anything to complain about, vampire strength, stamina, size, they all make human fumblings pale into insignificance in comparison.

'Don't you miss the, I don't know, the imperfections?' she asks quietly. I shake my head in bemusement. 'You know, that nakedness where their head joins their neck? The sigh caught between the soar of the shoulder blades? The hope hammocked between knobbled knuckle bones?' Her gaze is soft, unfocused, and she pulls at her toes as she speaks.

'You're the one who walked away from a steamy slow dance because you looked up and noticed the man had uneven nostrils,' I counter. 'You have a hatred of ugly feet and would not even talk to a man whose fingernails were too long. You hate imperfections.'

'Ummm, you're right.' She nods, musing. 'Imperfections is the wrong word. Vulnerabilities, that's what I mean.' And I instantly understand her. Damn her for finding the shadow in our new world so quickly, and putting her finger on it so precisely.

'Oh, I know,' I murmur. 'Like the ticklish spot that makes them wriggle and giggle like a little boy.' Her eyes light up and she nods.

'Yes, yes, like their scent, when they've worked hard, but are clean, that richness.'

'Like the moles in funny places.' Our words race and intermingle, bubbling with giggles.

'And that point on their tummy, just above the hip bone, where you can make the muscle flutter and jump.'

'Like that funny little dent James has got, at the top of his arse crack.' For a second, we laugh, until the impact of what I've said hits us both. Then the silence is like a vacuum. I can't be sure if the words just slipped out, or if I let them out on purpose, because she was ruining everything, finding the cracks when I have so little now. She looks straight at me for a long moment, and blinks her lioness eyes. I see her make the decision to be calm, to let bygones be bygones. And I know, in that instant, she is wrong, we vampires do still show our vulnerabilities, as much as we ever did as humans. You just have to look closer to see them.

'When did you sleep with him?' I'm almost insulted by her question, but can't really blame her for it.

'Before you met him. We were both on a heavy night out with work, and, well, the vodka made the decisions that night. It never happened again. I was never sure if he told you or not.'

'No. He didn't. Neither did you.'

'When would I? When you asked me to be Maid of Honour? On your Hen night? Anyway, it wasn't really my place, once you were together.' She's quiet for long seconds, pulling her lower lip while she thinks, then she forces her face into a brittle smile.

'Well, it doesn't matter now anyway, does it?'

But it's a rhetorical question, and not one I'll answer. Because I have a nasty feeling that maybe it does.

Chapter Five

Rae

I don't really notice Layla leave the room, I'm too busy reassessing my memories of my marriage refracted through this new nugget of information. James's face lighting up whenever Layla's name was mentioned, even as his enthusiasm for me waned with time and familiarity. His consideration to our friend had delighted me, been a factor in me staying too long. All those kindnesses, and jokes take on a new aspect now. Even with this new information though, there is no change in my memory of how Layla treated James, he was just a charming chump she could tease. She was fond of him, but she was not attracted to him.

The tick of the door opening startles me from my ponderings and I look up expecting to see Layla, here to apologise for her bombshell and to make things right between us. Or Matt, coming to see where I've disappeared to. Instead, it's Abigail sauntering across the room, a look of pious concern on her face. I think she's going to warn me off Mattie, despite the way she brushed him off. I'm preparing to fight my corner as she fixes me with her wide blue gaze.

'Rae, may I speak to you for a moment? I'm glad to catch

you alone. There's something you need to know,' she says, voice cloying with faux sincerity. My heart sinks, because I know that whatever comes next she's been savouring the anticipation of telling me. This is why she was dallying.

'What?' I ask, my heart pounding, my brain rushing around trying to work out what she has over me.

'I don't like to be a tittle tattle, darling, and I really have struggled with myself over whether I should tell you at all, but, well, I would want to know if I was you.'

My heart is so loud in my ears I can hardly hear her simper. I have a sudden terror that she is about to show me a photo of Guillaume with someone else; that's the only thing my brain can come up with that would upset me enough for this show of fake solidarity.

'I said to Seb, I said, it's her Pride, darling, she needs to know. But you all seemed so happy, and I can tell you've got no idea, and I just feel so awful that is me who has to tell you.'

The greedy way her avid gaze is guzzling up my distress makes a lie of her words. Not Guillaume then. So what? I look at her imploringly, too freaked out to speak. The whole situation has completely sideswiped me.

Five minutes ago, I was trying to make sense of the news that my best friend had slept with my husband, before I even knew him. Now a dangerous vampire is delighting in dragging out the delivery of news about my Pride, bad news. I am trying to save face by seeming unfazed, but inside I am spinning. I feel as if my world is being shaken like a snow globe, all the contents of my life flying around me in a swirling flurry. Who knows where they'll settle.

'You need to see these.' Abigail has pulled an Apple Tablet out of her bag, and flicks quickly through to the pictures she wants. They are dark, blurred, and fuzzy, but it only takes a second for my eyes to find Layla's face in shadows. Heavily made up in gothic disguise, half hidden by a bad black wig, and wearing her TOWIE veneers, it is still obviously her. I can't see David's face, but the size of the figure next to her means it must be him. Abigail flicks through a few more pictures. Layla is never in the foreground, she is always merging with the shadows, an unnoticed extra in other people's group souvenirs of nights out, but she's there.

I can't believe it. I can't believe they have been so stupid. A sobbing breath rips through me as the consequences of these pictures slams my heart. I look up at Abigail, as she pats my hand, and I see something that may actually be genuine sympathy in her eyes.

'Such responsibility, I know. That's why I almost didn't tell you. But they can't continue just mingling like that. The Council will find out.'

'Thank you, Abigail. I don't know how... I–I can't bear to think what might have happened if you hadn't shown me. I can't thank you enough.' My instincts tell me that she wants power over me. So I'll give it to her willingly, I will make sure she has no need to involve the High Council. I will be her supplicant. So I gush on.

'What do I do now, though? Who else will see them? Oh Layla, you have betrayed us all.' That last bit was true, and I am furious with her. So furious I fear the Rage will sweep through me at first sight of her. I can already feel the bones in my face tingling with it. 'What shall I do?' I implore Abigail, clutching her hands and letting her see how desperate I feel.

'Only I know.' Abigail is enjoying her magnanimous role. 'Not even Matthieu or Sebastian have actually seen the pictures, and I won't show them. This will be our little secret.' She pats my hand and squints up at me earnestly. 'You can sort it out, lovey. It can all go away, and no one will be any the wiser, yes darling? Just tell her not to do it again.'

'How, though? How did you find them? If you could, then the High Council's spies can.' My thoughts have turned to Darius and Agata, the Council's spies who had arrived at Guillaume's Farm and not left until they had the damning evidence that put all our lives at risk from the High Council. The basic rules of being part of the vampire community are simple. You do not kill your own kind; or at least not without permission from the High Council. It's a responsibility that is only granted to Pride Leaders, and only when the vampire kind are put at risk. The second rule is the one that brings the death penalty from your leader—you do not allow humans to know we exist, or even begin to suspect it. We need them to believe we are only murky figures of myth and legend.

'That nightclub is in my territory, sweetie. They hunted that area so often, and were so clumsy with tidying up after themselves I couldn't help but notice they were there. They came the same time every month, like clockwork. I needed to check on who these new vampires were. What with them having no respect for another's patch, you know?' She smiles like a Siamese cat who has found the canary with its cage unlocked.

'I followed her one night, to the club, and saw what she was up to. She wasn't being terribly discrete, so I thought I'd better check social media, just in case anyone had seen anything. I came across the photo. I was going to come and see you anyway, have a little chat about the hunting, but then I saw these, and well, I knew I had to come. I didn't want to just spring it on you, though. I wanted to get the lie of the land a bit first.' She blinks at me, savouring my discomfort and confusion.

'But I told them...' I start. I know no explanation will be good enough, though. Having seen what Megan had done the first time we went hunting, I should not have shirked my responsibility. I might have been trying to avoid a big full scale row, hoping to avoid the violence that simmered underneath all my dealings with Megan, but that will not excuse what has happened on Abigail's territory. Instead, I've just caused bigger, more dangerous problems. Now the blood shed could end up being my best friend's, instead.

Stupid cow. Stupid, stupid, selfish cow. Now we are all in danger because she was a bit bored and wanted to go dancing, and they were too lazy to look for new places to hunt. Now I know what she's been doing, it's my responsibility to contact the High Council, seek the relevant permissions, and then kill the two of them. A Council witness will need to be here to confirm their deaths. Megan at least had the sense not to go partying with humans, she only ate them.

If I don't report this to the High Council and we are found out, then Guillaume would be tasked with killing us all, since he accepted ultimate responsibility for us at our trial over the Farm Pride battle.

'I've spent a bit of time here, and I can see there's no malice, just inexperience. I was half expecting it to be clumsy territories grab, but I can see it's just stupidity.' She smirks, and I can't argue with her condemnation. 'Megan is running rings round you all, isn't she?' Abigail peers at me through her wispy fringe. 'Well, I'm so glad that's all sorted. We'll be off soon, and I'll take Meg with me, because, frankly, if you can't control Layla who is your best friend, well, she's going to be beyond your ability to manage.' Abigail smiles sanctimoniously. Her insults grate, but again I have to concede she's right. 'We are a bigger Pride and we hunt often. She'll be stimulated, and won't go looking for trouble. And if she does, well, I have no qualms in, ah, resolving the situation. I've been around longer than you, dear. I'm more experienced, and, I think, not so tender-hearted.'

Her smugness galls, but I can't deny the truth of it. If my best friend in the world, pre- and post-vampire infection, who was there when the High Council gave us one last chance to live within the rules, will not respect me, then Megan certainly won't. The Council was explicit about what happened if you chose to live outside their community rules; the community turns on you, and you die. They've spent centuries honing their systems, and there is too much to lose for a sloppy New One to put everyone's safety at risk.

The fizzing in my jaw becomes a dull ache, and my fingers grind with pain as they start to stretch. I struggle to hold onto my temper, but the surprised fear in Abigail's eyes shows that I'm not doing such a good job of it.

'Ah, I can see you're upset. We'll be off, and leave you to get your house in order.' Abigail has manoeuvred us so she is closer to the door, and now she slides hurriedly towards it.

'Abigail,' I say, and she stops and looks at me cautiously. 'Thank you for this. I promise you I won't waste this chance.' I am sincere, and I hope so badly that my gratitude will be enough for her. 'If I can ever do anything for you, to thank you properly, just ask.' It doesn't hurt to make sure she knows that I know I owe her, to make my debt explicit. For a moment, I think she's going to say something as she studies me assiduously, but then she smiles benignly at me, and leaves the room.

I wish I could trust her. I wish I could believe she means what she says, but anxiety has settled into my stomach like a great cold stone freezing any hope. I stand in the lounge doorway, hearing their fluted goodbyes as finally Lady Abigail and her entourage piss off. They make a big rigmarole of leaving, or at least Abigail does. I'm delighted Megan has decided to go with them, but Brian, it appears, is not so pleased to be joining the new pride. The only way I know this is by the way he's merging with the paintwork in the hallway periodically as they linger there over goodbyes. He doesn't look at me, and I'm too busy fighting back the Rage to spare him any energy. At last, they leave, and I stalk back into the lounge slamming the door behind me.

Mattie sticks his head in, takes one look at me, and freezes. I'm standing by the fireplace, and I know the Rage is rising, despite my attempts to control it. I'm so tall now that I can rest my elbow on the mantelpiece without lifting my shoulder. I know my face must have descended, and my teeth extended, but I can't bear to check in the mirror.

When we first arrived at the cottage, I told Brian to remove the mantel mirror from above the fireplace in the lounge. I hated catching sight of us all as we reclined talking and laughing, and feeling homely by the fire of a winter's evening. Because just as I relaxed, reflected back to me would be a cameo of monsters, smooth and freakish in the firelight. When Megan arrived, she insisted on returning it though, and now I keep my eyes lowered so I don't have to watch the nightmarish slide of my features.

'Tell Layla to come here,' I tell Mattie. Before he can slip away again, he nods, massive forehead drawing down over his eyes, so he looks even more like an obsidian gargoyle. He doesn't question me, and a couple of minutes later, Layla pops her head around the door.

'What's up?' She chirps. 'Mattie said you looked cross. And you do. Oh! You really do. What did Abigail do?'

'It's not Abigail. It's you. I know.' I watch guilt flit over her features, a sagging of the eyebrows, a flinch at the corners of her mouth.

'Rae, I...' she appeals to me. I look back at her, no rescue in my glance, no understanding. 'I was bored, I just wanted to dance.'

'So put a fucking CD on, and dance in kitchen, dance in garden. Dance on the roof for all I fucking care. There are photos of you, on Facebook. If Abigail can find them, so can the Council. We know several busybodies who will be all too delighted to point them out. We had one last chance, Layla. One. It hasn't even been a year.'

'I'm sorry. I just wanted to play. You're so serious all the time, and then you sent us on the hunts, and they fired me up. I wanted more.'

'Well, why didn't you hunt, then? We wouldn't have this problem...'

'Have you listened to yourself?' Layla's voice has curdled with disgust. 'I'm in trouble because I didn't kill anyone, because I didn't want to watch Megan hunting and killing people, and you couldn't manage your own feelings enough to do *your* job. But dancing, dancing is the end of the world? You disgust me,' she snarls and storms out of the room, leaving me stymied, heart pounding with leftover adrenaline.

'You know that isn't what I mean,' I argue with empty air. 'I just don't want to have to kill you.'

Rae

The next few days are awkward, I can't look at Layla, and she is ostentatiously ignoring me. David looks like a kicked puppy torn between us. He knows I'm right, and I can see him start to apologise several times, but each time his loyalty to Layla wins out, and I like him for that, even though it could spell his death penalty.

I spend my time with Mattie as much as I can. He sucks his teeth when I ask him if we can trust Abigail and shrugs, I can see his friendship with me battling with his loyalty to her Ladyship, and I don't like it. So we steer clear of that topic, because ultimately, whether or not Abigail shows the photos to the Council will depend on a whim, which side of bed she got out of, what she can trade for the information. Asking Mattie to predict isn't fair, and the fact he can't, tells me everything I really need to know.

We spend our time in bed losing ourselves in the incredible sensations that are vampire sex. Hours are lost to having the inside of my elbow stroked, the back of my knee kissed, the inside of my wrist nibbled. If my worries start to distract me, I just turn up my Glamour, and allow the whirlwind of Need to sweep us up and lash us frantically against the shores of desire until we are spent and exhausted. There is no shame afterwards with Mattie, not like there was with Brian. Instead, we share a childish glee, and cry again and again like we have just ridden a rollercoaster.

I am straddling his lap, his heavy erection glistening against his stomach while his tongue flicks my nipples, and his thumb strokes me to a throbbing climax. I attempt to slide myself down his cock, desperate to be filled as the spasms of orgasm ebb away and I want more, from the depths of me, but he stops me.

'Wait, let me bite you as I enter you, then I can feel what it feels like for you, when I fuck you,' he growls, holding my hips back, even as his cock jumps in anticipation.

'What?' What he's suggesting sounds much too intimate, like letting a man watch you masturbate for real, not for show. 'No.' I'm going off steam now, and he can feel the tension leave my body.

'Okay, okay, you bite me, it's good, I promise. So intense.' He's looking up into my eyes now, sunstone eyes sparkling and earnest. A big warm grin splits his face and he kisses my worries away. 'It's sexy, girl, I promise,' he whispers into my neck, finding my sweet spots to get me aroused again. I giggle and wriggle, and as he holds me so the tip of him is stretching the mouth of me, he tilts his head to one side, and slices quickly with his fingernail, so a small spurt of blood pools quickly in his clavicle.

Trusting him, I lean into him and drink, so my head is filled with the sensation of the hot silken cushions of my cunt sliding down the boiling, rigid flesh of his cock, while my body is filled with the feelings of solid fullness, utter, aching repleteness as he plunges up to meet me. I am lost in the dual sensations, his and mine, in a whirlwind of colours and images, fireworks and blooming roses, until like a bucket of icy water, my mind is filled with an image of Lady Abigail's face, coquettish and minxy, open-lipped and ready.

I pull back, spitting out his blood, and jerking away from his dick, which is left spasming and pumping his cum like glistening pomegranate seeds over his stomach.

'What the fuck?' he asks, as I grab my dressing gown, fling it on and flounce out of the room. I lock myself into the bathroom, and try to calm down. As I wash him from me, and swill my mouth with water, I ask myself why I'm so upset. I know he is in love with her. I'm not in love with him, why am I jealous? I accept that I've overreacted a bit but decide that the blood-sharing is too intimate an act to carry out with someone you're not in love with. I don't need my nose rubbing in the fact that he thinks of her as he cums. I opt to shut the whole experience away, and just don't think about it anymore.

When I go back into my room, Mattie is lying on top of my bed wearing a T-shirt and shorts, looking worried. I perch on the armchair by the pretty cast-iron fireplace, and tell him briefly what happened. He looks sad, and guilty, and I reassure him that I'm not angry. I don't blame him, I understand. I move back to his arms while we agree we won't try that again.

Layla

I am so angry with Rae. She is being completely unreasonable and a sanctimonious cow. As if any of the Council are going to stumble across my photo on Facebook. If they were even aware of fun, we wouldn't be in this predicament. And David can get over his whole eye rolling, silent apology bollocks too. I know he didn't really want to go, but he was there, he went too. If she hadn't made me go to supervise the hunt, it wouldn't have even happened. If she had done her duties as Pride Leader, instead of fobbing them off onto me.

I'm festering in the kitchen, scrubbing the grout between the kitchen tiles when Rae walks in, sees I'm there and wheels round to stalk straight back out again. Well, I'm not having it anymore; it's been almost a week that she's refused to speak to me for.

'Let it go, Rae, no one from the Council is going to see the photos. Abigail understands the need for fun, even if you don't, and we wore disguises, no one will even realise it was us.'

'Layla—' Rae heaves a deep breath, squares her shoulders and starts to count points off on her fingers. 'One, Abigail recognised you. You are a vampire, you do not look human anymore, I don't know what the hell you put on your face, but it was not a good disguise.'

I'm a bit offended by this, I'd ordered chunky permanent markers in black and purple and black wigs from Amazon specially because make-up does not stay on vampire skin. I'd scribbled on our faces until we looked like emos, along with the black wigs swept forward over our faces, and black hoodies pulled low; I think it was an excellent disguise. If the markers weren't permanent on vampire flesh, and ran as the evening wore on, well, that just added to the effect.

'Two, Abigail's idea of fun is twisted. This week it's turning up at a stranger's home, high on blood and causing mayhem, next week it could all too easily be watching the shit hit the fan as the High Council swoops. You hunted in her territory, repeatedly and messily. You pissed her off.'

'Don't be stupid, Rae, that's not going to happen. I just wanted to dance. I didn't want to hunt. I didn't want to watch the hunt. I just wanted to stand next to the speakers and feel the beat through my body and lose myself in the rhythm. Abigail understands that, she's a party girl.'

'Layla, even Mattie, who is completely in love with her Ladyship will not answer me when I ask him if she is likely to tell.'

'Really? Mattie's in love with Abigail? I hadn't realised. Why are you two at it, then? Is this why you're in such a bad mood?'

'Urgh! Oh my God! Layla, I don't care about Mattie, we're having fun, we both love other people, vampires, whatever. We don't care about that. I am devastated because you and David have put everything we have at risk.'

'Are you still in love with Guillaume? Really? Come on, Rae, you've got to let that go. Surely you are not going to lug this heartbreak around with you for twenty years like you did with Seb?' I see her flinch at this barb, but if we've having an all cards on the table row, she needs to hear this.

'Which is why I don't talk to you about it,' she snarls. Ouch, that smarts. The implication that I'm not a good friend rankles.

'Rae, I listened to you drone on about Seb for years, even after you married poor James, the moment you had a drink, out he came, in all his misremembered glory. I don't know why you're implying otherwise.'

'I didn't drink for fifteen years, and you lived an hour and a half's drive away. I saw you once, maybe twice a year, and that Dickhead you were married to hogged all the oxygen anytime we were in the same room.'

'We didn't come to see you because you were so bloody boring, just like you are now.' I'm yelling now, I know I'm saying things I'll regret, but I'm so cross with her, and her sanctimonious bloody attitude. 'Oh! Silly me. I've just realised what this is all really about. One minute I'm telling you I slept with your husband, the next you're totally overreacting to me going out dancing. Instead of killing people...'

'Layla, for the last time, I am not cross because you went to have some fun without me, or because you were a bit rebellious and broke a rule, like some naughty school girl up to a prank. I'm not upset because you shagged my ex-husband once, before I even knew him. Although I am disappointed you didn't tell me sooner. I am devastated because you have been seen on the internet around humans.' Rae holds my gaze unflinchingly. 'When the High Council gave us one final chance, they made it clear that the smallest of infractions will lead to the death penalty. I am the leader of this Pride. I should have phoned the High Council and obtained permission to kill you both already. I should just be waiting for their witness to arrive.'

Her voice is an icy contrast to my shouting, and sends the hairs up on the back of my neck as what she is saying sinks in. 'And if you don't?'

'Guillaume will have to take us both, and David, to the Council so they can witness him kill us all.'

While we have been arguing, Mattie and David have entered the kitchen behind us, and are watching us in horror.

'It's not all about you, Layla. It's not all about you being a bit bored, because your life is bloody perfect now you've found Mr Right. You've forced me into an impossible position. Murder my best friend, or force the man I love to murder us both. So fuck you and your dancing, fuck you and your fun. Excuse me if I'm just not in the mood to listen to your brattish whining about being bored. I'm busy trying to work out how to avoid killing you both.'

Chapter Six

Rae

So, no one's speaking to me this morning. I may have been a little too honest for everyone's taste, I'll admit. I go down to the river and float, resolutely naked in the deep pool. I am confident no one other than Matt will seek me out, and when he does, I don't want to talk. Eventually, I get bored of floating and climb up onto the bank. I choose a sun-drenched spot, golden with buttercups and settle myself for a snooze. I didn't sleep last night, too riddled with fury at Layla, and unable to relax without Matthieu beside me.

The sun strokes warm kisses over my limbs, while the softest breeze sways the flower petals against me. It takes me a moment to realise there is another touch there, and I open my eyes lazily to be treated to Mattie's naughty grin.

'I'm sorry I didn't come up last night, I just needed time to think...'

'Shhh, it doesn't matter.' I push him backwards, slide his T-shirt upwards, my eyes asking the question as my hands reach his shoulders. His slight sitting up, so I can slip the bunched fabric over his head is my reply. I leave the cotton tangled around his elbows and pin his arms above his head. His pupils are dilated with delight. I kiss and nibble his lips, his neck, his earlobes. He groans happily as I bury my mouth into the crook of his neck and suck and bite a love bite that heals faster than I make it.

I trace a line with my tongue down to his belly button, detouring to nibble each nipple softly with lip-clad teeth. With the heavy weight of my bust testing the bulge in his trousers, I look up at his lust-plumped face. Holding his gaze, I wriggle lower, unzip his jeans, pop open the straining button, and slip his jeans and boxers down over his hips. Lifting his hips to allow me to undress him bumps the burning velvet head of his cock against my soft, accommodating smile, making him groan his submission.

For an instant, I part my lips and allow the tip of my tongue to flit over him, just long enough to lap up a ruby seed of desire. He shudders all down his body, and his cock flexes and bounces, balls tightening and bracing against my breasts that hang sweetly against them. Head back, hands gripping the grasses above his head, he arches before me.

'Not yet,' I whisper. 'Not yet.' I slide myself up his body, to kiss his mouth, welcoming in his hungry tongue, as I lean on my elbows and use my feet to hook his jeans and pants and pull them further down, until he can take over with his own feet, and kick them off completely. I carefully keep my weight on my knees, while his cock has a chance to calm. At first, he bucks and rises towards me, hot with the lust I've inspired; eager to chase his fulfilment. I remain out of reach, and demand more from him with my mouth, deepening the kiss further.

He reaches up, strokes my nipples, and so it's my turn to gasp. He pulls me closer so he can nip and bruise my neck, delicious rivers of delight running from his teeth to my core. I lie down his length, legs closed while he wraps his great arms around me, and pulls me up, so his mouth can reach my nipple, and the burning tip of his cock is directly under the throbbing nub of my clitoris. Then I'm lost as he sucks and licks, teases and flicks each nipple in turn, while he lightly claws up my back from buttocks to my shoulders; I arch and moan and wriggle, and finally, hotly, come.

I open my legs then, slide him inside me. He grabs my hips, pulls me down tight, rises into me, filling me, completing me. Fireworks fill my brain, roses bud, bloom and lose their petals. I sob my orgasm while he bucks into me, groaning and calling, until it's just the ebbs, and I am squeezing him tight within me and he's still arching with each squeeze, panting and babbling, until finally he begs no more, and I laugh and let him slide out of me.

I lie besides him for a while, stroking his forehead as his breathing softens and deepens. Once he is fast asleep, I quickly get bored. I'm not at all sleepy, my brain feels like it's fizzling at a thousand miles an hour. I feel content and relaxed; I couldn't give a shit about Layla right now, fuck her. She can sort it all out herself. I sit in the river and let its cold fingers soothe and clean my burning blood pearled flesh.

Once I am clean, I decide I am going to return to the house for my book. I pull on my sundress and knickers, and tootle back up to the cottage. The awful atmosphere inside soon ruins my mood though, and I crash around making just myself a coffee. I grab my book and stalk back outside in the hope of the fresh air shifting my awful mood. I drag one of the cushioned teak sunloungers to the back of the garden behind the little orchard. I hoped the trees will act as a screen between me and the filthy looks coming from the lounge.

As I get myself settled, curved on my side with my towel serving as a pillow, Babette trots over, chirruping her happy greeting and leaps up beside me. She settles into the curve my legs make, purring happily as I rub her ears. At least, I still have two friends. I ignore the memory of Matt trying to talk to me before I seduced him. I don't mean to drop off, but the warmth of the late morning sun, gentled by the breeze that dances and tickles between the trees and over my bare skin soothes me, and soon Babette and I are fast asleep curled up together.

Layla

I am in a huff, ignoring Rae and trying to read Anne Tyler's newest on my Kindle when a creepy little man waltzes into our lounge. We don't keep our back door locked because, quite frankly, a household of four vampires in rural France doesn't need to. One minute David and I are happily minding our own business, and then all of a sudden there's a strange figure wriggling and jiggling with delight in the doorway. He's friendly at first, asking about what David is watching on the TV, then appearing utterly fascinated that the tiny Kindle could hold so many books. I almost show him it's a Kindle Fire, my chatty show-off nature wants to astound him with everything it can do, but Rae's voice in my head whispers caution and flashes the image of him in our doorway, uninvited, gleeful.

Despite his invasion of our home and Rae's contagious concerns, I feel remarkably accepting of his presence. My compliance triggers a distant alarm bell in the back of my mind, some smothered instinct whispering a warning.

'So, Sir, how can we help you?' David asks, and I'm glad he's taken the lead. Our visitor ignores him though, pointing to one of the novels on my reading list and calling my attention to it. When I look to see what he's tapping, worried his crusty nails might damage my screen, he grabs my throat, latching on and tearing with his razor teeth, gulping and sucking.

For a frozen moment, everything stands still, but then he has his bleeding wrist in my mouth. His blood tastes fusty and dank, and fills my mind with a million broken fragments of thought. In an instant, he has total control of me, and I slump back in my seat, glazed and bewildered.

I can only watch David shout, watch him dive across the room at the invader, watch how, despite his greater strength, he is quickly torn, drunk and fed too, crumpling onto the sofa next to me. My heart thunders with terror as I see my gentle giant slump, mouth sagging, eyes unfocused.

Alerted by our shouts, Mattie bursts into the lounge, only to be accosted from behind while he stands dazed by the sight of David and I sprawled on the sofa. He's bitten and fed in the same way we were, so he too becomes a stunned doll, lolling in the armchair.

Our decrepit attacker jiggles and dances, giggling and pointing, whooping with glee. He totters amongst us, poking and looking and snickering to himself. He stops in front of me and grubs at my breasts a while, leering into my face while I feel his blood thrumming through my veins, controlling me, subduing me.

'Where's the big one?' he asks. 'The one with all the hair and the tits? Proper woman that one, heh heh heh.' I don't want to answer him, and I struggle against his control, but despite myself my hand points towards the garden. 'Hee hee hee. Lovely, lovely.' He trots out of the room and out of the front door. Once he isn't in the house anymore, I expect his control to falter, but instead I am forced to my feet and drawn to the window, the two men dragged to my side. We are pinned, watching while his stooped and scuttling figure skitters across the lawn towards Rae. Rae, who lies innocently sleeping in the early afternoon sunshine.

Appalled, we stare in chained silence as he jigs around her, but as she awakens, I feel his control loosen minutely. I thank the heavens I trusted my instincts and didn't show him everything my Kindle could do. I'm still clutching it; unaware of its full capacity he didn't know enough to force me to drop it. Now I flick quickly to Facebook, hardly looking at what I'm doing, filling my mind with horror at what's happening to Rae, as the creature tears her top open and pulls at her breasts. Glancing at my screen only to confirm I have my messenger window opened, I tap Annie's picture, reopening a conversation about handbags from the previous week. 'HELP' I type now. Obediently, I look back out of the window as I feel our attacker's attention return to us and re-establish control. I keep my eyes glued to his attack on Rae until her memories draw his attention again, then I flick my gaze to the screen, and swallow the relief that floods me when I see Annie's reply.

'WHAT??????'

'Attack.' I type and click send just as his mind returns to me and starts snooping around at what holds my interest away from him. I stare stubbornly at my clenched fists, covering my actions with a surge of Rage against his control. Distracting him with the strength of my fury at what he is forcing me to witness, while my tablet drops unheeded to the floor. Hoping against hope that he won't notice it, won't notice what I've done, while I struggle against his command to watch.

Frozen at the window and unable to resist the invisible force that keeps my face turned towards the attack, I cannot respond when the phone rings. Once, twice, three times, it peals ten insistent chimes before cutting off and restarting. I ignore it, refusing to allow myself to wonder if it's the Pride responding to my plea. Instead, I fill my mind with what he's doing, and my horror, until I can feel his delight at my grief.

Rae

I become aware of a dark shape blotting out the sun which has been shining on my eyelids. At first, I think it's Mattie back from the river, and decide to ignore him. My head feels swimmy with sleep and stuffed with cotton wool, and the thought of opening my eyes and having a deep and meaningful is beyond me. There was something wrong with the scent though, vampires don't smell, but his arrival has brought the scent of dank caves and musty corners. I wonder vaguely if his clothes need washing, but the breathing is wrong too. Mattie doesn't breathe through his mouth like a child concentrating on doing something cruel in secret.

I struggle to open my eyes, it feels like they are glued closed. I manage to force them open a tiny crack and I'm able to see the outline of a figure bent over me. It definitely isn't Mattie, and it wasn't Layla or David either. My brain is trying to scream to my body. I should have been flooding with adrenaline, my heart pounding, so I can leap to my feet and run for my life, but I'm floppy and leaden. Babette is hissing and spitting in an arch of fury and terror by my feet.

The figure turns his attention away from watching my face, and looks towards my cat. The instant he looks away from me, I'm able to force my eyes open wider so I can see a shambolic figure bending over me. His skin is the colour and texture of Stilton cheese, with crusty grey warts caking his nose, cheeks and chin. His mouth hangs slightly open, and his liverish tongue pokes at the spittle crusted in the corners of his cracked bluish lips. He is wheezing directly into my face, his breath icy and smelling like the inside of a crypt.

He makes a sudden snatch at Babette with nightmarishly long gnarled fingers. They seemed to have an extra bulbous knuckle each and are tipped with long yellowed scythes. The little cat flattens herself, leaps off the lounger and streaks off through the orchard. He chuckles like the rustling of dry leaves and turns his empty eyes back up to my face. They are the colour of curdled milk, and utterly soulless.

'I'll have her later,' he mutters, as much to himself as to me.

He sees me staring at him and chuckles again, blasting me with his fetid breath. He turns his head to and fro as he looks at me, like a crow deciding which angle would be best for pecking out a lamb's eye. Then he slowly shimmies his shoulders, cupping his hideous hands in front of his crotch, so his curving nails click together like gruesome maracas.

'So, Pretty One, you're awake, are you?' He steps back a bit, and I can see more of his twisted body. He is stooped, and scrawny, but I do not think for one second that he is vulnerable or weak. He oozes evil from every pore, and his delight in others' agony washes off him in waves. I know he was in my head controlling me, so I can't scream or run.

'Go on, my dear, fight me, it feels soooo good,' he croons, giving another creepy shimmy, making his nails rattle in front of my face again. As he speaks, I see his teeth peeping over his lip, short and sharp, like the blade on a hacksaw, so I know that despite his rotten skin and corpse scent, he is a vampire. I realise he must have me Compelled, but it feels nothing like when Simon soothed us at the High Council. I didn't know one vampire could do this to another.

I watch in horror as he lifts my wrist, carves an incision with his yellowed talon, and latches onto my wound like a nightmarish baby at a tit. I can feel his crusty nails flicking through my memories as if they are files in a filing cabinet. Every now and again a memory of my unhappiness or humiliation particularly pleases him, and he'll spend longer on that one drinking in as much of my pain as he can.

I stop my internal struggle. I can't resist him, but if my

attempts to fight give him pleasure, then I can at least refuse him that delicacy. As I submit to him riffling through my thoughts, I feel a low, simmering rage burning off the terror, like the afternoon sun burning off the morning's mists. I find myself almost welcoming the fight. I learned how to fight the horrors of having my memories ravaged at the High Council, by pretending to comply, while distracting them with intimate memories, but not the real soul secrets.

A lifetime of nightmares has taught me there's only one way to win against a monster like this. By appearing to submit, then attacking when they think they have you beaten. The secret is not to care about surviving, only about beating the beast. I feel myself split inside, the furious, fierce core of me, curling around my decision to destroy this monster through whatever means necessary, while I feed him fear and compliance. His hollow eyes crinkle in delight as he feels my submission.

'Don't expect any help, my lovely,' he chortles, 'I am ancient, and I am immense, and I can control your friends as easily as I can control you. I fed on them all, and they sucked from me, and now my blood rules their veins. They stand at the window and watch what I do, but they cannot move, and they cannot scream, not out loud. But inside, oh, inside, I can hear them in there, and I can taste them, and it tastes so good.' He smacks his rubbery lips in delight. 'Oh, what fun, what funny, funny, fun, hee hee hee.'

He latches back onto my wrist, while his spare claw reaches out and traces a line down my cheek, down my neck, rips the top of my dress down to my waist. He traces back up to my breast, until his nails are holding my nipple tight, twisting it and turning it. In my head I writhe and sob and defer to him, while at my core the pain stokes my ire. He cackles and hops in pleasure, smearing my blood around his mouth like a messy child. He runs his fingers down my stomach, down my thigh, up under my skirt and into my knickers. He makes no attempt at gentleness, and scratches and tears at my velvet flesh. Still sucking my wrist, he withdraws his hand to scrabble at the buttons on the front of his mud-coloured trousers, tenderly bringing forth his wizened cock, so it sits between his thumb and index finger like a desiccated maggot.

I fill my thoughts with terror and repulsion at the sight of it, whimpering and begging to be released, while in my depths my essence roars with laughter at his shrunken manhood. He rubs his little dick, faster and faster, dry as tinder, trying to start his fire. Gripping the flesh of my wrist with his razor teeth, he frees his other hand to scrabble and tear at me, snagging the tender bud, and scratching the delicate lips.

Shaking his head to widen my wound, he sucks harder and while he reaches into my thoughts and finds the memories of my loves, and plays them back, not just for himself this time, but for me too, so I feel my body throb and swell despite myself as the echoes of arousal flow through me.

As he senses my body betraying me in its flowering, he dances a little jig of glee, waving his stiffening member in my face. Rubbing madly, determined to keep it primed, he clambers awkwardly over me, so he can keep my flesh clamped between his teeth, keep his cock hard with my mounting dismay. Finally, he is in position, between my knees, pushing my legs apart and yanking at my knickers. I know what he means to do, and I know I can't resist, so I turn his own strength against him. I turn the trickle into a torrent and open the floodgates of every erotic experience I've ever had, I wash every orgasm I've ever melted and throbbed to into him at once. I allow my Glamour to rise and peak, and he judders and shakes, and a feeble strand of thin slime laces over my thigh. I hide my jubilation from him and cry and simper beneath him.

He tugs and yanks at himself some more, face twisted in frustration, but quickly gives up, and tucks himself away again.

I make sure that when he looks back at my face, my eyes are closed, tears seeping out beneath the lids, letting him believe I have not witnessed his shame, have not gained strength from it.

'It's been a long time,' he snickers as he climbs back out from between my legs letting go of my wrist. 'And you are a dirty little bitch. Got an old man going, you did. Not a problem though, tee hee hee. I'll just get one of those nice boys from the house to help me.' Despite myself my eyes fly open. 'Oh yes, lovey, I'll just slide into his mind and I'll be able to feel everything he can. Be better like that anyway. Young man like that, bet he can last for hours.' He looks at me closely as he tells me his plans. I make sure I carry on showing the same level of wretched misery, as if unaffected by whom he'll chose to use, allowing him to savour my dejection.

My eye is caught by movement over his shoulder, and he turns to watch Matt stagger towards us like an automaton. As he gets closer, Mattie's eyes are screaming in his slack face. I hold his gaze for a moment and try to convey my blessing, to let him know I will not blame him for whatever this monster uses his body for, to tell him to do whatever he needs to do to keep himself and the others safe.

'Hello kind sir, and welcome to our little gathering. We are in need of your assistance.' The creature shakes another hideous shimmy, one shoulder dropping, then the other, nails clacking. Matthieu blinks slowly and stumbles to a stop before us. The goblin prances and jitters around us clapping his claws in glee, then he grabs Mattie's wrist and sinks his teeth into the underside.

A look of such horror spreads over Matt's face as he feels the monster invade his memories. I see the horror replaced with despair as it finds the memories it wants, and the arousal spreads through Mattie's face, lips plumping, cheeks flushing. His nipples enlarge and his jeans tent. The tendons stand out in his arms as he uses his immense strength to try to resist the invasion, granite slabs of muscle quivering. He fights against having his free hand forced to open his fly and take out his erection. I look resolutely at his face, holding his gaze, reassuring him as best I can.

The monster lets go of Mattie's wrist and his gaze prods at me again, and finding only soggy misery and acceptance of my fate, he returns his attention to his new exciting toy. He jiggles and chortles dancing a dance of repulsive joy. He walks around in front of Matt and pokes at his rearing cock, face twisted in envy. In that second as he teases and tortures himself as much as my lover, I feel his attention leave me. Complacent in breaking me, he is concentrating completely on Matthieu's penis.

In the second his attention is switched away, I reach under my lounger and grab the coffee mug I'd tucked there hours earlier. I jump to my feet pushing the teaspoon that had been in my mug between my middle fingers, so the concave head is cupped in my palm, and the handle pokes out between my fingers, as I curl my hand into a fist.

My other hand clutches the handle of the mug as I smash it against the top of the wooden lounger, so it splinters into savage shards. I spin towards the creature slashing and gouging, aiming for his throat and eyes, doing as much damage as I can as quickly as I can. He shrieks, and turns on me, curdled eyes glowing madly furious like burning coals. As his attention shifts to me, Matt is released, and he punches the fiend between the shoulder blades, and kicks his legs out from under him. Matthieu stamps on his neck, trapping him on the ground. I fall on our tormentor slashing and hacking, fury powering me on, overwhelming his enfeebled attempts to infiltrate my mind again.

'That will do. I'll take it from here.' A cold female voice says. I startle around and gape at the towering female that stands over us. She is as imposing as a statue, frozen face turned towards me. Her hair and eyes are as black as a raven's wing, her skin as white and smooth as alabaster. 'He slipped his leash. I'll take him now.'

'Who, what...' I blink at her, unable to reconcile her calm authority with the brutal fight for our lives Mattie and I had been battling only moments earlier.

'My name is Amunet,' she tells me, pride staining her voice. 'This wretched creature is Ahmes.' Ahmes is keening softly, curled beneath Matthieu's massive knee as he kneels on him. All fight has fled his ragged body.

'I...' I stammer.

'I must apologise for his behaviour. Usually we live on the fringes of life, avoiding others of our kind. He can't be trusted around company.'

'Then what the fuck was this about? We were here, minding our own bloody business and he just attacked us.'

'It's complicated...' She pauses a moment. 'I'm afraid Ahmes has corrupted himself. He fed on other vampires too often. He is addicted to memories, feeding right back to human memories, collecting all their knowledge, feeling all of their hopes, fears and heartbreaks. At the same time he has poisoned himself, like any addict will.' She has slipped an iron collar around his scrawny neck as she speaks, elegantly waving Mattie and I back away from him.

'He was my love once,' she murmurs, almost to herself. 'Majestic and beautiful, but he ignored my warnings and kept drinking, kept killing our kin, unable to resist and now he is a ruin, a wreckage. All that was regal before has been corrupted, until he is this snivelling wretch, humping like dog at a human's leg.' Her voice drips contempt and she yanks his chain, so he is hauled scrabbling to her heel.

'We are ancient, the first vampires, not those sanctimonious upstarts in Germany. He holds so much knowledge, he should be irresistible to others, one sip, and they could know so much, but his mind is coddled, and all that knowledge is beyond him, and anyone else.' As she snarls her frustration and hatred of what Ahmes has become, Amunet's face remains serene and smooth, only her tone giving away her disgust.

I look at her, bewildered by this outpouring of information, distrustful of what her openness means.

'It must be hard, not being able to put him out of his misery.' I decide to try understanding; maybe she wouldn't kill us all if I offer her sympathy. She turns her ancient gaze upon me, and sees right through me. The slightest smile touches her scarlet lips.

'I could kill him in an instant,' she says calmly. 'But I have loved him for millennia. When I look at him like this, I am repulsed, but I drag him behind me, so I cannot see him, and I remember who he was.' She looks down at her snivelling lover, and then back up at me. 'We seek a healer, a vampire who can make him whole again when he feeds on them, and then he shall be whole again, and his mind will be restored to him, and the knowledge of all the ancients will be his. We shall rise then, and rule the world together, my love and I.'

I feel cold terror wash through me when she says this. If she can unpick his maddened brain just enough to realise we know where to find a healer, she will be back to feed on us, and then they will rule. *So what?* a voice asks. *Would they be any worse than the High Council?* At least, I would have a way out of my terrible dilemma, and they would be so far removed, they would hardly influence me at all.

'Well, good luck,' I say, as she swirls away in her silky robes, swaying enigmatically out of the garden without a backward glance, although her husband glares balefully backwards, shimmying and snarling as she drags him away.

Chapter Seven

Layla

Finally, shockingly, it is over and I am cradled in David's arms again. I am stunned at Rae's strength, her resilience, her ability to manipulate her abuser. I'm sure that the attack will draw us closer again, overshadow the silliness about the photograph, and I beam at her, as she walks back towards the cottage in the wake of the ancient Egyptians. But Rae remains silent and aloof; she won't even look at me. David and I huddle together in the front garden watching down the lane where the ancient vampires vanished. I try to ignore the icy sensation on my right side where Rae should be standing.

I'm not sure how long we continue to stand there, dumbly staring after their progress as the high afternoon sun tips down to lengthen evening shadows. I don't know why we are even there, but we remain there as if turning back towards our cottage, to try to resume our usual evening activities is beyond us all. So we stay in position as shadows slowly lengthen, David grasping me to him, Mattie standing before us like a monolith, hands clenched behind his back; and Rae off to one side, oblivious to our presence, one arm wrapped tightly around her stomach, the other hand worrying unconsciously at her lower lip, pulling and rolling obsessively.

Simon screeches to a halt in the lane, startling us all. He vaults the gate, and flies into the garden, vicious-looking hunting knife drawn. Rae uncurls at the sight of him, and I can see she is gladdened to see him even though they are too late and we no longer need rescuing. He takes one look at Rae, and wraps his strong warm arms around her. He's never touched her before, no matter what they've been through, he's hardly even smiled at any of us really. Now he holds her snuggly for a few vital seconds before patting her back and pulling away. Even as she sagged against him in a second of surrender and smiled tightly at Elaine arriving behind Simon, I saw her gaze stretch beyond them, unable to resist looking for Guillaume; but of course he's not there.

Simon and Elaine usher us into the house. As we file in, Rae catches David's and my elbows, holding us back a step.

'Don't tell them about the dancing or photos. Nobody can know that bit,' she mutters. 'Plausible deniability,' she continues, at David's questioning eyebrow. He nods once. Then she drops back, and sits slightly separate from the rest of the group who gather around the table in the kitchen. David and I tell them what happened. We piece together that a group from the Farm Pride were hunting in Normandy when the Farm received my distress message and all further attempts to contact us were futile. It's only while we are talking that I realise that they have less than two hours to get here. It feels like several lifetimes.

Mattie remains standing, removed and silent, against the kitchen wall. Once I have described Amunet sailing off down the lane, like a stately barge, with Ahmes a subdued tug behind her, Rae speaks up.

'You have to take Layla and David away,' she says quietly. Her statement is met with shocked silence. 'They have been hunting in another vampire's territory with Brian's girlfriend, Megan.' Elaine gapes at Rae, her quick mind already slotting the pieces together. 'We cannot trust the Pride Leader not to return. She has taken Megan and Brian to join her Pride, but I am not sure she won't return to exact revenge. I don't want responsibility for them anymore.' I scowl at Rae in mute fury, and David is looking at his fingers, spread over the table top. He opens his mouth, thinks better of it and closes it again. He nods once and stands up, holding his hand out to me. I start to protest, to list all the reasons I need to stay with my battered friend, but he just shakes his head and leads me away.

Rae

'You're sure?' Simon asks once, and I nod. He looks at me a moment longer, then nods and goes to wait in the car with Elaine. I wait in the kitchen as Layla and David pack their cases, and David carries them out to the car. Layla pads silently into the kitchen, and stands for a moment in the doorway. I don't look up, instead I watch her little white toes squirm a moment, before they pad over to the cupboard.

'Do not tell Guillaume about the photographs. Let them think you are avoiding Abigail, and I've expelled you for trespass and our subsequent falling out. Stay there until I contact you. If the Council contacts me, I'll let you know. If they contact Guillaume and he comes to get me, you must leave before he returns. No one must know where you are, and he must be able to prove he did not know what you did. You know the Council will feed on us to make sure we are telling the truth.'

I still don't look at her as the cupboard opens and she takes her mug from the cupboard shelf. I've been too angry with her to put mine back next to hers, despite Meg moving out, and now it's smashed in the garden, so we avoid that sad metaphor at least.

After the front door closes, followed by feet crunching slowly over the gravel and the gate clanging shut, Mattie sits opposite me. I meet his gaze, glorious orange eyes bereft and ruby-rimmed. I reach for his hand and he holds just the tips of my fingers, stroking across them with the pad of his thumb. With a thud I know what's coming.

'This isn't going to work anymore,' he says softly.

I want to protest, I long to escape into his arms, so Need-fuelled sex can burn away the memories of the day, but something within me knows he's right. I won't say it though, instead I just look at him imploringly.

'You know I don't love you, can't love you, and to stay now would make this mean more than it does. We were fun, but this can't be fun anymore.'

I feel my chin wobble slightly, and he groans. 'Please don't cry, Rae, because I will stay, and wouldn't be fair on either of us. We both deserve to find someone who will love us.'

I pull myself together, paste on my biggest, bravest smile and nod for him, so he can pretend not to notice that my gaze slips over his and past his ear.

'No hard feelings?' he whispers.

'None,' I state firmly, meaning it. 'You are always welcome here.' I smile at him. 'Be happy,' I add softly.

Once he's gone, I make myself a coffee in one of the house mugs that were here when we moved in, but even the rich scent and cupped heat doesn't soothe me. I long to smoke so many cigarettes that my throat burns, and drink enough alcohol to find a place to hide, but those escapes are lost to me; which means I can't stop thinking about the one avenue of intoxication that's left to me. Blood.

There are two old ladies who live in the village, one is tall and thin, bitter as bark, while the other is short and plump, sweet-faced and jolly. They are often in their gardens when Layla and I drive past on our way to people-watch further afield. They have cream bungalows next to each other and stand in their own gardens or together at the fence nattering as they dead head roses or water their lavender. We drive slowly with our windows cracked open, so we can scent the twilight air like hunting hounds; mimosa and honeysuckle mingling with human and the burning coals of barbeques.

Through our open windows we listen to the thin tall woman sniff in disdain, insulted by the rude English, who have moved to her village and refused to join in village life; who live in such dubious circumstances, and are so rarely seen. Her sunny-natured friend waits though, until her haughty back is turned in high dudgeon, and then she peeks around and waves at us, her old hand clawed by arthritis into a scoop she can only waggle. And I, unable to resist her naughty overture of friendship, flash the headlights briefly.

Now I can't get her out of my head. Not the skinny mean one, sour with all life's disappointments, but the sweet chubby one, butter soft and cosy with a lifetime of love reciprocated thrumming through her veins. How easy it would be to slip through her window tonight, a silent shadow bringing release from her old body's aches. I could wrap her in the warm comforts of the Compelling while I shared her memories of a life well lived; only leaving her once she'd slipped into eternal rest.

I cannot bear it, though. I cannot bear the thought of the bitter old bitch next door waking up tomorrow morning and finding that the one person who can see beyond her gnarled wall of disappointments, to still love the girl she once was, has left her too. So I perch on the stairs, and clutch my coffee until it's cold, frozen with the thoughts of her, then I peel myself away, empty and rinse my coffee mug and retreat to the shower.

I tilt the bathroom window inwards, so the balmy evening air can kiss my naked skin while I run the shower hot. I climb in and drip my essential oils onto my natural sponge which tickles deliciously all over as I rub and scrub, and slough the day's horrors away, scenting the steamy air with roses. Slowly, the heat, the sponge's strokes, and the heady perfume relax me, so my shoulders finally drop from around my ears. I hum a little as I turn under the torrent of water, plunging my face under the stream, so at first I'm not sure I hear it. I step out of the water to listen.

SNIFF

There's no mistaking it this time, someone is outside taking great animalistic sniffs at the air, like a rooting pig, or a hunting dog. I freeze for a moment; heart thundering as anxiety crashes back, rushing through my veins like a high tide. Leaving the water running to cover my movements, I step silently out of the shower and slip over to the window, grabbing my towel from the rail as I pass. I clutch it to my chest to protect my modesty as I peep around the side of the window frame, and jump like a surprised cat as I come face to face with Mattie squatting on the window sill, face poking into the open gap.

'What the fuck, Mattie?' I yell as he grins at me. 'What are you playing at? Why didn't you knock at the door like a normal person?' His grin splits wider, so his eyes disappear into the crinkles and he chuckles hoarsely.

'Heh heh heh, I wanted to surprise you.' He chortles. 'Let me in.'

'Well, you did that. Arsehole.' I unclip the window and pull it the rest of the way open. He slides in, arms first, roly-polying into the room, and lying on his back laughing up at me. I've never seen him like this before, playful and a bit manic, he's always had a sweet, solemn air about him. Suddenly, he reminds me of a teenager with attention deficit disorder, as if he has lost his impulse control.

'What are you doing?' I ask, and he leaps to his feet in a nimble twist.

'Shall I get naked too?' he asks, snatching at my towel.

'No. Go and wait downstairs, I'll be there now.' I scowl at him, studying him closely and sniffing at him for the scent of human blood, wondering if that could be the reason for his change of heart and boisterous behaviour.

"Kay.' He leaves the room and I hear him clatter downstairs. I turn the shower off, and shut and lock the bathroom window. I'd normally leave it open to disperse the steam but I don't want any more surprises this evening. As I pull my clean cotton sundress over my head, I admit that despite his strange behaviour, my heart is gladdened to see Matt. I didn't want to admit to myself just how much his rejection had hurt, even while I agreed with his reasons. I'm glad he's back, glad we can hide from life in each other for a while longer.

I skip downstairs, into the lounge, where Mattie is waiting with his back to me while he preens in the mirror, oblivious to my arrival. I watch for a moment, taken aback, he's never shown the slightest vanity before, has called his big slabby vampire features ugly, despite my reassurances that I find him intensely masculine, and sexy. As I watch now, he turns his face from side to side, engrossed in his own reflected profile. Then his shoulders slide into a to and fro shimmy, fingertips clicking against each other in front of him, and my heart stops. At that moment he sees me behind him, and turns beaming towards me.

'There you are,' he cries, delighted. He skips across the room and grabs my wrists. 'Look how lovely you are, all fresh from the shower, and smelling of roses.' I scan his face frantically, what I feel and what I know fighting inside my head. I try to reassure myself that it's just some sort of post-traumatic shock, brought about by the fright he gave me, but even as I tell myself this, his shoulders slide again. What was a creepy little wiggle in Ahmes' scrawny frame has become a sinister predator slide of muscles under supple skin in Matthieu's massive body, reminding me of a panther dropping into a stalk, shoulders rolling into combat.

I swallow and look up into his eyes, still desperate to deny what I'm seeing. His orange eyes are cold, and his playful grip on my wrists tightens. I know I only have seconds to fool him, to play stupid, and buy myself time like I did this morning.

'I'm so glad you came back,' I coo, watching him through my lashes as I raise my Glamour, carefully, only taking it to a level where I cause disruption to his thought processes, not enough that the Need will engulf us. I lean forward and kiss his neck, nipping his skin until a low growl of lust rumbles through him, his big hands spreading over my back, and pulling me closer. At this sign of consent I bite his neck, drawing as much blood as I can into my mouth before he pushes me off.

Maddened flashes of memory flicker through my mind. I catch snatches of Matthieu leaving the cottage this afternoon, gratifyingly downhearted. Then somehow the scent of his blood changes and I can taste the crypt, and he is back under Ahmes' control, then Ahmes is feeding on him, and feeding, and feeding, until Matt is weakened, and Ahmes is raving. Then Matthieu is being made to feed on Ahmes, and there is less and less of the cocoa and nutmeg scent of Mattie and more and more of the maddened, staticky thoughts of the crazed ancient vampire. It shouldn't be possible, but the last memory I have from Matt is Ahmes' empty body crumpling to the ground, and there is no more Mattie, and Ahmes has possession of his body.

Ahmes' grip on me is hard now; he is using all of Matthieu's massive strength, and has raised my arms above my head, gripping both of my wrists in one huge paw, while he fumbles for knickers I'm not wearing with his other hand.

'Oh, you were pleased to see me this time, weren't you, my pretty, weren't you, my little flower?' he mutters on, drool collecting in the corner of his mouth. He pulls at his own trousers and pants, until he exposes Matt's final gift for me.

Where there should be a massive ebony erection, there is only a small smooth stump. My mind fills with the memory of Matt's struggle against the control of the blood filling his veins, his recoil of horror from the intention he could feel stealing his will. Matt always carried a small lethally sharp blade, and this was his last act as his own mind was swallowed by the greedy needs of the Ancient One. With one quick slice in the confusion, he removed what Ahmes wanted most and there was nothing for his vampire body to repair. It could only stop the bleeding and scar over, like the flesh on my face did after the battle at the Farm.

Outrage twists Ahmes' features, and he starts his Rumpelstiltskin dance of rage, stamping and roaring his frustration, spitting and swearing in a language so ancient I have no idea what he is saying, but his meaning is clear. In the second that his grip on me is slackened, I get a flash of memory of Matt slipping the flick knife back into his trouser pocket, and while Ahmes is distracted by his loss, I reach forward as quick as a flash, and slip the slender knife into my palm. One flick of my thumb extends the blade, and before I have time for doubts, I have plunged the blade between his ribs, his startled orange eyes meeting mine, and I hold them as I swish the blade quickly through the heavy mass of his heart, one fast flick of my wrist after the other, the blade's deadly sharpness slicing through arteries and chambers effortlessly.

Ahmes gnashes his teeth at me once, as I see the idea of taking my body next flash through his eyes, but almost instantly the blood stops flowing to his brain and he drops to his knees. I've watched too many horror films to take any chances, and with a quick wrench I have pulled the blade from his heart, and *swish, swish*, I've slit his throat into a bloodless maw, and his expressionless face drops back, over his shoulders. *Swish, swish, yank* and his vertebrae are severed, and his head rolls away from his slumping corpse.

Chapter Eight

Rae

'What have you done?' I don't recognise Amunet immediately, her lustrous liquorice hair is coarse and white, her golden skin is the matt white of chalk, and her eyes have faded to sun-bleached cotton from smooth conker brown. She grabs my arm and tows me, shell-shocked and stuttering, out to where she has dropped Ahmes' bloodless corpse in the front garden. She must have found it on the verge where he shed his old body and took over Matthieu's.

'He did that,' I say, pointing at the crumpled body. 'Ahmes,' I'm trying to explain, but I don't know where to start. Her dusty eyes don't leave my face while I fumble round for words. 'He took over, he was in Mattie. He killed Mattie and then was in his body.' Her eyes stray over my shoulder, back towards the lounge. 'Then I killed him. You promised. You promised to keep him away,' I ferret around for the right words.

'I should kill you for this. I should rip out your heart and enjoy every second,' she snarls, but her threats are as muted as the roars of an old caged lion. Her shoulders slump in defeat. 'I had to feed. I have to feed often now, and he just feeds from me, so I don't, didn't, take him to hunt. He just gets in the way, so I left him... and he escaped.' She's tugging at her hair as she speaks, rocking gently from foot to foot. 'He did it you said? He was in your lover, in his body?'

'Yes, I recognised that thing he did.' I sway my own shoulders and clack my nails, and her lip curls, repulsed, surprising me.

'Oh yes. But are you sure? He tried so long. We were never sure he could. It was such a risk.'

'I bit him. I could feel the memories change, he was still mad.' I gulp and glance at her, hoping she won't take offence, but she nods. She has experienced the fairground swirl of his thoughts, loud and unfocused, bright and broken. 'How? How could... that... happen?' I'm struggling to find the words to describe what he did.

'That was his Gift, one of them, or rather, a concoction of many. We didn't know for sure, though,' Amunet replies. She walks away from his corpse and lowers herself onto the bench beneath the kitchen window. 'He could absorb the powers of other vampires when he fed on them. That's why he became addicted to the feeding, not just the memories. We are different from you modern vampires; we were the originals. It was us who created the virus. It was an accident, but it changed everything for us. The virus continued to evolve and mutate over the years, so we are different, although reinfection from feeding on other vampires has brought a lot of the changes, we... I am still not the same, physically.' She rubs her forehead and sighs deeply. 'It's all terribly hard to explain, and I'm desperately hungry. I need to feed far more frequently than you younger vampires. Do you have anything here?'

'We don't eat human, but I can run and get you some cow blood if you like?' I am still distrustful, but she seems to have decided not to kill me. Or not immediately anyway.

'Yuk. That's very dull. Go on then, that'll have to do, but be fast and bring plenty.'

I rush to fill a kitchen mixing bowl with blood from several of the heifers in the nearest field. I feel guilty not bringing their usual snack in exchange, but I Compel them into a bovine stupor and take what I need quickly and cleanly.

Back home, Amunet snatches the bowl off me, and drinks the blood in big gulps, grimacing and gurning at the bottom of the bowl as the thin bitter flavour registers.

'Awful, I really don't know why you do it to yourselves.' She sighs. As I watch colour rises through her, returning her skin to honeyed travertine, her hair to ebony waves, and her eyes to smoky quartz. She shudders from top to bottom and then pins me with her freshened gaze. 'Now, come here and feed on me, it's much easier than trying to explain it all.'

I'm startled by her suggestion, and not entirely amenable. She has a regal way of expecting her commands to be obeyed, and I'm anxious she's about to rip my head off for killing her consort, but I still don't want to drink her blood or explore her memories. Tasting one Ancient's coddled thoughts is enough for one day. It's enough for one lifetime.

'You aren't considering refusing, are you?' she's bemused. 'My husband is the only one I have ever allowed to feed on me; my late husband, whom you murdered, less than one hour ago.' I open my mouth to defend myself, but she wafts her hand at me, brushing away what I was going to say. 'I am offering you the precious gift of understanding. Something I've never offered to anyone else, and I am only doing that because there is something about you that I recognise, from myself, when I was still more human.'

I remember the frustration I felt at the Farm, trying to find answers to the question of what I was now, how even the High Council had not been able, or willing, to satisfy my curiosity completely. Now that knowledge is being offered to me as a unique gift—knowledge that others do not possess—I fear the cost, troubled by the nightmares I sense will be lurking in our history, but like Eve, or Pandora, I am powerless to resist. Amunet sees the decision in my eyes and pats the bench beside her. I sit and she elegantly slices into the artery beneath her thumb, then cups the back of my head and pulls me into her lap to feed in a gesture so shockingly intimate I struggle to pull away, but her blood has slipped between my lips, rich and sweet. As her memories start to fill my mind, I swoon into her arms, grateful for how they catch me.

Witnessing the Ancient One's memories is not like the experiences I've had with other vampires, which I could control to some extent, and were projected like a film into my mind's eye for me to watch. Instead, Amunet takes my soul and slips it in beside her own. I relive each experience as vividly as she does; each thought, every emotion is as intense as when she first felt it. Every doubt, every desire exposed to my appetite to learn. Unlike with other vampires, I cannot look around these memories, noting things that were seen but not registered. I cannot feel my own interpretation of what she experienced, I see exactly what she saw, feel exactly what she felt. I become she, and she becomes I as we smudge and merge together.

The air is warm, tickled with delicate breezes from window slits positioned to entice even the faintest movement of air into my chambers. My room is scented with pungent perfumes and filled with the lilting chatter of my ladies as they dress me, paint my face, and arrange an elaborate wig and towering hairpiece over my own neat braids. I'm looking in a mirror of polished metal, and I am preening. Today is an exciting day, I am to meet my proposed husband.

He is a little beneath me socially, new money not old, but, I have heard, beautiful. My eunuch, Kha has advised me this will be advantageous, I will retain my power, and he will be grateful if I will take him, and propel his family to the top most echelons of society. Whispers from my slaves, who have spoken to slaves from other households in the marketplace hint at tales of mischief and fun loving, and I like the sound of this. Mine is not a sombre home, I love to dance and sing and feast.

My parents are dead, but I was much loved before they died. My father was Ramses II, the all-powerful, much beloved brave Ozymandias, conqueror of the Hittites. My mother was his darling minor wife, Ornament to the King, as he loved to call her. She caught his eye with her dances, and kept his heart with her sage advice and careful counsel. Although he was ancient beyond all expectation when he saw her, she revived his flagging will, and I was born soon later. My father died ten years ago, but I clearly remember being dandled on his knee, a darling of the courts.

My mother died young, just two years ago, and I miss her still, but her clever Kha is my advisor now and he loves me even more than my father did. I have many siblings, and no claim to the crown, so my life is not at risk. Instead, I am loved for my singing and dancing, like my mother, and am often invited to parties to play my harp and sing mournful love songs as the evenings grow long. I join my brother for diplomatic duties, aiding in the honeying of the cogs that make his reign glide. My brother is a fair king and I am lucky to live in a time of peace and plenty. People are content and loving towards their new monarch, after their terror when my father died. Into this happy world of abundance, I shall bring my husband, and together we shall have fat babies and live a prosperous life in my brother's court.

Kha comes to escort me to the reception chamber, and my tummy ripples like tiny fish in the shallows, I feel my cheeks glow. At the sight of me in my flowing linen gown, exquisitely beaded, and cinched tight with a wrought leather belt, my eunuch's eyes fill with loving tears.

'Ah, so beautiful,' he whispers, cupping my chin. 'Right on the cusp of womanhood and about to select yourself a husband.' He traces my full lips, wiping a tiny smudge from the carefully applied paint, and turning my face from side to side to check the perfection of kohl painted thickly around my eyes. My eyebrows have been plucked into sweeping arcs, like crane wings, widening my already huge eyes. We laugh and clutch each other briefly, a last moment of childhood play before the regal woman returns and he leads me to the hall where my future awaits.

As I enter the room, the young man does not turn. Instead, he continues a whispered conversation with his father, who stiffens at my entrance and makes big eyes at his son to turn towards me. I see the hoped for future fall from his eyes and ruin darken his cheeks. This boy's insolence flames my face and flares my nostrils, I lift my chin and clear my throat. The boy turns to me, too slowly for me to believe the hesitation is accidental, but when he sees me before him, his painted eyes widen appreciatively, pupils darkening with lust. He looks at me with frank approval, and I am lost.

He is more beautiful than I knew a man could be. His eyes are huge, as dark as dates, and blackly fringed with lashes that make my own seem sparse by comparison. His noble nose is long and straight, leading to a mouth of such soft prettiness I am filled with the desire to suck his cushioned bottom lip. His bare shoulders are broad and muscled; the dark golden skin of his chest is decorated by a line of dark hairs that disappear enticingly under the cloths he wears belted around his waist in the short skirts of fine linen that rich men wear. I have never felt desire before, and the heat and power of it surprise me, taking my feet from me and rattling my ribcage with the heavy beating of my heart. I can feel the heat in my face, the swelling of my lips, my vision feels sharp and crisp, and I can see the details of him as though I am standing beside him already. My only experience with loving has been in the arms of my Nubian slave, my childhood playmate, who slipped velvet soft into my bed and into my arms as the moon brought our menses within months of each other. Comfort turned to play and darkness ripened with spice and musk as fingers slipped and slid in secret folds. Such games seem innocent now, bereft of the wanting, flavoured only with curiosity and mischief.

I have no idea what is spoken of in that room, I only attend my spinning thoughts, whirling like sand around the central cyclone of him. Eventually, it is agreed that he and I should spend some time together in the gardens with my nanny as chaperone. The brightness and the heat after the shady cool of the hall make me stagger, and he catches my elbow to steady me. His touch scorches, it is all I can feel, all the rest of me liquefies and I struggle to breathe. I heave a gasp of sun-soaked air into my lungs, and force my spine straight and knees locked, determined not to give myself away any further.

'My lady, are you unwell?' His voice is honey and gravel.

'I–I got the sun in my eyes and stumbled, I will be perfectly fine now.' I radiate my broadest smile at him, but he does not let go of my arm, instead he holds me to him as we wander the grounds pointing and exclaiming over the beauty of the terraces, laughter trickling with the water of babbling brooks, and breath mingling with the perfume of sunned flowers, herbs and fruit.

We stop at a walled boundary, my old nanny huffing and panting behind us, wiping her sweaty brow. The valley spreads out before us, and in the distance my brother's pyramid grows incrementally upwards.

'I would spend some time alone with you,' Ahmes whispers, looking out over the fertile lands bordering the Nile. His mouth hardly moves, words no louder than a sigh, ensuring only I can hear. 'Could this be?'

'Oh, oh...' I set up a coughing and spluttering, doubling over, gasping for breath, knees betraying me so I sag against the wall, choking and swooning. I cannot speak, can only croak desperately to my nanny, 'Water... oh water... please...' She dithers for a moment, torn between fetching a drink and leaving me alone with a man; we are a distance now from the kitchens. I gag and retch, sagging further into a slump, Ahmes' arms supporting me, horror written stark across his face. He had not been warned I am sickly. My nurse looks appeal at him and he nods to her to hurry off to fetch refreshment. As she rounds the corner, after one last anxious glance, I leap to my feet, grinning.

'You were shamming?' he gasps. For a second, I think he is angry, but then I see the smile at the corners of his mouth.

'I wanted to be alone with you too,' I whisper, suddenly coy.

And then his head is thrown back in a great roar of laughter, and he has slid his great hands under my buttocks, and has lifted me, effortlessly, to spin me around, and I am laughing too, wrapping my legs around his waist, and leaning back into his grip like a child. I feel the aching, secret core of me meet a hard ridge in his robes that burns with an answering heat of its own.

The laughter stops, and my back is against the wall, one foot dropping to the floor, sandal lost, tippy toes reaching to push me tighter to him. My arms circle his neck, his mouth explores mine, an intoxicating mixture of heat and softness, firmness, and teeth nipping, tongue sliding. His hands slide up from my waist, so tightly I can hardly breathe, until he reaches the sweet rise of my breasts, and then his thumbs are stroking and teasing and circling my nipples, making my breath catch, and melting me further, so I push harder against him, sighing my longing.

He groans his reply, pushing back, lifting me up to meet him. Only the fabric we both wear is preventing him sliding completely inside me. I know I shouldn't, I know someone might see, I know this should be saved for our wedding night, but I don't care, I don't care, I don't care. I rub the heated nub of mine harder against the burning rise of his, panting, and intent. His thumbs answer me, flicking over the swollen knots my nipples have become, tied so tightly to that central jewel that I cannot divide the sensations, and as he sucks and nips my neck, my shoulder, my ear, the waves of pleasure build, and suddenly I am lost, boneless, gasping as stars explode and fade behind my eyes and my body twitches in his arms.

I have hardly recovered myself, vision still clouded and blurred when he is guiding my fingers down under the belt that secures his robes, until my hand touches a stick of such heat I jerk back gasping. I look up at him startled, but his eyes are closed, breath coming in fast pants.

'Oh, hold me,' he gasps. 'Stroke me, my little vixen, my little she-wolf. Squeeze me tight.' So I take it in my hand, burning, rigid, as hard and hot as a stone heated in the evening fires to warm my bed, with the softest silk covering, stretched tight. As my fingers explore, it quivers at my touch. I slide my grip down the sleek ripples of the shaft, and then trail my fingertips back up to the pulsing head. His breath hitches and jumps as my nails trail over the raised ridges and experience the new textures at the tip hotter, smoother, with a dimple at the top. As I stroke the dimple, he gasps and groans, cursing softly under his breath, so I start to snatch my hand back, afraid I've hurt him.

'Oh dear gods no,' he moans. 'Oh, don't stop now.' The tip of his opens then, and a hot gobbet of liquid, spurts to meet my fingers. 'Ahh, ahhh,' he cries. Blindly, he butts against my hand, and I open my screwed closed eyes to look down at his manhood, rearing purple and furious before him. He stands over me, arms against the wall above my head, forehead against them. His eyes are closed, and I snatch this stolen moment of his lost control to watch as he shakes and shudders as I stroke the head of his. I grasp the shaft, and squeeze to try to close my fingers around it, marvelling at the feel of him, the textures I've never felt before. He bucks against my squeezing, but I know better than to let go now, instead I rub against his thrusts.

'Ah, you sweet, sweet, little bitch.' His breath sobs as I feel him swell even further, his whole body spasming into an arc before me. And then we hear it, faintly, a footstep coming towards us, not around the corner yet, but close, so close.

'Stop, stop,' he hisses, and I am unsure whether he is begging my busy hands or his own body, because even as he commands the halt, his body breaches. His knees sag, and he collapses onto the ground, pulling his clothing back up to protect his dignity. I fling myself into the hammock of his folded legs, so he grunts with the force of me. I rest my head on his shoulder and watch through slit eyes as my nanny turns the corner, walking slowly towards us, trying to preserve the horn of water she carries, that threatens to slop with each uneven step.

'Oh my wicked little kitten,' he croons softly into the top of my head, as he rocks and pats this invalid in his arms, even as the last tremors shudder through his loins at the weight of me in his lap. 'What a marriage we shall have.'

* * * *

There follow the happy days of our marriage, while everyone waits hopefully for children, and we happily oblige in aiming to fulfil their hopes. Golden, honeyed days, until I notice whispers hushed before I walk into a room. I see the times he is missing when I returned from dealing with the business of the court. At first, I am delighted that he does not attempt to interfere with my diplomatic life, but then I took count of how often entertaining himself involves beautiful women. Too often I turn a corner calling him, and find him, over-smiling, while a woman with bruised lips slips away.

I seek the sympathetic, always discrete ear of Kha, who can only offer the dry consolation of his removal from the kingdom, or to ignore his dalliances. Whichever option I choose, cautions my old friend, I need to decide for myself before I find my evidence. I spend days questioning my mirror, unable to understand why I am not enough for him, like he is for me.

One day I find him pinching a prettily plump girl to make her giggle and squeal, calling me to join the game when he sees me approach, which I decline. So maybe he wants me plumper? I eat extra for the following days, forcing down so much my belly swells painfully, causing people to laugh and ask if I am eating for two already. Days later, I catch him stroking the willow limbs of a calm beauty, calling me to admire the length of her fingers, and so the next days are spent starving.

It has to happen eventually, my concerns flavour my approach to him. No more the pretty singsong of his name, now silent feet steal softly towards smothered giggles, until I turn a corner and find him deep in an associate's daughter. A woman I do not count as a friend, who could be spiteful and cruel to other women in our circle. I freeze, watching his familiar rhythm before they realise I am there. I had not believed that he would fling away, with such disregard, our love, not really. Not in my heart. Now though, I stand before the shuddering evidence of his pumping buttocks, and white cold rage rips through me. I fling myself upon them, my only thought that he will not finish inside her. Using the advantage of surprise I pull him free, pushing her over onto her face, kicking her ribs for good measure. I turn on him like a beast, clawing his face, and neck while he staggers backwards, stunned by my onslaught. I scream my hatred and pain at him while I gouge and rip, tearing at his clothing, scratching at his hands when he raised them in defence. He finds his senses, and grabs at my hands to still me, crooning and laughing at my fury.

'Hush. Hush now, my little tiger, hush, my angry queen, this is nothing, just a game while you are busy. You know it's you I love.' So, like a tiger, I bite him, hard on his mealy mouth, feeling the firm flesh crush and split and my mouth fill with the hot coppery gush. I clamp my teeth and keep hold as he yells and tries to pull away, until he submits, and stoops to me, panting, his lip held in my teeth, while I snarl my disgust. Finally, I let go, and step back horrified yet quickened at the harm I have done, his blood soaking both our faces as I taste him. His eyes are as dark as that first day in the gardens, when I'd fooled Nanny for him. The next second, I am caught up in his arms and he is kissing me, undressing me, sliding inside. I smirk triumphant at the girl scrabbling to her feet and scuttling off, staring at us open-mouthed as we consummate my triumph.

My solution is not perfect, but it will do. He adores the physical pain, and he loves to see me fight for him. Other women may offer a diversion, but none of them offer what I do. I acquire a tiny knife with a jewelled handle, and write my love in hieroglyphics over his body, lapping the blood from his wounds. I would prefer our games to remain a secret, our secret, but he likes to boast to his closest friends. So, in these replete, lazy times, we set the tastes of our era.

One afternoon, Ahmes returns from a hunting trip, flushed with excitement. He bursts into my chamber babbling and catching me up in his arms.

'Come and see what I have made for us.' He pulls me to my feet, and tows me to where his groom is already preparing my chariot for me. We cross the Nile by ferry, and drive East to a small crevice in the rock face of a mountain which offers a secretive entrance to a large cave, as big as our entertaining hall at home; with arched ceilings so high the flames of our reed torches do not reach to light them. Soft white river sand covers the flooring, and blacksmiths wrought stands hold torches aloft around the edges. Big smooth pebbles have been used to build a fire pit in the centre, and thick couches encircle it. I believe this is a haven he has created for us, just us, and love and excitement blaze inside me.

The evening paints the sky with rose and gold as we set out to return to our cave. In dizzy anticipation, I am naked under the flimsiest of robes, covered with a thick cloak to protect my dignity as I walk through the villa. Already aroused, and blushing with it, I let him lift me from my horse, heart pounding at his touch. He lifts the large wine pouch onto his shoulder, beams a grin of pure mischief and leads me into the cavern. I have been into cathedrals since that have not been as awe-inspiring or holy as that room seemed to me that first time.

I grip his hand, gazing around me in delight, but then I hear giggling and laughter behind us, and my heart sinks with the realisation that this was not to be a secret lovers' escape after all. A group of revellers bound into our sacred space, desecrating it with their noise and high spirits.

I turn my face from him then; remove my cloak so the flames shine through my fine linen robes, rendering them invisible. After a beat of stunned silence, my husband follows my lead, and flings his own clothing over his head, forgetting he still has the wine sack over his shoulder. I go and untangle it, not to save his blushes as he thought, but to take ownership of the wine. Around me the other men also begin to strip, their tumescent excitement already showing. I swig the wine, too fast, while I unlace the cord at the front of my dress, so I can slip it from my shoulders, wiggling it down my body. I watch the other girls; they are reticent at first, but driven by jealousy as their men gaze at me, they strip naked too.

Power and fury dance together with the wine in my heart making me reckless. When wine spills from my mouth and dribbles in rivulets down my throat and between my breasts, Ahmes steps forward to lick it from me, but I push him away, discarding him. Instead, I beckon forth a dark young man, burnished muscles kissed by the firelight, proud manhood reaching right up his belly to his umbilical indent. He glances first at Ahmes, but sees me lift my chin and raise my eyebrows so comes to me; his body already tells me how much he wants to, he only needed my permission. I pin Ahmes' eyes with my own, daring him to protest.

His warm, soft mouth laps the flesh of my throat, and down between my breasts, obediently licking me clean of the wine. So I pour more over first one breast, then the other, gasping as he sucks clean each nipple. Then I pour more, down the curve of my belly, into the soft fuzz of hair beneath, so the cool wine trickles between my secret lips, and his tongue soon follows so my back arches above him. Still I hold my husband's eye as the boy's strong hand slides up the inside of my thighs, softly spreading my legs and centre, so he can suck at the source of me.

My fingers knot in his hair and my mouth softens into a moue as my eyes' focus slips, but still I watch my husband. The other men are whooping, banging drums and shaking rattles they've brought with them. Both men and women are swigging wine, as the music finds the rhythm of my heart, and they set up a humming and keening wordless song of lust. My husband's face does not look so pleased, and I am thrilled at stealing his night as I dance and writhe to the animal song. I rub against the young man's mouth until I see something spark in Ahmes' eyes, his mouth going hard, then I step away from the boy on his knees. I pull him up, kissing him hard on his big soft mouth that tastes sweetly of wine and my own spicy perfume, still holding my husband's gaze.

Finally, I sway towards him, lost in the beat of the drums, stopping only to scoop up my little blade. As I reach him, the baying rises higher, the pace of the drumming picks up, everyone is dancing now, naked and circling around us. I dance the blade over his skin and lick up his blood, drinking from him as he swigs from the wine sack I hand him. Unable to resist, he pulls my mouth to his, tasting wine, me, and his own blood, mingled. And then we are writhing together on the floor, I am astride him, riding him to completion, while all around us our friends join us in copulation. So his glory is mine, is theirs, and our pleasure, all our pleasures, are intense, dangerous, addictive.

After that evening the group of us meet in darkness in our secret cave often. We drink and dance to the beating drums and wordless songs, and once we are in a roused frenzy, with me at their heart, we cut and bite and drink and fuck, sharing lovers, cutting friends. We pass the days in polite pretending, but with increasing frequency we cannot resist the draw of our secret place. We invite visitors to the region, favoured traders and diplomats.

None of them appear ill, but someone must carry some infection, something that swells and grows, twists and changes as we pass back and forth between us all. We first know that something is wrong when we receive word that one of our friends is ailing, bed-bound and listless. I do not like the woman, she always makes sure she is close to Ahmes when we play, so I distract him, persuade him to wait until she is better before he sees her. By the next day she is dead, she is the first, but she is not the last. We blame bad water, rotten meat, anything other than what we enjoy. Our numbers dwindle, but still we play. We refuse to admit that mixing blood and sex between us has created a new disease.

I hear that the beautiful boy I cavorted with is sickening. I visit him taking tinctures of herbs and honey my mother taught me to make. I am shocked by his deathly pallor, and shake while I prepare the medicines. I slice my thumb, but ignore the wound after wiping it with a linen. I feed them to him slowly, one sip at a time between slack lips, hardly able to look at him; he is so changed. So I do not notice at first that the cut has opened back up, and blood is running down the back of the spoon, and I am feeding it to him with the tinctures.

Embarrassed, I wipe his mouth and leave. At home I am greeted by the news that two other friends are ill as well. I take them the tinctures, and spend my afternoon feeding them. My wound is dressed now, and no blood mixes into theirs.

The next morning he is still alive, still clinging to this world all be it weakly, my other friends are dead. I suspect my blood has helped him, and as I go around our newly fallen friends that morning taking the tinctures, I slip them a dose of my blood too. Once the tinctures run out, I hold the cuts against their mouths and drip my blood straight onto their tongues. By the time the shadows are lengthening towards nightfall, I am ill. I remember only feeling light-headed, hot and cold, every cut on my hands and wrists that I have fed my friends from is throbbing to a deep and heated beat. I start to ask my slave to bring Ahmes, sure I am about to die. But then I am waking up, and the world is different, colours brighter, sounds clearer, the moonlight like liquid silver flowing through the window. I rise from my couch where I have lain in my sickness, and slip through the sleeping house and into Ahmes' rooms. The perfume of him stuns me and creates such a hunger in me. I try to eat dates from a dish in his room, and swig wine that's been left in a goblet by his bed, but they taste of mud and rotted fruit, and as soon as they hit my stomach, it cramps horribly. I am forced to dash to his commode as my bowels rip open and my whole body convulses with its ejection of my meal.

When I'm finished, I try swigging some water to wash the flavours out of my mouth, but the water tastes stagnant, and I'm immediately crippled with cramps, and squatting over his pot again. All this time the scent of him rises enticingly, my ears throb with the sound of his heart beat, and my hunger digs its fierce claws deeper. As I remove the chamber pot from his room, leaving it outside the room for his staff to deal with, he awakes and seeing me, smiles in delight. He opens his arms to me and I slide into his bed beside him.

We kiss, and I hope to stave off my craving by cleaving to him, but as our kisses deepen, I hear his heartbeat rising, singing its lure to me. I kiss across his cheek to his ear, and nibble the lobe while he growls in pleasure. I find myself kissing and biting his neck, my tongue tracing the throb of his pulse, so near under his skin. I do not mean to bite deeper, but he meets the pain not with cries but gasps of pleasure, and as I lap the nick I've torn, he enters my body and in the whirl of lust and pleasure that engulfs me, I tear deeper, and drink my fill.

The pain of my first feeding drives Ahmes into a frenzy and he pumps and arches, and then lies beneath me spent and weakened. I am terrified I have killed him, and sit above him sobbing and begging him to speak to me. He raises a limp hand and strokes my cheek before slipping into a deep dark sleep. I still hear his heart, weak and thready but constant. I can't bear to be found with him, but I can't bear to leave him either, so I hide in a shadowy corner amongst his wall drapings, curled into a ball, and keep vigil, listening as his tired heart fights for his life.

While I wait unseen and stricken, to see if he will wake, his retinue come and go chattering with concern when they see his pale malaise. They think my leavings are his, and that he is now gripped by whatever malaise ails our friends. They do not wish to risk contamination, so they do not untuck the linens I have wrapped around his bite. In the two days I wait, I hear whispers of concern about my whereabouts, but in the muddle everyone assumes I have died and someone else has arranged for my body to be taken to the embalmers.

As time passes, their whispers became more urgent and scared, they speak of terrible things. Corpses taken to their tomb only to walk back out days later, bodies carried to the embalmers only for them to sit up and drink the blood of the medic. They mutter of the demons of the underworld risen into corpses to drink the blood of the living, no longer satisfied with just the dead. They are afraid I will return and drink their blood, so I hide carefully, afraid of what they will do if they find me, wondering if I am possessed by greedy demons. As the stories worsen, and my own hunger rises its vicious head once more, I come to my own conclusions. When Ahmes awakes, I am waiting for him, with the half drained body of the boy who had painted his eyes and dressed his hair. After that I listen no more, for there is no one left for me to hear.

Chapter Nine

Rae

Suddenly, I am back in France, the light, the scents, the sounds so different from ancient Egypt. I am light-headed and dazzled, unbalanced from the contrast of the two times, the two minds. Amunet looks at me and smiles vaguely, and then tells me the rest of her story.

'We were an abomination, a shame upon our people, unable to die, unable to return to our gods. They believed we were demons and fled without looking back, and they wiped us from their history in shame and horror. We too believed we were vessels for these dark demons, and waited to see what that meant. New and sickly we had no energy to go after the families who abandoned us to our fates. Instead, we fed on the loyal few who remained, and raided the prisons and dungeons where the criminals had been abandoned by their jailors. When they turned, they fed on us in return. We no longer needed to travel to our secret cave, instead we could recreate our theatre in my villa itself. We discovered the bliss of drum beats and blood to the vampire senses, feeding and fucking to our hearts' content. We did not know what we were, demons or gods, but we soon learned to love being whatever it was.

'Every now and again someone would become ill again, some died; most often the deaths were those who had only fed on vampire or animal. They never seemed as strong as those who fed on human first. Those who did reawaken would be a little different each time. Slowly, as mutations corrupted the virus that we re-infected each other with over and over, it became closer to the infection modern vampires know. Our features changed, becoming the big eyed, pale-skinned, purple-taloned creatures you would know today. There were many unsuccessful mutations over the years that lead to horrible deaths for the vampires afflicted, wings and a yearning for flight the bones were too heavy for, an exoskeleton that crushed the organs. Their deaths were brutal and prolonged.

'Eventually, we noticed the Gifts developing, the Compelling had been apparent for a while by then, a blessing for those still squeamish about killing. It would have been the fourth or fifth time I transformed that I awoke and found myself much changed. I discovered that I could feel whatever someone else felt. At first, like every new vampire, it overwhelmed me, but over time I learned to manage my Gift, choosing when to be an Empath. The Gift allowed me to gauge how others felt, their motivations, weaknesses and fears. I was able to use this knowledge to decide how best to manipulate situations, pre-empting individuals, understanding their desires before they did. As the only vampire with royal blood, and this ability to please and appease, I became their Queen. By now we had decided that we were not the underworld damned, escaped to wreak havoc; instead, we believed ourselves gods, a race superior to humans, the race entitled to rule the world.

'We discovered Ahmes' Gift accidentally, when he fed on a man who had been a kitchen slave when human. Our new society was remarkably egalitarian, criminals, diplomats, slaves and priests mingled and played together, happy with our godly new existence, blessed with the Gifts, and empowered with divine strengths and drives. However, with my Gift I had become aware of some small number of malcontents, individuals who still bore grudges from their human lives they could not move on from for the greater good of our community. This vampire was one such soul, indeed, I suspected him to be the ring leader. Whenever I came into close contact with him, I felt itchy and uncomfortable, almost suffocated with unsatisfied rage. I called for an audience with him, with just my husband and closest friends in attendance.

'I tried to speak to him, to find solutions to his discontents, to soothe his agitations, but he would not be won over. The more I offered and contrived to find solutions, the more furious and resentful he became, as I offered him exactly what he yearned for. I realised his resentments went deeper than I could calm with gift and glory, and so my patience with him snapped. I clicked my fingers to order my friends to take him to our dungeon, but he spoke out against me, and I discovered his Gift as he did so. My people fell back at his Command, unable to carry out my orders. As an Empath, I could feel his effect on them while not being influenced myself. His insolence outraged me, and where before I had felt dismay at his inability to settle with the rest of us, now I felt fury.

'I strode past his arrogantly pointing finger, as he Commanded my friends, and tore at his throat before he knew what had happened. He was not used to vampires able to resist the control of his whims, so his surprise prevented his defence until it was too late. It was I who started the attack, and our friends that held him down, able to move again as soon as I disabled him; but it was Ahmes who actually fed on him until his heart stopped. It was Ahmes, so enraged by the slave boy's insolence, who fed while he tore the empty heart from the ribcage. It was the first time we had seen a vampire die, other than during transition, or due to some unfortunate change wrought by the virus. That was how we learned about separating the heart and the head.

'It was also how we learned that Ahmes could absorb the Gift of any vampire he drank from as he killed them. After the slaughter of the slave boy with the Gift of Command, Ahmes could dictate another vampire's behaviour with a click of his fingers. He went from being my consort to my King. I could not be Commanded, but everyone else could; our love allowed us to create an invincible alliance, where without it we may have faced an unholy enmity.

'Once he had absorbed the powers of Command, Strength and Stealth, Ahmes was almost undefeatable. If he had stopped there, he could have ruled the world, both vampire and human. But he saw a Pretty One, and wanted that Gift too. Then he saw a Psychic and took that, he took Speed, and Forgetting and Distraction, and anything else he saw that he wanted. He started off only taking the Gifts of those vampires who broke our rules, but then he created more and more obscure rules to ensure that the vampire who had a Gift he wanted could not help but contravene them. As time passed however, he did not even bother with these flimsy niceties, but just took what he wanted.

'We first discovered the Rage when he tried to take the Gift, and therefore life, of an exceptionally beautiful vampire who had been a slave and now had the gift of Siren Song. I remembered the days he would have just wanted to bed such a woman with nostalgia. She would not give up easily, and when he sidled into her bed chamber one night, his Stealth powers allowing him to mingle with the shadows and move so silently that even vampire senses could not detect him, she met his eventual onslaught and attack with the towering transformation you and Layla experience. He overpowered her eventually, but he became fixated on the Rage.

'He would scare our comrades, attacking them from hidden corners, dropping on them from great heights, and flickering into existence besides them as they innocently went about their day. He had stumbled onto every vampire's weakness to attack from behind, and used the advantage mercilessly. He'd slash them with curved blades and watch their Rage reactions. No matter how dear they were to me, or how important within our Court, he would murder the vampires that exhibited the biggest reactions.

'He never inherited the Rage, though. I noticed that the vampires who had had difficult lives as humans, torn from their families, bereaved, or beaten by husbands or masters, these were the vampires with the greatest Rage transformations. I realised he had been too pampered, his life had been too easy, as had mine. We only experienced the subtlest of changes. He would not be advised though, and his pursuit of Rage increased his consumption of the other vampires until there came the inevitable uprising against us.

'Fear had meant they left it too late to revolt, though. He Commanded our guard to protect us and howled with maddened laughter as civil war ripped through our community. This is when I realised that in chasing the Rage, he had found madness. When he was hard with battle triumph, I took him to my bed, and drank from him for the first time in months. His thoughts were a flickering morass, incoherent, bloodied.

'A gentle female friend of mine awoke as a Healer, and I brought her to him, begging him to feed gently, just a little each day, so he may be healed, as her husband had when he'd been poisoned by the blood of a Destroyer. He would not listen, and he drank the healer dry, determined to steal her Gift. That night he lay in wait, and stole the Gift of the Destroyer too, almost poisoning himself in the process. Only the Healer's blood awash in his system saved him. That night as I sat beside my squirming love, wracked with poisoned agony, I realised that we were not earthbound Gods. We were after all the demonic abominations, aberrations too powerful for this earth. I decided I would allow my husband to continue his greedy trail of destruction. Vampires should not exist, and he could destroy them. Then I would destroy him, then myself.

'I stood with him, implacable, as he tore through our people. His appetites knew no bounds. When vampires tried to flee his desires, he hunted them with his friends, taking whooping pleasure in the chase. He would feed his friends his blood before the hunts so they were as hysterical as him, their horses eye-rollingly terrified beneath them. His closest consorts and allies remained uneasily safe in their inner circle, and we still danced our moonlight dances of lust and madness. They were no longer a pleasure to me, just one more cold, grey chore to be play-acted to cover my true intent. As each friend fell back into the transformative sleep, and their Gift became stronger, Ahmes' hungry gaze would fall on them, and they would disappear.

'Until only our closest few friends remained, and my beloved Kha came to me, my friend, my protector, and begged me to leave with him, secretly, that night. For a moment, a different life, with my gentle friend shone golden in my future, but Ahmes would never let us go. He would hunt us as he'd hunted the others, mercilessly. When the scarlet tears trailed down my cheeks, Kha held me in his arms and begged. I spluttered out my fears that we were indeed the demons, troubled and tortured in the underworld, lured into the upper world by our wicked behaviour in the cave.

'He did not contradict me. He rested his forehead on mine, and promised me there was another way we could exist. He told me he had started feeding only on animals, foraging for flocks and wild life. He promised we could live without spreading our infection further, hidden from humans. That we did not even need to kill the animals we fed on. He told me that Ahmes massacres were not my fault, his gentle brown eyes gazing into mine. I could read him with my Gift, and I knew he spoke the truth, as he saw it. He didn't understand though, it was me who had infected Ahmes, and so I was responsible for him. Kha had been infected later, when he would not abandon me. He had not partaken of our wanton wickedness; this was not his mess. He did not need to remain and remove the blight from the earth. I drew on every regal resource left in me and ordered him to leave immediately and follow the path he described.

'He begged to be allowed to stay with me, to help me. I forbade it. He begged to be allowed to wait for me, hidden far away, so when it was over, I could join him. I started to refuse him, to tell him I would be ending my own life after my husband's, but one look at his pleading face, and I knew that if he realised my plans, he would never leave. So I agreed I would find him later, once the monsters were slayed, and finally he left.

'Soon afterwards the rest of our court fled too, snatching their chance while Ahmes hunted his best friend. His brother at arms had just awoken from another distorting sleep to discover he was a Chameleon, and my husband lusted after that Gift to go with his others. When he returned on his exhausted horse, dragging his friend's bloodied mount behind his, he found me alone. Oh, how he raged and tantrumed when he realised they had left him. But then his guile rose, and he turned on his stolen Seeker Gift, and made to set out to hunt them that very night. I bade him to wait though, to let the horses rest. Wearily, I promised him he could find them all so easily, pointed out that a head start would allow him to enjoy the chase even more.

'The next day was the first day of our nomadic life. We chased across the continent, and then the world as he fed on our fellow vampires, and their new kin. He savoured every second of every kill. Eventually, there was only one vampire left, Kha. I thought, hoped, Ahmes may have forgotten. He was so maddened now, but he hadn't. When we found Kha, he was living alone in the Romanian mountains. I persuaded Ahmes to wait instead of rushing into the kill, and we watched him for a week or more, living alone and peacefully, feeding only on his livestock. For the first time I questioned my belief that all vampires are ravenous monsters, blinded by their own lusts.

'Silently, my fury rose as I watched his peaceable ways, as he made a liar out of me. "I want to kill this one," I told Ahmes. He was shocked, some deep memory of my lifelong friendship stirred. When I snarled my contempt for his farming and pacifism though, Ahmes jiggled with laughter and urged me on. I strode across the clearing in the pine forest around his home, making no attempt to silence my footsteps. He spun at the cracking of a twig, and his face lit up with such delight at the sight of me, such open-hearted pleasure, that my fury evaporated, and I felt grubby and unworthy of his adoration.

'"RUN," I mouthed silently, the only warning I could offer, and in an instant he took my meaning, and terror crossed his face like a slap, his gaze flitting over my shoulder to where Ahmes bounced and clapped like a maddened monkey. Kha curled away from me, sprinting into the forest, dropping his feeding bowls as he ran, and I bounded after him in pursuit. In the days we had watched him, we had explored his environment and I knew that about a mile away, through the pine forests, there was a jagged ravine with a fast river roaring along its floor. I herded him towards it, I could hear Ahmes howling and screeching in the trees behind me as he leapt from bough to bough, intoxicated by the game. Kha glanced back over his shoulder at me once, aware of where I was chasing him. I had one second to hold his gaze, to nod a comfort and hope he would trust me still. As we reached the edge of the ravine, he wheeled to face me, and I grabbed him.

"'Hide," I breathed into his ear, then tore into his throat, messily ripping his flesh so my face was coated with his blood. I held him for a few seconds longer, my face tucked against his neck as he struggled and writhed, attempting to push me off, but never once hurting me. "Collapse. I will push you, fall, then hide. Do not ever let him find you," I whispered quickly. He suddenly went limp in my arms a dead weight, so I staggered, dropping him down the cliff face more convincingly than I'd planned. I watched him tumble and crash down over the jagged rocks, and Ahmes arrived at my side as he splashed into the river and was washed out of sight.

"'Dead?" he asked me.

"'Yes." I used the wiping of his blood from my mouth as an excuse to slightly avert my gaze. "We should stay here," I added, remembering to lick my fingers with forced relish. He refused, he missed the golden light and open skies of our homeland, but I persuaded him to stay for one night. As I curled around him, tucking my legs into the back of his, and wrapping my arms around him, ruby tears slipped down my nose while I took advantage of his inability to protect himself from behind and bite his neck, feeding and feeding, until his struggles became feeble, and finally stopped. I knew it was time for the killing blow, but in his blood I'd followed the muddled avenues of his mind, traced the fractured thoughts, and always, in every minute of every day, my own dusty lily perfume scented his every moment.

'His love for me was as imperfect as mine for him, but every bit as intense. I held him in my arms, unable to strike the killing blow. I do not know if it was my feeding on him that brought another changing sleep to him, or if it would have happened anyway, a consequence of so many feedings. This time he slept for many days, and when he woke, he was utterly addled, and none of his Gifts worked anymore. Initially, he was difficult to care for as a disobedient child, but I welcomed my new life, safe from inflicting further harm on the world.

'Together we found a sort of peace, in our hidden mountain home feeding only on travellers that strayed too close to our farm and would not be missed. I discovered that I could entertain Ahmes for hours merely by scattering the livestock's corn or oats in front of him. He would become engrossed, separating and sorting, counting and columning the seeds for hours on end, unable to leave them until he had sorted them to his own satisfaction. This made my life immeasurably easier, and allowed me the hunts I needed to keep us both fed.

'Occasionally, he would have a spell of coherence, and disappear from my guard, racing me to local villages to seize the unwary. He would hide with them, infect them and let them change. Once they were vampire, he would kill them, still chasing the elusive Rage. I learnt to let him finish his cycle with them; otherwise, I was forced to kill them myself, and he simply repeated the process until allowed to kill a vampire.

'In an attempt to restrict his escapes, I fed from him again, deeply, until he was unconscious, hardly breathing at all. Then I thickly veiled myself, and rushed to a remote town to commission the blacksmith to make me the heaviest, strongest chain and shackle they could. I claimed I had a monstrous dog, bigger and stronger than a bear, that I needed to restrain, and I promised a gold and turquoise ring from my own finger if he could complete the work in a month.

'A month later, I fed from Ahmes again, even though he'd hardly regained his strength from the last time I fed on him, and once he slept, weakened and safe to leave, I travelled to the forge at night. I wanted to take the chain without being seen, so questions wouldn't be raised when I could so easily sling the great roughly worked links over one shoulder and walk away. I left the ring for the blacksmith though; he had a family to feed and he had done a good job. The restraints were not ornate, but they were sturdy and honest. When I returned to our farm, I lined the shackle with sheep's wool for comfort, then bolted it around Ahmes' throat and attached the other end of the chain to a mighty fir tree close to the hut. He had the freedom to roam our home and the clearing surrounding it but could not wander further.

'We settled into a strange peace, my love and I, dreamy days that drifted first into years, and then decades. Although he was completely maddened, he always knew me, babbling incessantly, and we kissed and loved each other passionately. Over the years his physical beauty faded as his madness grew, but I did not care; he loved me now, only me.

'Occasionally, the whirring cogs of his brain would click into a sort of order and he would be clear-headed for a while. I usually discovered this when he escaped, because he quickly learned to hide his coherent times from me. I would trace his progress by the trail of bloodied animal corpses, and sorted seeds. Then the distressed cries of families missing a loved one would confirm I was close. He never killed the humans immediately; even mad he would lure them away, infect them, and then murder the freshly turned vampire while they were weak and confused. Still chasing the Gifts, my megalomaniac darling. I learned to let him have these hunts, the fresh dose of the virus quickly tipped him back into fractured thought and coddled ideas, so I could guide him weakly home.

'Mostly, though, he fed from me. I would fill myself to brimming with blood from wandering individuals, mad old folk, or disgraced girls. I would approach silently and Compel them, so they slipped into a comforting sleep as I fed, a delicious escape from their troubles. Afterwards, I would wrap Ahmes in my arms and let him feed from me while he slipped himself inside me, taking and giving with such abandoned lust. I did not think his damaged mind would be able to make sense of the hidden memory of my friend's leap that I kept so carefully hidden from him, squirrelled in the furthest corner in my mind. I never thought of Kha, never, not even when I was alone.

'One spring evening, when I returned from feeding, he was gone. This time there was no blundered trail for me to follow, so I was forced to seek and search, and follow from finding only the faintest clues. I found scattered row of pinecones, where he had fallen into his counting sorting trance, but then roused, and recognised the trail he was leaving and tried to hide the evidence. I scented the fading scent of blood, listened for the echo of a last gasp. There were few clues to follow and I took too many wrong turns. Days stretched into weeks, which rolled into months as we travelled far, far from home, into hot arid lands so like home. I realised for the first time that I have missed the blessing of the sun's heated kiss on my shoulders.

'As dusk fell one evening, I settled at a safe distance from the nearest village to feed on the elderly shepherd I'd taken, knowing that scavengers would have destroyed every sign of my blood draining by dawn. As I wiped my mouth on the soft fleece he had worn around his shoulder, I heard a scream. It was so faint, so far away, but pitched so richly that I could only believe a vampire could make the sound. It made my own blood run cold. I have never run as fast as I ran that night, but I was still too late. When I arrived in the rural homestead, far from the nearest village, Ahmes had already torn Kha apart. His bloody entrails were spread around his headless corpse, and Ahmes stood amidst the gore, holding Kha's head by its blood-matted locks.

'His eyes were cold as they met mine, and though he submitted and followed me home after I had buried deep the remains of my friend, things were never the same between us again. He could not forgive my betrayal when I only pretended to kill my friend, and I couldn't forgive his murder. We remained hidden; moving further into the mountains as humanity encroached, losing ourselves in the deepest European forests, their dark cold days a redemption of sorts.

'I had no idea Kha had turned others. I did not believe he would ever do such a thing. I had not accounted for his loneliness. I did not stay long enough at his home to discover any trace, and then I avoided all contact with the outside world for many, many centuries. It was only when Ahmes got loose again a few years ago that I discovered traces of a vampire kill that was not his. The corpse was still human.'

Without another word, Amunet stands up startling me. I had been transported to her life with Ahmes by her rich stories. Her regal bearing is only faintly betrayed by the beginnings of the fading to her colouring in the thin dawn light. The hours of talking have drained her, but they have left me overwhelmed with memories, facts fighting for attention. Overlying all is the deep grief that throbs through me for the death of my friend who still lies in a pool of blood in the lounge. Stunned and glutted with information, I don't try to stop her as she leaves. I watch her glide away, her husband's withered corpse in her arms, disappearing around the corner of the hedged lanes. Slowly, her footsteps fade, and the morning bird song and animal calls are the only sounds above the eternal bubbling of the river and song of the breeze in the orchard.

Chapter Ten

Rae

Sitting in the early morning sunshine, contemplating all I have learned, it takes me a little while to realise that I haven't seen Babette for hours. At first, I think she has been avoiding the Ancient Vampire, distrusting the stranger, so I call her. She doesn't come. There is no answering chirrup, no gentle weight arriving in my lap, accompanied by the deep bass purr. I try to banish the memory of Ahmes' grab for her yesterday when she spat at him. I try to remember if I saw her after he returned, but I can't pinpoint seeing her in amongst everything else that's happening. I walk towards the hangar with a sickening foreboding gnawing at my stomach and speeding my heartbeat, and there she is. She is curled on the hay strewn floor, too still. I don't need to walk closer, to see he's stamped on her skull, shattering her head into an unrecognisable mound, but I do. I don't need to tenderly smooth the curve of her back with my thumb to feel how cold she is, but I do.

As my scarlet tears run down my nose and drip onto her fur, a memory stirs from the tangle I drank from Ahmes when he inhabited Matt's body. I struggle not to witness the memory of him spotting her engrossed in hunting in the barn, and catching her up in one grab. The hand that dropped to her neck was not seeking her ticklish spot between her shoulders, instead the massive fingers she trusted snapped her fragile spine in an instant. Then he tossed her corpse onto the ground and stamped once on her head.

Watching her death is torturous, and my mind skitters over it, circling back to watch, and flinching away. My heart aches with the sense of betrayal she must have felt, her final seconds of confusion as the fingers that she trusted to feed and tickle her hurt her instead. My only comfort is that his mind was so full of me that he did not linger on my cat and draw out her death. Over and over, my imagination runs her fear through my head while I sob over her little corpse, my heart breaking.

Slowly though, my grief morphs and twists into a fury so absolute; so deep and dark that I forget who I am. I am absorbed into the moment, staring out of a black tunnel, spiked red with pain, betrayal, loss. I have no one. I have nothing. My rational mind tries to throw up images to slow my descent into maddened Rage, but each picture it sends just makes the pain worse. Layla laughing up at me from her sofa in Splott—betrayed me, gone. Mattie reaching his arms towards me, grin splitting his face—gone, at my own hands. My mother patting my hand at our last meal together—lost to me. Simon and Elaine—gone with Layla, as are David, Brian, Annie and Georgette. Everyone always prefers Layla, my desolate heart screams. Then comes the picture of Guillaume in the library, refusing to look at me for the wanting of me, and my demons laugh and laugh at my brains futile attempts at comfort. There is none.

The pains of the Rage transformation rip through me, physical pain lancing and searing the emotional agony, as my ribs tear through my sides, and bones extend through my fingertips, raw and ready for defence. But there's nothing to defend myself from, it's too late for that. So instead I destroy. I tear all the hay out of the bales and fling it around, stamping and kicking it. That's not enough; the lack of resistance makes me worse. I punch granite lumps out from the stone walls at the sheltered back of the barn, so the skin splits over my knuckles and the blood mixes with my tears, as fast as I heal, I split them again.

The sunlight spilling through the gaping holes in the wall that lights golden the dust from the settling hay feels like a personal insult, and I kick a wooden strut holding up the roof of the hangar, so it creaks and tilts. It's not enough. I am furious at how fast my wounds heal, I need to see the blood and feel the physical pain to drown out the emotional desolation. I gouge and tear at my face, my arms, and my chest, in between kicking and punching. I start headbutting the remaining walls, splitting my head open over and over again, then tearing at my hair, pulling out chunks, only for them to grow back, removing all the satisfaction of the pain. My tears now are thick clotted lumps and my sobs just the driest of rasps.

All the destruction I wreck does not touch Babette, though. She remains stiff and cold at the centre of my storm. Until finally I have blown myself out, and I collapse into a cross-legged heap beside her, and cradle her in my tattered lap, rocking and humming as my limbs retract and my body finishes healing. I am blind to my surroundings. I do not see the nest of hay surrounding me, matted thickly with my blood and hair, stomped into a clotted muddy circle around me. I don't see the fallen roof, which remains propped in only one front corner, or the rear and side walls that are hardly more than rubble now, littered with my nails and teeth where I tore them out without noticing.

I do not know how long the destruction lasted, or how long I sit afterwards, rocking, singing softly, empty. I don't notice when it is light, I don't notice when it is dark, or the pink flush of the dawn again. I don't notice anything at all.

'Dear God, Rae.' His shocked voice startles me out of my reverie. I didn't notice when he arrived, and I'm startled to see him standing in the triangle which is all that is left of the open front of the barn.

'What the hell happened here? Are you okay?' Guillaume continues questioning me as he crouches in front of me, lifting my chin with his fingers. I ignore him, fascinated by his lack of fear now, when it's so much too late. Too late, too late. It's all too late. I start to laugh, a whooping hyena howl of hysteria so he jolts back from me, appalled. Which makes me laugh louder. I consider for a moment, unbridling my Gift, forcing him to feel the Need for me in my repulsive state. Hiding from all that I have become in the fucking, but until when? Nothing is going to change. There's no point. My laughter dries up, and I return to rocking, ignoring Guillaume as I sing my dead cat a soft lullaby.

The next thing I know he has grabbed me under my armpits and is pulling me out of the barn. I cling to Babette and go floppy in his grip, not assisting him at all. When we are in the early sunlight, he looks me in the eye.

'GIVE ME THE CAT,' he Commands. I have to hand him her body, and he lays her gently in a flower bed on a soft bed of mint. 'NOW GET UP.' He is using his Gift on me, after I resisted using mine on him. I would Rage against it, tearing myself from his control, but I have no energy left, and I can't see the point anyway. 'COME WITH ME.' He leads the way to the house, but stops as soon as he enters the front door and sees the blood crusting the floor that has leaked out of the lounge.

'What the fuck happened here, Rae?' he asks, his eyes scanning my ravaged face; even his eternal calm is ruffled.

'He came back,' is all I'll say. 'I'm going to have a shower.' I walk past him, past the lounge doorway, turning my eyes away with Mattie's splayed legs. I turn back to Guillaume and look into his bewildered face. 'You know, Layla once told me I was good at negotiating the dance of life. She said I could always turn the one step forward and two steps backward nature of things into a Cha Cha Cha. But she was wrong. I'm here, all alone, just darkly dancing in the shadows.'

I turn away from his baffled eyes and slowly climb the stairs. In the bathroom I stop by the mirror and look at my smeared and clotted reflection impassively. My eyes are opaque, dead behind the blood-spiked lashes. I turn the water as hot as it will go, tear my dress off and drop it into the little white bin by the toilet that has never been used before. I stand under the full force of the shower and let the water cleanse my skin and hair. I stay in there for an hour, until I feel almost clean.

When I step out and grab the towel I left on the dresser during my last interrupted shower, I wrap it around me, and then survey the state of the bathroom. I wipe my gore footprints off the white floor tiles, with the toilet roll that has gathered dust from disuse. I am moving slowly, as if I am under water. Everything feels so far away. All I want to do is sleep. When the cleaning up is finished, I stop and gaze at myself in the mirror. I notice my skin is healed, even the scar on my lip from the battle at the Farm has been torn and re-healed smoothly this time. My hair, dry already, falls in lustrous curls and waves down my back, and my smooth implacable face is as unreadable as a doll's. I am perfect again.

I go to my room and dress in men's Levi's and a white T-shirt. Then I just sit on the end of my bed for a while, in a reverie as I consider my options before I finally go down to join Guillaume. While I've been showering, he has built a bonfire from the hay and patched together the struts supporting the roof, and fumbled the walls back into something resembling walls. The floors of the hallway and lounge are moped and bleached, and the ruined rug is smouldering on the bonfire too. Even for a vampire he has worked fast, and I vaguely appreciate the effort he has made to restore my home.

I wander out to where he has dug a deep hole in a sheltered corner, just behind the barn. He's thrown Mattie's body in there, separated head chucked in beside his trunk. I jump into the grave and, ignoring the look Guillaume gives me, I roll Matthieu onto his back, and position his head as close to his severed neck as I can get it. He almost looks as if he is just sleeping. As I climb back out of the hole, I catch sight of Babette's body, lying on top of the final pile of hay by the wide barn doorway, ready to be thrown onto the fire. I hiss and snatch her up glaring at Guillaume.

I jump back into Matt's grave, and tuck Babette's little body under his big hand. Getting back out of the grave, I give Guillaume a look, and run to the house. I return with the toys Matt made for her, feathers tied to twigs with ribbons and balls of tin foil that they played with together for hours, and lie those next to them. I take the shovel from Guillaume, and load it with earth. I look one last time at my two fallen friends, and then scatter the gentle earth upon them. He looks bewildered throughout the burial, but does not try to stop me, or ask any questions.

'You can go now,' I tell Guillaume without looking at him, hefting a second scoop of soil to scatter over them. I continue scattering the earth until their bodies are lightly covered, then I start to shovel in earnest. Once the grave is filled, I look up at him, where he is still standing watching me.

'Come on, you need to come back to the Farm with me, and on the way I need you to tell me exactly what happened here. We need to decide what we do next.' His voice is calm, confident, assured, brooking no argument.

'No,' I reply equally calmly. 'And do not even think of using that Command on me again, or I shall make you sorry.' The quietness of the threat serves to reinforce the promise. '*We* shall do nothing. There is no *we*. You will return to the Farm and ensure Layla and David are safe from Abigail.' Lying would take effort I do not have, so I say no more.

'Rae, I was told that you were all attacked, but they left you here. I came to get you...'

'Well, I'm not coming with you. I have things to do.' I pick up the shovel and walk away from him towards the house. I prop the shovel against the wall in the barn, then walk into the house and close the front door behind me. After a few minutes, his engine starts and he drives away. Once I'm sure he's gone, I retrieve my dress from the bathroom bin and carry it to the bonfire too. I look for the can of petrol that Brian kept filled in the stone outbuilding next to the house, in case we needed petrol in the daytime. We could fill the car at self-service stations in the night, but needed a backup supply for the days, especially since Layla never remembered to refill the car after she used it. Guillaume has left it next to the final load of hay that still needs to go onto the bonfire.

He's used most of the petrol to make the damp hay burn, but there's enough left to sprinkle over the final bundle of blood-soaked hay and hurl it onto the fire. I shake the last few drops over the dress and fling it into the flames too. Then I slowly, carefully, collect a big arm full of sleepy pink peonies from the garden, mix them with scented white roses and place them on the turf I've laid back over the grave, stamped into place so you can hardly see the disturbance. Only once that is done, and the fire has burnt out, can I finally crawl into bed and allow the blackness of sleep to welcome me. For once, I am glad vampires don't dream.

Layla

I'm still reeling from the fact she hasn't come with us when David and I arrive at the Farm. It takes me a while to notice that most of the Pride is missing; Simon tells us that several Farm vampires were still hunting in Normandy, and Guillaume and the rest of his inner circle have been unexpectedly called to assist a fellow Pride leader to make a judgement in an Italian Pride. I can't say I'm sorry; I'm deeply dreading the disapproval in his cold aquiline features when he hears what's happened, and that we've left Rae behind. Guillaume manages to make me feel like a stupid girl at the best of times. I really don't see what Rae sees in him, I don't think he's ever laughed in his life. His absence gives me time to lick my wounds a little.

I still smart from Rae attacking like she did. I've seen her turn on other people in the past, but she's never treated me like that. It doesn't happen often, but once she decides she dislikes or distrusts someone, she cuts them off. She never normally forgives the person she's turned cold on, but it'll be different this time, I'm sure. This is us. We've fallen out before, squabbles over silly things like forgotten bill payments at university, or someone using the last bit of milk and not replacing it. As long as I gave her time to calm down and start to miss me, she's always been fine, and we've resumed our friendship with only the tiniest blip. I'm confident she'll calm down once she realises the High Council are never going to find out what's happened. They aren't interested in me, and anyway, I was in disguise.

Even if they see the photos, they aren't going to recognise

me. Vampires often go into human environments to hunt. I didn't even kill anyone. When I try to talk to David about it, he just runs his fingers through his thick hair, blows his cheeks out and shrugs, looking haunted. God, sometimes he is just as bad as Rae. No wonder those two get on so well. Instead, I go to find Annie and Georgette.

They are such a sweet couple, slender fingers interlinked, shy giggles at each other's jokes, it makes me miss those tender early days with David. The days before all this blew up, and he got all serious and boring. The girlies are delighted to see me and we chatter and laugh while we work in the gardens and fed the livestock together. I find myself falling quickly back into the easy routines of country life. There's a lot to do with so many of the Pride absent, and I'm glad of the distractions. I don't want to think about what's happened, never mind talk about it.

It takes an entire day for them to realise this is more than a long promised visit to see them. We are sitting together in the rose garden after finishing the weeding, and the scent of roses is almost overwhelming on the gentle breeze. The air is busy with the buzzing of bees collecting their pollen. When I tell them about the attack from the Ancient Ones, their eyes become even bigger in their narrow faces and their mouths drop into hoops of astonishment.

'Have Rae and Brian gone after them with the rest of the Pride?' Georgette asks breathlessly. Their eyes remain huge and they gasp as I filled them in on Brian's betrayal, his awful fiancée, and our dreadful visitors. They giggle when I tell them about the incident with the pickles and clap in glee at my tales of Rae and Matthieu's trysts.

'So just Rae and Matthieu went with the rest of the Pride to get the old vampires then?' Annie asks when the laughter dies down.

'No, the rest of the Pride stayed where they were hunting,' I hedge.

'Just Rae and Matt went then? Gosh is that enough to deal with them when he can get into your head like that?'

'No one's gone after them. Amunet promised to keep Ahmes under control,' I explain. They stare at me, eyebrows raised.

'So it's just Rae and Matt at the cottage? What if those monsters go back? Why didn't they come? Did she think Guillaume would mind that she's got a boyfriend?' Annie probes, worry turning the corners of her mouth down.

'Rae knew perfectly well that our esteemed leader would not give a flying fuck if she had a whole harem of lovers,' I argue forcefully.

'So why didn't she come?' whispers Annie.

'At least she's got Mattie,' Georgette consoles her worried girlfriend. They both looked to me for confirmation, and spotlit in their innocent gazes, I have to confess the truth.

'Ah, actually no. I asked Matt to look after her while I was away, and he told me he was leaving too.' I can't meet their gaze.

'She's on her own?' Annie shrieks, causing a cloud of rooks to rise cawing from a nearby field. 'How could you leave her?'

'She wouldn't come, because I'm here,' I mutter.

'What did you do, Layla?' There is an edge of steel in Georgette's voice that I haven't heard before. The teenager really has grown up fast. Both of them look at me, stone-faced. All smiles and giggles vanish, so I tell them about Rae asking me to manage Megan's hunting, about how they could barely stand to be in the same room as each other, and Rae's fear that it would turn to violence between them. I explain how boring choosing a different spot each month was, and so we kept returning to the same area, and how that lead to Abigail's visit.

I want to tell them about the dancing; my reluctance to move away from the one town doesn't really make sense unless you knew about the huge three-storey nightclub with pounding beats, and sultry corners. About losing yourself in the vibrations from the speakers, and letting the rhythm flow through your entire body. Even still, I'm sure they'll agree that Rae is overreacting. I hope they'll agree to ring her and tell her to come. Tell that she's being silly sulking up there on her own when it's so dangerous.

Instead, they draw back from me, confusion in their eyes.

'But why, Layla? Why couldn't you just do as she asked?' I don't have an answer.

'I've heard of Abigail,' Annie says. 'She's not nice. Not nice at all. She hurts other vampires, controls them so they do what she wants. I heard Elaine and Simon talking about being worried that your cottage was too close to her when Elaine was looking for somewhere for you all to move to after the fight. Abigail was the reason they discounted it to begin with, but once Rae decided she needed to get away from Guillaume immediately, after she drank his blood, they decided they had to take the risk. They thought it would be okay, because you guys don't drink human. She thought Abigail wouldn't even realise you were there.'

'Bloody Megan,' I start. 'We were okay until she came along.'

'But you were asked, weren't you, to manage the hunts, to do them like Rae showed you. If you had done that, there wouldn't be a problem now.'

With that, they stand up to leave, shaking their heads and muttering to each other. I'm horrified. I can't believe they're judging me so harshly, and they don't even know the worst of it. I sit alone for a while, worrying that maybe Rae was right, maybe Abigail did have bigger plans for her knowledge. I feel a creeping unease at my vulnerability to her whim.

To dispel my unease, I jump up to return to the house, to see if David's in a better mood. I hope he's ready to kiss away my sudden fears. As I trail forlornly across the side garden, I hear a car approaching, and freeze; I recognise the throaty growl of the Land Rover. Guillaume is home. My heart sinks further. After the way the girls responded to my explanations, I'm really dreading seeing him now. Instead of going in, I linger in the shadows of the honeysuckle hedge and watch Simon and Elaine greet him, and accompany him into the house. It takes less than two minutes for him to slam back out of the front door again and climb back into his vehicle. Gravel spurts as he accelerates away. Simon leans in the doorway, face grim as he watches Guillaume leave.

'Where's he going?' I ask nonchalantly, remembering Rae's warning to leave with David if Guillaume suddenly went to go and get her.

'He wasn't pleased when he heard we left Rae behind after that attack. I tried explaining that it was what she requested, but, well...' He gestures to the lane where the dust cloud from Guillaume's departure still hangs in the still summer air and shrugs expansively.

'So, there was er, no phone calls before he left then?' I ask. Simon looks a bit confused. 'From, um Abigail, or, err, anyone?'

'No, he tried to telephone Rae, but there was no answer at the cottage. That was when he left.' Simon looks at me sceptically, and I try to nod wisely as if this is the information I was really after. Simon seems about to draw breath, and I fear he's going to ask me what's really going on. I feel his suspicions and if there's one person I want to confess to even less to Guillaume, it's Simon. He's of the implacable morals, minus Guillaume's holier than though attitude. He's not someone you want to disappoint. So I plaster a big smile on my face, and allow my Glamour to rise a little so Simon draws back in discomfort.

'Well excuse me,' I tinkle, batting my eyelids. 'I best go and check on my man.' I have no idea where the simpering cowgirl appears from but it does the job and makes Simon step out of my way, although he gives me a very odd look as I shimmy past and scamper upstairs.

Maybe Guillaume does care about Rae after all, I muse as I climb the second staircase up to our attic room. I feel my heart lift; he'll be able to persuade her to come back with him. She will do anything he asks. Then she and I will be able to sort things out properly. I can tell her I'm sorry, and promise not to do it again. We'll be fine. We should stay here at the Farm until the cottage sells, then find a new home somewhere far away from Abigail. Once Abigail sees she has succeeded in driving us away, she'll see our retreat as a victory and leave us alone. Then the three of us could settle somewhere near the Farm, so we can see our friends more often. Then we wouldn't get so lonely. So bored. I'm humming happily as I reach our bedroom. I can't wait to tell David everything is going to be okay after all.

I'm in a great mood all evening and all the next day. David and I make love, slowly and gently, and then cuddle in bed, talking about where in the world we'd like to go next, once Rae gets here. He fancies Puerto Rico to explore the rainforests, and I want to go to Thailand for a Full Moon party. Neither of us is sure how we'll get there, but we are confident we'll find a way. Later, I pad around the house and gardens, barefoot, enjoying the sunshine and breezes and steady hubbub of busy vampires now all the Pride is back together. I look for Annie and Georgette to tell them the good news, but I can't find them. I ask the others Pride members if they've seen them, but no one seems to know where they are. I'm just starting to wonder if I should worry about them when I hear a car approaching.

* * * *

I start to hurry to the front garden to greet them, but then I decide that I might be better letting Rae come to me in her own time. She can maintain a sulk that girl. Instead, I linger with the other vampires in the garden, apparently engrossed in some pruning, but really I'm watching the Land Rover pull up and park neatly. Guillaume climbs out with a face like thunder, brows draw and jaw clenched. The passenger door doesn't open. As my heart sinks, Guillaume scans the garden like a furious eagle until his gaze rests on me. He points at me and gestures abruptly at me to follow him as he strides into the house and into his study. I trot sheepishly behind him, ignoring the muttered queries from the rest of the Pride who have drawn closer to watch.

Guillaume is courteously but coldly holding the study door open, and he gestures to a seat opposite his desk as I enter, then slams the door behind us, making me jump and squeak. I decide that commiserating with him is probably the best policy. I know what Rae can be like and while instinct may make me take her side, indeed I can't help admire her for turning him down, the look on his face tells me this isn't the time to gloat.

'Did she do her sanctimonious shit on you?' I ask. He looks at me silently for several long lonely seconds, then sniffs and changes his gaze to just over my shoulder, and rests his chin on his clenched fists, elbows on the desk.

'You need to tell me what happened,' he states.

'Well, Rae was in the garden, and this awful little man arrived, and...'

'I know about that. Why is Rae on her own?'

'Okay. Erm, do you know about Brian?'

'Brian?'

'The Chameleon?'

'Oh, him.' Guillaume sniffs again, rolls his shirt sleeves up to his elbows, then rests his chin on his fists again. I do have to concede he does have the most beautiful forearms, broad and muscular, but not lumpen. 'No.'

'Err, okay, well, it turned out that Brian had made contact with his fiancée, and invited her over, in secret. Rae found out and went and put her into a trance and brought her back to the cottage, but when she came round, Brian lost control of her and she ran away, so Rae ran after her, and she punched Rae in the mouth, which cut her hand.'

'So she was infected?'

'So she was infected, and she hates Rae, and Rae hates her.' I look at him to check he's following me.

'And then...'

'And then she insisted on going hunting, so Rae organised one of her hunts—you know the ones she does?' Guillaume nods silently. 'It didn't go well. Megan was, um, disobedient. Rae was worried that things would escalate between them; Megan just has this ability to press Rae's buttons. She just doesn't seem to care, she deliberately wound her up. It was like she wanted to destroy our Pride. Rae was worried she would lash out in a Rage and kill her.'

'So,' prompts Guillaume coldly.

'So, Rae asked me to take her,' I mutter. 'Look, I'm not the Pride Leader, I couldn't see the point in all that messing about, so we went to a town near Calais, one with lots of tourists passing through, and I let her get on with it. Megan was the one that wanted to hunt, why should I have to watch? Rae was the one with all the rules that other vampires don't bother with, why should I have to do it?'

'I suspect Rae just wanted you to make sure Megan carried

out the safe procedure, rather than you having to lay the trap yourself?' Honestly, Guillaume is behaving like a headmaster with a disappointing five-year-old.

'Well, what do you think would have happened if I told her that Megan hadn't done the checks?' I ask.

'I think you wouldn't be in the situation you are in today,' he says drily.

I open my mouth to argue, concede he is probably at least partially correct.

'Anyway, these strange vampires turned up, Lady Abigail?' I wait to see if the name means anything to him. He thinks a moment, and then grimaces. 'Well, she arrived with two other vampires, Sebastian, who is one of Rae's exes from university, which was all a bit awkward, and Matthieu. Rae got together with him, Mattie. Pissed Sebastian off a bit I think.' I watch him to see if Rae's dalliance affects Guillaume at all. His face remains completely smooth. 'It turns out our hunts had been in her territory, and she wanted to know who we are. Rae hates Abigail too, she's actually a bit scared of her I think. Anyway, when Abigail left, she took Brian and Megan with her.'

'Rae is right to be frightened of her. She is old and dangerous, and does not appreciate strangers blundering into her territory. How did she know you'd been there?'

'Ah, it turns out Megan wasn't very good at getting rid of the bodies,' I explain, smiling my most beguiling smile at him, but he remains stone-faced. I'm tempted to turn my Glamour up, just a little, just to lighten the atmosphere.

'So you didn't even bother checking that was done properly?'

My smile freezes on my face, and I shake my head. 'No, I thought... well, I didn't like to keep checking on her. She was very convincing,' I gabble.

'So you just fucking let this disobedient and malicious New

One hunt on someone else's territory unsupervised, and brought an old and viscous vampire to your home seeking retribution.' Guillaume swearing is as shocking as his assessment of the situation. I nod. I can feel my bottom lip quiver, but he doesn't seem to notice.

'So,' he continues, taking over the story. 'You and Rae fall out, so she is outside when these other vampires attack?'

'Yes, that's when I messaged for help.'

'Which arrived too late. Rae had already fought her attacker off, and his wife had reclaimed him, promising to control him better. Simon told me that much. So, Rae arranges for Simon and Elaine to bring you here, so Abigail can't find you, and so she doesn't have to see you. Yes?'

'Um, well yes,' I nod. It's a somewhat negative summary, and I don't come out of very well. I was expecting more credit for summoning help. Nothing I can actually disagree with, though. And at least I haven't slipped up about the photos. Not that I have any desire to tell him. Guillaume is so furious already, I'd hate to see his reaction if he knew about that.

'So you leave Rae, all on her own, knowing there's a massive vampire, like an obsidian cliff face with it in for her?'

'What? No. Ahmes, the vampire who attacked us was wizened and grey, fetid. He stank. He was like, ugh, awful. The big black vampire is her... that's Matthieu. Why? He told me he was leaving after we left. Ahmes controlled him, he could do that, make us do what he wanted, all of us at the same time. Mattie almost had to rape Rae, but she attacked Ahmes while he was distracted. It was awful, and I don't think he could look at her afterwards. They didn't love each other...' I stop, a twinge of guilt making me wonder if I'm betraying Rae's confidence telling him this, but then I realise it's a bit late for such niceties. 'He told me that it was just supposed to be fun, something to make them both feel better. You know, because he'd had his heart broken too.' Guillaume has the decency to look slightly shame-faced. 'So he was leaving.'

'You were leaving her completely alone then?' he asks.

'I didn't want to. She refused to come. I didn't know what else to do. I thought you were bringing her back. I thought she'd come when you asked.'

'When I arrived, she was sitting in a smashed-up barn, a dead cat in her lap and blood everywhere...'

'A little silver cat?' I interrupt in horror.

'Grey,' he concedes, a look of horror passing over his face as I start to sob. 'Then, when I went into the house, there was a large black vampire dead, decapitated, on the floor.'

'What? No! Babette's dead? Mattie's dead? Oh my God! Oh, Rae! What the fuck happened?' I shriek.

'I have no idea. She refused to tell me. At least I understand why she wanted him buried nicely now. I thought she was just making sure he was actually dead when she jumped into the grave after him and started rearranging his body. And now I see why she wanted the cat in there too.'

I don't listen to anything else he says, I push my chair back and run up to our room to find David. He's horrified by what I tell him and wants to go and get Rae immediately, but I stop him. I can't bear the thought of her being all alone; the creep must have returned and killed Matthieu before he had chance to leave. And Babette. I have no idea what she's just been through, but even after all of that, with Guillaume there to get her, she's refused to come here. I have to respect how seriously she takes the threat of the High Council catching us together.

'But they don't know yet,' David reasons. 'We could get her, look after her for a bit, then when, if, the call from the High Council comes, we can disappear.'

'I'm going to ring her. Try to persuade her to come. It might be easier if she and I have cleared the air? She might come then,' I'm muttering to myself as much as David, and he pulls me into his lap and kisses my tears away.

* * * *

'Rae?'

'Yes.'

'It's me.'

'Yes.'

Oh dear, she is still fuming; I can hear it in her voice. It takes real fury for her voice to go completely flat and cold like that. She isn't going to make this easy on me. Usually when we're cross with each other, we can just ignore one another for a few hours, then whoever was in the wrong makes the other a cup of coffee, and everything is okay again. I swallow.

'Rae, Guillaume told me about Mattie, and Babette. I'm sorry, I'm so, so sorry. What happened? Did he come back?' There's a long cold silence while she decides whether or not to speak. When she does, her voice is empty, expressionless.

'Matthieu left just after you. I went to have a shower. Matthieu came in through the bathroom window. He was doing that thing with his shoulders Ahmes did. That jiggle.'

As soon as she says it, I know the shimmy she is describing, and an image of him flashes into mind, giggling and shifting in manic glee.

'I fed on him to be sure, and confirmed that Ahmes had attacked him on the road a few miles away. He subdued Matt mentally again, then drank his blood until he was almost empty. Then he made Mattie drink him completely dry, and somehow that allowed him to spread through Matt like a virus. So he could take him over completely, becoming him, snuffing Matthieu out.' Rae pauses for a moment, the short silence the only sign of any emotion.

'Ahmes then returned, intent on using the fitter young body to finish what he had started earlier, but Mattie had managed one last act of defiance before he was totally deleted. He had cut his own penis off.'

I gasp, but Rae doesn't echo my shock, she rejects my overture to commiserate again.

'When Ahmes saw that all that remained was a stump he was so shocked, so furious, I was able to take the knife Matthieu had slipped back into his pocket, unnoticed during the takeover. I stabbed him, and then slit his throat, decapitated him.'

'But, what if, what if Mattie...? Are you sure...?' I can't finish my question. Rae is silent again.

'Yes,' her voice is cold. 'He was gone. I could tell the difference.'

'And Babette?'

'She couldn't tell the difference. It was quick. I hope.'

'Oh Rae.' I'm sobbing again. 'Please let us come and get you. If the Council finds out about the photos, David and I will go with you when they phone the Farm. We can all go together and explain to the Council. If anyone should die for what happened, it's me. Only me. And if they don't, we can all go back to the cottage again in a few weeks, you, me and David. We can make it home again.'

'No.'

'What? Okay, we'll sell it. Live near the Farm again. Leave all those memories behind.'

'No. Listen, Layla, yesterday I buried two of the creatures I loved most in the entire world. Don't make me responsible for killing you too.'

'I thought you didn't love Mattie?'

'I wasn't in love with him, but of course I loved him, he was my friend.'

'I'm your friend, and I love you, and I'm begging you to come here. To face whatever comes side by side.'

'No.'

'Rae, *please.*'

'Layla, if they find out, they will demand I kill you and David for your disobedience. Both of you. We will not get to pick and choose who pays the price. And then Guillaume will probably still have to kill me for my inability to control you, and my abuse of the last chance they gave me last time. If we are very lucky, Guillaume may survive because he doesn't know anything about what's happened, and we no longer live under his protection. They may decide to summon Brian and Megan too. Why do you think I asked you to supervise the hunts rather than let her go alone?'

'I... you, why didn't you explain it this clearly then, when you asked me?'

'I thought I had.' So cold, so supercilious. 'Layla, you are happier now than I have ever known you, with David. Don't throw that away. Go, the two of you, hide, and live.'

'Please, Rae. I can't bear to think of you on your own through all this.'

'I am absolutely fine. I have to prepare. I have bought a pay as you go phone. I don't know its number. I will ring your number from it later. Write the number down, and delete it from your call log. Buy a pay as you go phone as soon as you can without anyone seeing. Ring the number I called you from, and then completely destroy the paper you have written it on. Hide the phone. Delete all of your social media accounts, and destroy your old phone. Destroy anything they could use to trace you.'

'Do not let anyone see you have the new phone. It is only for complete emergencies. I will only contact you if things are even worse than I thought and I truly believe they know where you are. Do not use it to contact anyone else at all. No one, ever. You know the Council collects vampires with every Gift, so they will be able to make anyone do anything they want. They will feed on me and raid my memories, so I can only hope this will protect you, and Guillaume since he has no part in warning you.'

Finally, as she talks about Ula and the others feeding on her, ransacking her mind, I detect a faint quiver in her voice, but then she swallows and continues.

'You must leave soon, tomorrow. You put them all in danger...' She is quiet for a beat. 'Goodbye.' She puts the phone down. I can't believe it. I can't believe it's over, just like that. I ring her back, choking on my sobs, determined to make her change her mind, sure there must be somewhere in the world we can hide together, must be someone, somewhere who can help us. Her phone is turned off, and the landline just rings and rings, so I am sure she has unplugged it. No one could sit in an empty house listening to a phone ring for that long without answering it, especially not a vampire.

Later, I hear my phone trill once with an unknown number, I try to answer the call but I'm too late, and when I ring it back, the phone is switched off already. So I write down the number, and memorise it. Then I destroy the paper and delete my call log, incoming and outgoing. David tries to persuade me to go back to the cottage anyway, but I just shake my head and order a cheap handset from Amazon for next day delivery. Then I set about posting comments on Facebook, Twitter, and Instagram that I've had enough of social media and I'm having a detox, choosing a simpler way of life.

Chapter Eleven

Rae

After I hang up the phone on Layla, I mooch around looking for things to do. I weed the flower beds and vegetable patch, but I'm unsure whether I'm actually pulling up weeds or David's carefully nurtured seedlings. I put a fresh bunch of flowers on the grave, which is hardly visible now that the turf has reknitted into the meadow. The extra effort Guillaume took to first remove and protect the top layer of grass, so I could relay it once the grave was full has paid off. I don't like to think about how he learned to do this to disguise burials so quickly, it is likely to be from his times with Patrice. Afterwards, I start scrubbing the kitchen and bathroom. The bleach burns my nostrils and normally I recoil from it, preferring to use the gentler eco products that are needed for the septic tank, but today I feel the need to really cleanse everything, even scrubbing the grout with the tooth brush Megan left behind.

I pack my rucksack to take with me when they come, slipping my small sharp flick knife into the inner pocket. I add emergency supplies, including a second sturdier knife with a curved and vicious blade I've sharpened to a razor edge. I dither a while over Layla's disguise, but eventually decide that it's better to have her wig and veneers with me, reasoning that it's better to be safe than sorry. Finally, I carefully fold my only smart outfit, so I have something respectable to wear when I am before the Council.

When there is nothing else at all I can clean or dig or mow and the inky sky is scattered with stars, the first blush of dawn just kissing the woodland at the top of the surrounding hills, I go down to the river. Naked, I slip into the icy water and float in the deepest pool and let my mind float with my body, the sensations of the cold water lapping against my skin keeping me present as I contemplate what to do. It would be best for everyone if there was a way I could kill myself. Guillaume could not be blamed for what I allowed, and Layla would be gone, untraceable. It is hard for a vampire to die though, the usual techniques would not work and I'm not convinced I could hack my own head off. I suspect that my body would heal as fast as I could hack. I consider hanging myself with cheese wire, but don't think even that would be sharp enough to cut through my vampire flesh, muscle and bone before it snapped.

Eventually, I give up and climb out of the river, striding nude and dripping diamond droplets back up to the house. I resist the temptation to ring the Farm, to check up Layla has left, and is no longer dawdling and putting the whole Pride at risk. I leave the landline unplugged and my mobile turned off. When the Council's henchmen come, there won't be any warning anyway, they will just arrive. I am cold into my very bones, but it is not an unpleasant pain like it would be if I was still human, rather it just serves to keep my mind on the sensations in my body rather than replaying over and over the slice that took Mattie's head off and Layla's voice asking 'Are you sure?'. I wipe the last of the water from my icy limbs and wrap my hair in a towel, then I climb into my bed and meditate so that as I warm up and my muscles relax, they feel heavy and softly, finally, I float into sleep.

I sleep for a long time, diving back into the comforting depths of my slumber every time I start to surface, until finally my eyes spring open and terrified thoughts whirl around my head. Has she gone? Are they safe? Will the High Council think I might try to hide her and go to the Farm first, rather than come after me? It is bright sunshine outside, I guess from the heat of the day, and the angle of the sunbeams sliding through the gap in my curtains that it's late afternoon. I have no way to check how long I've been asleep because I don't know what day or date it was when I went to sleep, but I have a sense it's been more than twenty-four hours.

'Rae.' I realise it was his voice that woke me up initially. He's downstairs, calling me. Of course they've sent him, not strangers. A final cruelty.

'Coming,' I call. I put on jeans, a cotton vest top, and hooded top I'd laid out ready. It's a man's top, so the sleeves cover my hands, combined with the hood, and sunglasses, it protects me from casual observers.

I pad downstairs and Guillaume stands in the hallway, hands clasped behind his back, pale face still and sombre. It's sooner than I hoped, but no worse than I feared. There is only Guillaume here, no High Council Henchmen have accompanied him. I attempt a smile, but it dies on my lips and I nod to him, instead.

'Why didn't you warn me to expect this?' he asks quietly.

'Plausible deniability,' I mutter as I glance around one last time to make sure there is nothing I've missed, no last evidence of our stay I haven't removed. 'Your Pride needs you to survive this. We will go to the Council, and when they tell you to kill me, you will do so without argument or discussion.' He opens his mouth to speak, brow furrowed. 'Please respect my decision on this matter, I have considered every option, and it is the only one. And Guillaume, if there is a chance to kill me before they feed on me, please, please take it.' Again, he starts to argue, but I hold his gaze. 'Please.'

His dark emerald eyes glitter as he looks back at me for long moments, looking, and really seeing; for the first time he drops his defences around me. It feels like he's reading my soul. Finally, he nods, once, and I grab my carefully prepared bag from by the door. We leave the cottage for the last time in a tense but strangely companionable silence.

He drives his Land Rover out of the garden and I follow behind, closing the gate securely before climbing up into the passenger seat. On the dashboard in front of me is a neatly opened brown envelope addressed to Guillaume, with a German postmark. I can see the sheen of photographs through the opened end.

'They posted the photos to you?' I ask, surprised.

'They sent them by overnight courier,' he replies.

'But... why didn't they just email them? It would have been quicker, and more secure.'

'It wouldn't have had the same impact, though. They do love to orchestrate a situation.' Guillaume smiles at me wryly.

'Can I look at them?' I ask, and he nods grimly. He doesn't pull away from the cottage, instead we sit with the engine rumbling idly. There are only three glossy photographs, but they are far worse than I was expecting. These are not the pictures Abigail showed me, where Layla was a shadowy glimpse in a far corner. In these photos she is in the centre of the group, arms draped over human shoulders, ghastly grin mocking me from the page. I flick quickly through the photographs, horrified. Then I shove them back into the envelope and put them into the glove compartment.

'They aren't the photos Abigail showed me,' I tell Guillaume. 'In the ones I saw she was just a blur in the corner.

There was a real possibility they might never find them. The internet is a big place.'

'They didn't find these. They were sent to them. Anonymously.'

'Oh.' Finally, he puts the Land Rover into gear and pulls away.

When we reach the T junction on the outskirts of the village, a farm hand is blocking the junction. I realise it's milking time, and they are moving the cows from their field to the milking sheds. Guillaume's breath hisses through his teeth, and I think for a moment that he is going to nudge through anyway, but then the first lumbering cows arrive in the road, and he sinks back in his seat, fingers tapping the steering wheel to his own agitated internal rhythm.

Despite my anxiety I can't resist looking beyond the swaying morass of bony black and white backs, up to the gardens of the two old ladies I like watching. To my surprise the skinny one has visitors. They are sitting around a table on the front terrace outside her bungalow. There's a man who looks in his early thirties, and is unmistakeably her son, although he is chubby and comfortably worn in a way she isn't. The plump pretty woman beside him, clutching his hand, is obviously his wife, and the mother of the boy and girl of about six and seven, who are busily drawing on the other side of the table. I watch the mother pass them another packet of coloured pencils from her bag before taking a nervous sip from her glass of water.

'...just after my money... sell this place... keep the money...'

I can only hear snatches of what the old woman is snarling at her son, over the grumbling engine and complaining cows, but his grey face tells the rest of the story. He shakes his head empathically.

'Mother... live with us... build an annexe... look after you...'

The plump neighbour is in her garden, and the pained look on her face shows she can hear what is being said all too clearly. She hurries to the fence that divides their gardens, hers as colourful as a child's colouring book, with roses and peonies, camellias, and gerberas spilling from beds and pots; her neighbour's is just a neatly mown lawn. The children see her coming and jump up to run to see her, clutching their drawings. She passes them sweeties through the fence and listens intently as they excitedly describe their drawings to her, while she exclaims delightedly about how clever they are. She carefully keeps them distracted as the adults at the table continue their heated conversation until finally the man shoves his seat back and stands, fists clenched, head drooping.

'Fine, Mother. Whatever you wish,' he says sadly. His mother crosses her skinny arms and tilts her bony chin in victory, while his wife scrabbles the children's art supplies back into her bag.

I feel Guillaume depress the clutch ready to put the Land Rover into gear, and realise the cows have passed, and pat splattered road is free again. I reach over and pat his hand on the gearstick.

'Wait. Please,' I whisper.

The mother and father have left the table; chairs neatly tucked back under it and are standing at the fence with their children. The plump neighbour says something that clears their faces and makes them laugh. Then the man reaches over the fence and wraps her in a warm hug before herding his family down the garden, calling and waving back to the sweet lady whose face is alight with love. I lift my hand from Guillaume's, and he shifts the vehicle into gear and pulls away.

'I got it all wrong,' I say. 'I thought the plump sweet one was the one with the family who loved her. I thought the thin one was bitter because she didn't have anyone, that life had disappointed her at every turn, so she became sad and sour in response. But she had it all. She had everything, all that love, and she was still mean and pithy. It was her friend who life let down, but she didn't let it spoil her. She still offered friendship to everyone, and was big-hearted enough to love that bitter old bitch anyway.'

Guillaume glances at me, a pinch of confusion between his brows.

'I could have been happy anyway,' I explain. 'I could have found a way.' For a moment, he looks like he's been punched, and I start to reassure him I wasn't talking about just him, I meant everything I'd lost, my family, my job, even Layla to some extent, as she and David became more and more of a couple. But then his face closes back up and he drives on, face as serene as a statue.

I think I've lost him; that the feeling of connection we made in the house has evaporated, but after a few miles of silence, he turns to me.

'We could run,' he suggests. 'Just drive away, go to the coast, and swim for Africa or the Caribbean, somewhere far away from them, and then hide. They would forget us, eventually.' My stomach and heart bunch into a big lumpy knot, I can't believe he's offering me this. I'm filled with love, and grief.

'We can't,' I reply. 'You know they will never stop. Layla and David's only chance is if they can exact their punishments on me. And your Pride needs you. My death is the only solution. I am so sorry you have to carry it out, but you must. And thank you. For offering.' I take his hand from the steering wheel and squeeze it hard. To my surprise, he squeezes back, and then laces his fingers through mine, resting our joined hands on his thigh. I turn and blaze a huge smile into his face, and he opens his mouth to say something, but then his dashboard starts to flash and bing an irritating chime.

'Bloody hell!' he exclaims, startling me with his venom. 'I meant to refuel on the way up to get you. I totally forgot. Dammit, we'll need to stop to get diesel soon.'

'Wait a second,' I say, digging my old phone out of my coat pocket. I connect to the mobile data, and click onto Google Maps, calling up the directions to the nearest service station a mile and a half away. A part of me is giggling, slightly hysterically, at the absurdity helping the man who is driving me to my death. It's the little voice that's calling on me to run as he stops at the back of the queue for the pumps. But I won't. I remind myself again of all the reasons why.

I'm surprised by the queue, you so rarely see queues in Brittany, but it's a tiny self service station, with only two lines of pumps. One of those is out of order, and in front of another an angry Englishman is shouting at his wife as she tries to make sense of the French instructions. I settle back in my seat to wait, and almost burst with happiness when Guillaume reaches over and takes my hand again. I turn to look at him and find his green eyes closer than I expected. My stomach sweeps and swells, my heart races. I swallow back the Glamour that threatens to rise like a blush, and then his other hand is cupping my chin, his thumb stroking my cheek, while I quiver under his touch.

It feels like his gaze is magnetic, my eyes drown so deeply in his, and I don't think I even blink, as slowly he lowers his lips to mine. Then my eyes are closing and I am lost in the petal soft sensation of his lips on mine. Our first kiss, and it is everything I dreamed it would be, and more besides, as he keeps his touch featherlight even as I long to open to him. His tongue teases my lips, and I answer him with my own, and it feels like my mouth is my whole body, every nerve sings as his exploration deepens, his touch becoming firmer. He sucks my bottom lip into his mouth and bites the plump flesh gently, running his teeth down it as he pulls away to look into my eyes, forehead pressed to mine, eyelashes tangling. My breath is sobbing in my chest, and I lean towards him, taking his top lip into my mouth, hand sliding under the soft cotton of his often washed hoodie, desperate to feel his flesh.

And then the car behind us beeps angrily, and we leap apart like naughty children. I see a pump is free, and we are holding up the cars behind us. Guillaume takes a shaking breath, raises his eyebrows at me, and shoots me a stomach-melting grin. I'm delighted, I thought the disturbance would crash him back into his staid persona, instead he is grinning at me like a co-conspirator. I beam back at him as he eases the car forward. He pulls his hood over his head, and sleeves over his hands, then puts his sunglasses on, and I swallow a giggle at his transformation into a moody Goth. While he fills the tank, I wriggle in my seat, my entire body aflame with running currents of desire. I lick at my lips and stroke my jaw where his hand held me.

I can't believe we've finally kissed. I don't know what's changed his mind about me at last, and part of me wants to shout at him, why now? Why did you leave it until it's too late? But another part of me understands the freedom my imminent death offers him, the erotic thrill death flavours my final hours with. I'm just going to enjoy it. And as soon as it's dark, I'm going to persuade him to stop driving, so finally, finally, I can make unrestrained love to my brooding vampire.

The jangling tune of his mobile phone ringing startles me out of my filthy reverie, I watch him answer it in the wing mirror. The tensing of his shoulders and his sombre tone are enough to tell me this is serious, even though all I can hear him say is 'yes...yes...getting diesel...yes.' Then he finishes paying for the fuel, and slides back into the car.

'That was the Council,' he explains grimly. 'They want to know why we've stopped. They have a trace on my phone.'

I stare at him, a sluice of icy fear washing away the bubbling exhilaration of a moment ago. Stopping to slake my lust is not going to be an option.

The phone call has brought both of us back to earth with a bump and Guillaume drives grimly onwards, diagonally across France towards the border with Germany. He joins the auto-route as soon as he can and drives consistently at five kilometres an hour over the speed limit, which makes him invisible with the other cars. I sink back in my seat, and stare out of the window, watching the evening fade to darkness, while my mind worries at the edge of my problem. I can't think about it directly, as I can't risk the Council reading my memories and discovering how to trace Layla.

My new phone, the one that contains only her number is in my bag. I dropped it in casually when I walked past my bag while I was preparing to leave, all the time busily thinking of other things. Things like whether the bleach would thoroughly destroy Matthieu's D.N.A in the lounge, just in case the police ever came looking for the strange English who had lived here temporarily, and whether the Council members' security staff will check my bag as well as my pockets, and discover my carefully stowed knife.

Later, I covered it with the smart outfit I would wear to present my case to the High Council, while I begged and pleaded for leniency, furious with Layla and David's betrayal and escape. I know full well the Council will not believe that for long. I just want to interweave other thoughts, other plans for them to chase to distract them from the phone in the bottom of my bag. I employed a similar trick when I hid a third devastatingly sharp filleting knife inside the lining of my bag. I hope they will find this and believe this is what I was hiding.

Now whenever my mind circles back to my worries about the phone, I picture the knife, distracting myself from that instead. Maybe, just maybe it will work. I need to get the phone out of my bag though, and leave it in the Land Rover. It cannot come into the Council's headquarters with me. They would definitely find it then, but if by some miracle I get out, or if I think they know where she is, I can find the phone in here, and warn her.

'Can we stop in Orleans please?' Guillaume looks at me incredulously.

'What?'

'I haven't eaten for days and days, and if it's to be my last meal, I want human. I want the hunt.'

'Really?' He shakes his head. 'After all that fuss about your first meal?' He's referring to the homeless man Patrice and Suzannah brought to the Farm for their New Ones, and invite Layla, David, Brian and I to feed on too. My disgusted refusal supported by my friends had been seen as the start of the deep enmity that led to the dreadful Pride battle that left Patrice and Suzannah and their New Ones dead, and my friends and I facing the High Council's punishment for breaking rules. Personally, I always felt the enmity started when Patrice and Suzannah allowed their monstrous new family to feed randomly at the party in Tours where my friends got infected, leading to me and Layla getting infected later at the hotel. None of the older vampires seem to feel I have the right to bear that grudge, though.

'That was our first meal, setting the precedent for the rest of our time as vampires. This is my last. And I won't be slaughtering a vulnerable innocent, I'm going to find myself a people trafficker, or pimp, or someone like that. Someone who deserves to die. Take me to Rue Du Faubourg-de-Bourgogne please, according to this article that's where the prostitutes are to be found,' I say, flicking through the articles on my phone. Guillaume doesn't answer me; he just raises his eyebrows and flicks his indicator on for the next junction.

We thread smoothly through the side streets, heading

towards the river in the dim light of the evening.

'Wait! Stop! He'll do,' I cry, pointing to a man who is standing on a patch of grass near the closed gates of a park. He has a medium-sized ginger dog on a lead and he is shaking it and shouting. Guillaume slows, scowling, then drives past him as he kicks the dog. At the next corner Guillaume turns right, then takes the next right, and again, circling back around so he can approach slowly. He stops the Land Rover quietly, a few metres behind the man, who is screaming abuse at the huddled dog, oblivious to our approach. He nods in grim satisfaction, approving my choice.

'Go and tear the padlock off the park gates for me please,' I ask softly, already humming with the chase, hunger roiling and coiling inside. I do not attempt to calm it or swallow it down as I open the vehicle door. I stopped only to remove my hoodie, and adjust my vest top underneath, pulling it down so the top hem rests just above my perky nipples, blushing aureole only just covered. I shake out my hair, flicking a wedge of curls over one shoulder, and lick a line of shiny red saliva over my lips. My Glamour thrums, coursing through my veins with the hunt and the hunger, making my eyes sparkly and my cheeks plump. Guillaume glances back over his shoulder at me and gawps a moment, making me smirk, before he turns back to pulling undone the padlock that protects the park from nighttime abuses.

'Excuse me?' My voice is a provocative croon, every straight man's fantasy and the man startles, stops kicking his dog and turns to me. He's met by waves of Compelling and Glamour so his clenched jaw drops, and the beet of fury is replaced in his cheeks and throat by the blush of lust, and his eyes soften and dilate. His poor wretched dog is not so easily fooled, and tries even now to protect him, a deep growl rumbling in her throat, hackles rising. He yanks her lead, pulling her off her feet, and making her choke.

'Ah, excuse this silly bitch,' the man smarms. 'I don't know what has got into her, won't do a thing I tell her. Don't know why I keep her.'

'Quiet, good girl,' I simper. I send her a wave of gentle compelling, so she drops to a relaxed crouch beside her owner, panting widely, tail thumping once, twice, and then stills as she glances anxiously up at her owner.

'You've got a way with them,' he mutters. 'One bitch to another.' He could save his life even now by asking me if I want her, and handing me her lead. Instead, he kicks her in the ribs again, sneering. 'Stupid little cow doesn't know what's good for her.' He laughs as dry as a cough to cover her yelp. The little red dog cowers besides him whining softly, one front leg raised and tongue licking in futile submission. I swallow my answering snarl, quench my rising Rage. Not here, not yet.

'Could you help my neighbour and I look for his dog?' I ask, smiling sweetly, and nodding over to where Guillaume waits with his back to us, peering through the now opened park gates. I can see he's on the phone, talking quietly. I can guess who it is. 'He got in from work to find her gone from his garden; it looks like she chewed through the fence. She might come if she smells your doggie.'

'Eh? Well, I should be getting home for my dinner.' He frowns, not a man who is used to being asked for favours. I flutter my eyelashes, turn my Glamour back up, swallowing down the Rage that had reduced the effects of the Glamour too.

'Oh please,' I beg. 'With three of us searching the park it won't take long at all. Her name is Belle.'

'The park will be closed at this time of the night,' he starts.

'No, it's not, look.' I nod towards the gates and Guillaume's disappearing back as he strides down the path, calling his imaginary dog.

'Ah, okay. But you'll owe me.' The man smirks, staring blatantly at my breasts.

'Oh yes, I'll have you for dinner to say thank you.' I smile.

'What's your dog's name?' I ask, as we walk through the gates, my shoulder deliberately brushing his, so he shivers with lust.

'Marie,' he says. 'After my ex-wife, silly bitches both of them.' He barks his dry and mirthless laugh again.

'Oh, so you are single then.' I smile at him, and lick the corner of my mouth, careful to keep my pointy teeth covered, so his eyes boggle. 'Well, why don't we lend Marie to my neighbour so he can use her to help look for Belle, while we look over there, together?' I cross my arms, squeezing by breasts so they almost pop out of my flimsy top, and tip my head prettily in query. No need for the poor dog to witness her owner's death. He hands me the lead without taking his eyes from my cleavage, mouth slack and shining with desire.

'Robert,' I call Guillaume, and then run the little dog down to him. His own eyes have trouble lifting from my bouncing breasts, and I grin at him wickedly.

'Everything okay? With the Council?' I ask.

'Well, they aren't impressed,' he grumbles, and I smile at his understatement. I hand him the lead, and he stoops to pet the frightened dog's ears, so she sighs and leans against his leg.

'Will you be okay with him on your own?' he whispers to me.

'Ah ha ha, yes. Very! I'm going to enjoy this. Meet me back by the gates in half an hour. Unless you want some?' I see the temptation cross his face, but then he shakes his head quickly and moves away, Marie trotting happily by his side, as decidedly his dog now as if she had said so.

I turn and trot back to her previous owner, who is just starting to look thunderous without the effects of the

Compelling and the Glamour to sweeten his bilious personality. He is not a stupid man, he knows that pretty girls do not stop and offer men like him fantasy favours in should-be closed parks, but the sight of my bobbing bosom as I skip back to him soon wipes all other thoughts from his mind. Blood for one major organ at a time, I've always laughed scornfully with Layla, brain or cock, a man can't be expected to operate both at the same time.

'Come on,' I pant breathily, grabbing his hand, and swamping him with the Need, so he shudders with a pre-climax surge. I tow him behind a large rhododendron, away from the view of early morning joggers. It's not fair they should always be the ones to find bodies. Not much I can do about dog walkers, though. I turn my back to him, rubbing my bum into his crotch, taking his hands and putting them on my breasts, where they start to mangle my nipples and twist and maul my breasts. If I was human, it would hurt a great deal, but as a vampire it is only mildly annoying.

'Ohhhh, kiss my neck,' I beg, shifting my mane of hair to one side.

'You love it, don't you, you dirty bitch... you look all angelic... but look at you, panting for it... you filthy fucking whore,' he gasps and pants into my neck. He doesn't kiss as I requested, instead he licks with a slimy tobacco-scented tongue and then bites me. No lover's nibbles, but nasty, abusive bites. I reach my hand down and squeeze his crotch, just hard enough to hurt a little, like I'm overenthusiastic, not furious. While his back is arched away from me, and he chides me viciously, I slide my knife out of my pocket.

'Oh sorry,' I coo. 'I thought you liked it rough.' I sidle back against him, then lift one of his hands away from squeezing my tit like a breakfast grapefruit, and suck his finger, so he gasps and pants, and pumps his rigid cock against my arse. While he's lost in his ecstasy, I feel his wrist for the deep throb of his pulse, and then make the fatal slice up his forearm. I grab the spurting wound to my mouth and gulp his terrified memories, hot and sweet while he struggles behind me. As he draws breath to scream, I send a wave of Compelling over him, so he sags to the floor, a quick push sends him toppling to one side. I slice his other wrist, and allow that one to bleed into the ground, while I feed sloppily on his arm in my grip.

When he's drained and still, I rub his empty wound into the sticky blood that's covering the other wrist. Then I squeeze his right hand over the knife handle, and leave it by his hand, as if it dropped from his grip as he lost consciousness. My smooth vampire fingers leave no fingerprints or scattered DNA to tell tales on me. I take his phone out of his jeans pocket, open it with the passcode I can remember now and search for 'Dirty Bitches'. I flick open a range of sites with girls rubbing each other, themselves, men, and finally find one with an actual dog involved. I don't look at it for any longer than the second it takes to confirm it's what I was looking for. I enter his credit card details, and then leave it playing on the ground beside him.

This will serve as explanation for his cum-soaked pants, his missing pet, and his suicide. I saunter back to the park gate, wiping my mouth on my T-shirt. His memories have shown he was as cruel to women as he was to animals. He's no loss to the world. Those who will mourn his passing will mourn their memories rather than him, and enjoy the attention his death brings far more than they enjoyed him.

Guillaume is waiting by the gates with Marie. He looks at my blood-smeared top and just raises one eyebrow sardonically.

'Hello Marie,' I call as the scent of the blood on me sends her tail between her legs, and her scurrying between his legs.

'She's called Flicker now,' is all he says, rubbing her silky ears so she's soothed.

192

When we get back to the Land Rover, Guillaume settles Flicker into the back seat while I grab my bag out of the foot-well of the front seat and open the boot. It's full of tools in there, tidily stacked and bagged off, the tools a farmer might need on the daily tours of his land, or a vampire in the protection of his Pride. I dwell luxuriously in the blood memories, high on them. Carelessly, drunkenly, I shake my belongings out of my bag, so they scatter and clatter around, making me giggle. I grab my clean clothes, and change as quickly as a vampire can, ignoring the shocked O of Guillaume's mouth at his split-second glimpse of my nakedness.

I grin at him mischievously, then I reach between his coils of wire and twine and pick my knife out. It's too big to fit in my pocket, so I slide it into the back of my black linen trousers I selected for my performance for the High Council. Along with the black silk T-shirt I've replaced my blood-soaked vest with, it's the smartest outfit I own as a vampire. I don't have much call for dressing up nowadays. I screw my dirty clothes into a bundle, and chuck them into my bag. While I'm at it, I check with a quick prod that my hidden knife is still there. Then I jump into the passenger seat besides Guillaume, and yawn theatrically.

'You don't mind if I doze a while do you?' I ask him.

'It doesn't look like I have much choice,' he sniffs. 'Look at the state of you.'

I smile sleepily. 'I don't indulge often. Got to make the most of it when I do.' I let my head loll against the window and let my mind swirl and swill amongst his memories, secure in the certainty my mind won't linger on the clatter of a phone slipping under a pile of plastic feed sacks in the boot.

Chapter Twelve

Layla

W
e don't leave the next day. I still hope she'll change her mind, and I'll get a phone call. I've destroyed my old phone like she told me to, and David's done the same. I have to wait until late evening for my new phone to actually arrive. It's an old Nokia brick, with no location tracking, no internet, nothing fun at all. The only number I programme into it is Rae's new one. Then I keep it hidden in my hoodie pocket all the next day, as I mooch around, waiting for it to ring. It doesn't. That night David and I brutally delete all the books we've already read off our Kindles, and then fill them up with as many as we can squeeze on, we use our SD cards, and every USB stick we can find too. Between the two of us we will have enough to keep us going for several years, before we need to worry about restocking.

The following morning I accept that we have no reason to hang around, and Rae might be right, I might be putting everyone in danger. I don't want to make a big performance about leaving, so we put a change of clothes and our Kindles into a rucksack each, and then saunter off down the lane, looking like we are just going for a walk together.

We don't have any sort of a plan, we just wander down lanes, across fields and through woodland for the day, chatting about what we will do.

'Well, Barbados is out,' I muse. 'Too overpopulated.'

'Canada is too bloody cold,' replies David.

'Russia?' I ask. David ponders a moment and then shakes his head.

'Not really my cup of tea. Hey, how about Morocco? I've never been, but I always fancied it. We can dress like nomads and live in a tent in the desert. There will be plenty of goats to feed on, and not much internet or CCTV.'

'That could be perfect. How will we get there?'

'Find our way to the fast trains to Spain, get to the Spanish coast, and swim over from Gibraltar, it's less than eight miles at the narrowest point.'

'Oh my God, yes, yes. This is going to be amazing. It will be so romantic.' I'm so excited I grab his hand and skip down the road, pulling him laughing and protesting behind me.

We decide that the easiest way to get into the big station at Lyon unseen is on top of one of the small local trains. It's easy enough to find a local train line and wait in the early dusk for a train into central Lyon. We grab the guardrail on the final carriage and leap lightly onto the roof. Lying under the canopy of the sky, watching the leaves of overhanging trees whizz by, I'm filled with exhilaration.

'Why haven't we done this before?' I ask, spreading my fingers to glory in the sensations of the rushing air. I started to think about how it would feel on my naked skin, and turned a lascivious glance towards David.

'Shame we didn't,' he says sadly. 'It might have kept you entertained, so you didn't need nightclubs.' There's a sadness to his voice that tears me apart.

'I'm sorry,' I whisper.

'I just wish I'd been enough for you. I loved our life in that cottage, I know Brian and Megan were pests, but you and I, what we had, that was special. That was the happiest I've ever been in my whole life. Ever.'

Hearing him say that douses me in icy regret. I had just always assumed he enjoyed the thrill and the adventure as much as I did. But suddenly I realise that my thirst for excitement, my determination to find thrills, it was all a way of avoiding intimacy. I love David, more than I've ever loved anyone, but with a sudden lurch I realise that I haven't really let him in, not like I thought I had. Shame smothers me, and I feel a burning tear trickle down my cheek.

'You were enough. You are enough. More than enough. You are my true love. I was being a selfish brat. And it's time to put that right.' I stand up and step to the end of the carriage to judge my jump. Landing wouldn't harm me, but I'd rather not tangle with a fence, and risk livestock on the tracks. I have quite enough on my conscience as it is without causing a train crash.

'Come on,' I call to David, who's looking at me in stunned bewilderment. I wipe the tears from my cheek and grin at him through my wiping hair. 'We're going back to the Farm, borrowing a car, and going to get Rae. Then we are all going to Morocco together.'

And with that, I jump.

It takes all night to get back to the Farm, even at the loping run a vampire can maintain for hours. As we pant up the field from the river, I hear the roar of a big engine pulling away and as we reach the farmhouse, Simon is walking across the parking area looking grim. When he sees us, he freezes for a long moment, and then shakes himself, and rubs his hands roughly over his face.

'What the fuck do you want?' It's not the welcome I was expecting. I can feel David bristle besides me. I put my hand on his wrist to calm him.

'Um, ah, we want to borrow a car. We are going to go and get Rae. We've got a plan...'

'I don't want to hear it.' Simon's eyes flash with fury, and his wiry frame shudders. I realise with surprise he's actually containing the Rage. 'We have just received a courier delivery of some very damning photographs, and a dreadful phone call from The High Council.'

'Oh, fuck no!' I burst into tears. 'Oh David, come on. We have to leave now. We have to go and get her.'

'Don't be so fucking stupid,' Simon snarls.

I'm shocked to my core. He is always so restrained and efficient. The only time I've ever seen him this agitated is when he held Guillaume, dying in his arms, after the battle with Patrice and her New Ones.

'Rae has sent you away to keep you safe. You selfish little bitch. Don't you fucking dare undo that now. Guillaume has to go and get her, and then take her and kill her. Don't make him have to kill you too. And me, for knowing you were here.'

He's losing his struggle to control the Rage, and he shrieks as his jaw twists and extends. His transformation is nowhere near as awful as Rae and I experience when we are swallowed by the Rage, but still, seeing smooth and calm Simon, gripped by the pain and the fury is terrifying.

'Get the fuck out of here, now. No car, no trip to Brittany. You two just fuck off, and don't come back, ever. Don't tell anyone where you are going, and keep away from cameras. Go on, for Rae's sake, FUCK OFF.'

So we do. We turn and run, and run.

Rae

I swim through his grotty memories as thoroughly and distractingly as I can, then I decide to explore Matthieu's memories. Now Guillaume has kissed me, all my jealousy of Abigail being so apparent in Matt's aroused thoughts has evaporated, and I realise I can explore my lost friend, truly know him. This will be a fitting tribute for his bravery I decide, to know him, and remember him with love and acceptance. I slip past the coddled thoughts that Ahmes polluted his mind with and use the high hyacinth scent of Abigail to guide me to the past, to his time living in her Pride. It takes a while to wade through his erotic snapshots of her, going about her day, and then the bitter and hurt feelings that accompany her playful attachment to Sebastian.

At first, the snippets I am glimpsing and hearing don't make much sense, they didn't really interest Matt, he was too caught up in his heartbreak, but I catch mutters and suggestions, tail ends of phone calls, and slowly I can put the pieces together to form an alarming picture. They did not come to our cottage because of the untidy hunting on her patch. They came for me. The hunts were a welcomed reason to visit, although the annoyance at the invasion into her territory was genuine, Matthieu's memories show me her crowing jubilation at her opportunity, as well as her snarling disgust at the sloppiness of the messes Megan left.

Abigail has spies in the High Council, but only lowly administrators, no one who is allowed into the inner sanctum. But one of those spies had heard a whisper that a new vampire had been offered a place within the Council's tutorage; and been stupid enough, arrogant enough, to refuse it. Abigail was jealous of the offer, and even more so of the will to walk away, although she would never admit such a thing. I recognised the sneering venom that twisted her face as she spoke about me, as she prepared Sebastian to seduce me, to feed on me, to raid my memories, with Mattie there as a backup plan in case I was still angry with Sebastian for disappearing all those years ago. But why? Why did they want my memories? I dived deeper, pushing into secret corners and barely glimpsed scenes.

What I find terrifies me. There is Ahmes, and Amunet, just dim shadows, reflections in mirrors. Abigail had kept them well hidden, only she and Sebastian had spoken to them directly, and it is jealously alone that sent Matthieu to snoop at doors, and it is purely accidental that he overheard the snatches of conversation about there being one who does know the layout of the hidden inner halls of the High Council's headquarters. One whose blood would allow them to glimpse the secrets that would help them to plan their attack.

Attack? I try to calmly piece together everything Matt knew, and saw or heard. The picture is awful, a plan to seize power. The age of the Egyptian vampires, and the fact they were the first, the creators of the virus, is their flimsy excuse to stake their claim. Worse, these two ancients would only be figureheads, the power would be held by Abigail and Sebastian, and all decisions about the future of vampires, and their interactions with humans, would be made by this megalomaniac pair. Already, first inquiries have been made, dissatisfactions with the current system sought and exploited. Visitors from around the world were seen by Matt, despite him not being invited on those hunts, or subsequent blood oiled conversations as allies were sought, and found.

'Oh my God!' I shriek so loudly that Guillaume jumps out of his skin, and steers the Land Rover across the lanes of the empty motorway. I realise I've been lost in blood memories all night, and it's light again, although luckily it's still early enough for the roads to be almost empty. I wait while Guillaume wrestles the vehicle back under control, and then point out a junction just ahead.

'Pull off, you have to stop the car, I need to talk to you.' I'm thrumming with distress, and need to walk about as I explain. I cannot have Guillaume distracted by the road while I try to describe what I've seen. Actually, it will be easier if I get him to feed from me so he can see what I saw, all of it, the ancient memories of Amunet, as well as Matthieu's memories. I baulk at what else he will see and know, but there is no time for quibbles, and he has let me explore his mind, so maybe it is only fair.

'What are you on about, Rae?' he asks in annoyance. 'The Council are already furious we've taken this long.' But even as he argues, he's indicating and taking the slip road off.

'Just get somewhere you can stop,' I say. 'I can't tell you, I have to show you.' I am resolutely silent for the ten minutes it takes him to find a quiet lane with a layby in front of a field gate. As soon as we've stopped, even before he's turned the engine off, I've opened the door and leaped out, hopping easily over the metal gate into the empty pasture. Guillaume follows behind me with Flicker under one arm.

'Time she had a break anyway,' he mutters reproachfully.

'They are planning an attack,' I tell him.

'What? Who? Where? What?' He shakes his head in bewilderment. 'What are you on about?'

'Abigail and Sebastian, and lots of others, along with the Egyptians. They claim the Egyptians are the oldest vampires, so they should be rulers. But they plan to just have them as figureheads, they know Ahmes was mad, and takes up all Amunet's time, so Abigail and Sebastian will have the real power. Oh God, just imagine what they will do...'

'Wait, wait, slow down, what makes you think any of this?'

'I have been exploring Matthieu's memories. I never really had a chance before.' I see Guillaume's brow lower.

'Oh yes, Matthieu, your lover,' he growls.

I refuse to be ashamed. 'He persuaded me to feed off him when we fucked, it intensifies the experience,' I explain stiffly. 'It turns out I was supposed to let him feed on me in return, so Abigail could feed on him and raid my memories of the Council's headquarters.'

'What?' Guillaume is incredulous. 'And you are only just realising this now?'

'I got jealous before,' I mutter. 'Matt wasn't aware of what he was doing, he was a stooge. Abigail was abusing his love of her, she just told him she wanted to know why I turned down their offer of a place with them. She was genuinely fascinated by that so it was believable. Anyway, the fact that he was in love with her meant that when I fed on him I could tell that as he approached climax his mind filled with her. That made me cross, and I refused to ever feed from him again, or let him feed from me, and I never looked at his memories again. I just shut them away.'

Guillaume is stroking the dog's ears as I speak, so I can't see his face.

'After what happened earlier, when you kissed me, everything felt different, I wasn't jealous anymore, and I wanted to fill my mind with distracting thoughts, so...' I pause for the tiniest moment, but then decide to protect my secret, not from him but from anyone at all reading either of our blood later. 'So I didn't have to think about what's going to happen.'

The look of grief he throws me is startlingly raw. I gabble on.

'So, I started going through his memories, just to fill my

mind, and now I don't care about her smug face popping up all the time I could go beyond her, and explore her Pride, and I started to notice things that worried me, firstly about her interest in me, and when I went deeper and wider to find out why she wanted access to my memories, I managed to piece her intent together.'

'Are you sure? Is there no way at all you could be wrong?'

I feel a tiny flare of frustration. He's not being as sanctimoniously sure of himself as he was when I warned him about my concerns about the three bitches at the Farm. He'd decided I was wrong about them telling the High Council's Spanish spies about the battle, and ignored my warnings. Of course I'd been right, and given my propensity to be accurate about horrible things, my Cassandra fate, I wish he would trust me now.

'It really will save a lot of time if you feed from me, you'll be able to see what I saw. She smells of hyacinths, just keep following that. First, you need to ring The High Council though, and warn them. I can drive us there while you're under the influence of the blood.' I tilt my chin and challenge him to argue.

'I can't.'

'What?' That deflates me. 'Just ring them back on the number they keep ringing you on.'

'It's a blocked number. Nobody has direct access to a Councillor.'

'Just them to you,' I grumble. 'Okay, you'll have to ring their main number, and get to speak to them that way.'

'Oh joy,' Guillaume mutters, but he's already got his phone out and is flicking through his contacts list. He sets his mobile to speaker phone while it rings. Within six rings it's answered and I feel a contradictory surge of relief that nothing has happened there yet and gush of icy adrenaline that we have to try to persuade them of the danger they are in over the phone. We have to convince them it's not just a scam to avoid my death sentence.

'Hello,' a snooty German voice says. 'How may I help you?' There is no mention of where we've reached.

'It's Guillaume Monserrat, need to speak to the Adelfried, urgently.' Guillaume fills his voice with authority and Command.

'Hold please,' the voice sounds bored, and the tinny hold music fills the air. Apparently, Command does not work on the telephone. Guillaume looks a little sheepish.

'Snooty bitch,' I comment. 'Do you think they'll listen to you? It seems unimaginable, impossible. But she was so sure in those memories. So sure she could defeat the Council and seize control.'

Almost immediately the music stops, and we both draw breath to explain what I've discovered, but the sanctimonious voice is back.

'He said to get her here now. No more excuses. No more delays. Now.'

'But, this is urgent and of extreme importance...' Guillaume starts to explain.

'Have a nice day now,' the voice chirps with deliberate pleasure before hanging up on us.

'Arsehole!' I snarl. 'Well, I hope they kill her first.' As we hurry back towards the Land Rover, a sudden thought stops me in my tracks. I run to the glove compartment, and pull the photos of Layla back out of their envelope; I flick through them all, rechecking the details I should have spotted earlier.

'It's not Layla in these photos. They've been photoshopped,' I gasp in triumph. 'Look, see here you can see her fangs, and there you can see her talons, but Layla was always very careful. She wore a clip-in set of veneers, and gloves, and stupid magic marker eyeliner. It wasn't a very convincing disguise, but it was a disguise. These photos have been well done to fool the Council, but I should have noticed the discrepancies immediately.' Guillaume flicks through the photographs but doesn't seem especially convinced by my explanation. It's one more piece of the puzzle for me to try to work out. I settle the dog in the back seat, then I kick off my shoes, and chuck them into the boot over the back of the seat. My toes stretch and wriggle appreciatively. Knowing we are approaching trouble, I want to be as unimpeded as possible. Finally, I climb into the driver's seat and settle comfortably besides Guillaume.

I don't ask him not to rummage through my embarrassing moments, and difficult days. He did not set any limits on me when he let me in to explore his hideous past with Patrice. He knew I needed the freedom to explore his memories so I would be able to understand why he could never trust another Pretty One, and why he couldn't love me back. It wouldn't be fair to set any in return, not now he finally trusts me like this. I don't think I would have been able to resist looking anyway even if he had set limits, and I don't want to sully our final hours together by setting a test I myself would fail.

'Do you know the way?' he asks, ever practical.

'I'll just type the address into google maps, and ask my phone for directions.' I waggle my old handset at him.

'Technology, it moves so damn fast now, it's hard for a vampire to keep up.' He laughs.

'Hey, don't worry, it's hard for humans to keep up. At least, vampires can learn how to use it easily, as a human I felt permanently overwhelmed.'

Once he is settled in the front seat, reclined as far back as it will go, I give him my wrist, and tender as a kiss, he slices the flesh and feeds on my blood. His green gaze holds mine in an almost unbearable intimacy, until the blood high unfocuses his eyes and his breathing deepens. I slip my wrist out of his slackened grip and set up the sat nav app.

I shouldn't let hope flare, but it's as prevalent in vampires as humans apparently, and despite myself I feel a thrill frond uncurl in my heart. Surely, if I can save them, they will pardon us all?

Chapter Thirteen

Rae

I can't believe my bad luck when I hit a huge traffic jam on the autobahn just outside Frankfurt Oder. I'm so close I bounce in my seat in frustration. A long way up ahead I can make out flashing lights of various emergency vehicles and I realise I won't be going anywhere for a while. Guillaume remains oblivious besides me, still lost in the blood fog of my memories. I try not to think about what he might be witnessing, but mortifying memories from my past keep popping back into mind, causing icy washes of embarrassment to sweep me from head to toe, quickly followed by boiling bursts of shame.

I try to reassure myself that Guillaume won't be interested in the time I got really drunk and tried to give Sebastian a lap dance, but fell over instead, flashing my knickerless state to all and sundry. He won't care about the time I sneezed on the bus and was too embarrassed to wipe my snot off the jacket of the man stood in front of me, instead leaping off two stops too early and trudging through the drizzle to get to my appointment late. It doesn't stop the thoughts annihilating me, though.

After a few minutes of self-torture, I become aware of a persistent buzzing and realise Guillaume's mobile is ringing. He remains oblivious. I can guess who it is and screw up my courage to answer. Then I realise this could be the perfect chance to warn them of the danger they are in, and I rush to scrabble his phone out of his hoodie pocket and end up flipping it into the air and snatching at it as though it's suddenly become as slippery as a live fish. It ends up in the footwell, and cuts out before I can pick it up again. I curse and hit the steering wheel in frustration, catching the horn, and making a series of aggressive beeps that draw disgusted scowls from the drivers around me. I pull my hood closer around my face, and sink down in my seat. Guillaume dozes on.

I sit clutching the handset, waiting for it to ring again. I'm so intent that I scream a bit when it does buzz into life. I answer hastily and hear Adelfried's sanctimonious tones demanding to know why we've stopped.

'There's a traffic jam. There's been a big accident just outside Frankfurt Oder. Nothing's moving.'

'Rae? Why are you answering Herr Monserrat's phone?'

'He's having a sleep. Listen, that doesn't matter. I need to tell you, you're under thr...'

'I beg your pardon? You are not the one to tell me what does and doesn't matter in this situation. Put Herr Monserrat on the phone immediately.'

'I can't, I told you. He's asleep. He fed on...'

'Don't you dare argue with me. How dare you. Enough of this nonsense, get here immediately. I don't care how.' And then he puts the phone down. I stare at it in astonishment. What a stupid self-righteous little man!

'Well, he's just signed his own death warrant,' I mutter grimly. Around me the traffic starts to move slowly, but I don't edge forward with the rest of it. Instead, I remain in exactly the same spot ignoring the frustrated horns and screeching of tires as tired and irritable drivers pull around me to accelerate the twenty metres down the road that have opened up. I wait for the phone to ring, but it doesn't, so after a few minutes I pull back into the flow of traffic and shove and bully my way through, pushing to get to the Hall as soon as I can.

When I pull into the broad expanse of clear ground at the front of their small, plain schloss, it is as unprepossessing as always, but I'm worried to see a lot more cars parked in the vicinity than there was last time we were here. There's even a cattle truck with all its slats locked closed. Has the High Council given up human? I doubt it, but I don't have time to ponder now. I reach into the back seat and pull a blanket over Flicker. She should be taken for a quick walk, but we need to get in to speak to the four ancients. I reach over and shake Guillaume's arm urgently.

'We're here,' I say. His eyes open slowly, and take a few soft moments to focus on me, then he beams broadly.

'You weirdo.' He chuckles. It's the loveliest thing anyone's ever said to me, and I feel my Glamour rise in a delighted blush.

'Come on,' I bluster. 'We're here.' I'm out of the vehicle and around to his side before he's even undone his door. I open it for him, and he puts one heavy hand on my shoulder and slithers out, stumbling slightly. He giggles as he finds his footing, surprising me. Then I watch him scan the parked vehicles over my shoulder, and his face sobers. It's uncannily silent, there isn't even any bird song. It feels like the hush of held breaths, of shock after a terrible scream.

'Shit,' he breathes, grabbing my hand. 'We need to hurry.' We stride into the big house, casting uneasy glances at each other as the heavy front door swings open unimpeded, the multitude of bolts and latches all undone. The wooden panelled hallway seems even darker than usual, the dark oak absorbing all the light from the small high windows. There are none of the huge vampire security staff we expected to be there to greet us in sight. Everything is quiet in here too, but the air is agitated, as if turmoil has just frozen.

We cross the hallway, and approach the broad curved staircase, but as I put my foot on the first step, I freeze. Blood oozes up from the deep burgundy carpet runner, and paints a carmine outline on my naked toes. We both stare at it for a horrified moment, I try the next step, and the same happens. We jog up and turn towards the Council's inner meeting hall. The grand double doors are closed, Guillaume opens them and we peer inside. It takes long surreal seconds for my brain to accept what my eyes are telling me. The room looks like it has been decorated for a nightmarish Christmas. It is bedecked with streamers of guts and innards, and blood is sprayed over the walls in great festive sweeps. The big ugly slabs of vampires that used to guard the inner sanctum are spread around it in lumps and clots, their heads stamped into mush.

The energy and Rage it must have taken to decimate those

immense killers is terrifying. Worse, at the great black oak table, where the Councillors sat in judgement, their headless corpses sit in grim mimicry of their usual prim posture. Limp hands cross neatly on the table before them, as if patiently waiting for their own heads, placed neatly in front of them, like a last supper.

'Fuck,' Guillaume mutters again, before we spin and start back towards the staircase, but as we reach the top of the stairs and start our descent, Lady Abigail, Sebastian, and several other vampires appear at the bottom of the staircase. Abigail ascends the bottom few steps, grinning up at us, while Sebastian remains on the ground floor holding a handful of chains which restrain several grotesque creatures. They scurry about on all fours, gnashing and flinging themselves against their shackles as they try to follow Abigail up the wooden stairs.

'Ah, there you are, darlings,' Abigail singsongs, swigging from a bottle of blood. I sniff discreetly, but there's no honeyed scent of human blood. There's no smell from it at all. I shudder internally. Abigail wears another party frock, the dusty rose pink splotched with blood and dirt, and delicate silk and lace torn and rent, but I can't give her more than a passing glance, before I'm staring at the creatures gibbering and straining around her ankles again. Translucently pale and naked, smeared in blood and filth, they screech and chatter. They are all awkward angles, and twisted limbs, and it takes me assessing seconds to confirm they were once human.

'Remarkable, aren't they?' Abigail crows manically. 'My secret weapon. Clever, clever Sebastian.' She giggles, swinging carelessly from the bannister with one arm, the other holding the bottle of blood tilted carelessly so globs slosh and darken the burgundy carpet runner.

'Well hello,' I enthuse, squeezing Guillaume's hand. 'What on earth are you doing here? Any idea what's going on? We can't find anyone left alive!' I grin manically, turning up the thrum of my Glamour just a little, carefully masking the insincerity of my words.

'We've killed them all,' states Abigail bluntly. I don't bother to hide my surprise, but I'm careful to keep it politely startled rather than the shock and horror I'm really feeling. 'We have seized power, and taken over. We rule the world now.' She swigs a gloopy mouthful from her bottle, but spits the blood out. 'Ugh, that's cold. Go and get me some fresh.' She shoves her bottle towards one of the vampires in her group. I watch him enter the code to the lock panel on one of the doors on the ground floor that leads to the offices where the workers were based previously. As the door swings open, I hear a desperate scream that is cut off to a gurgle before the door slams closed, enveloping us in silence again. I hadn't realised they were soundproof, but it makes sense. The High Council were shadowy secretive beings.

Abigail's eyes meet mine, calculating as she begins the climb towards us, her harem following in her wake. I have seconds to convince her I am an ally. I frown slightly, she tenses.

'Does that mean we're free to go? Guillaume doesn't have to kill me?' I ask, hope adding a tiny sob to my voice. Abigail flings back her head and laughs a tinkling peal.

'Oh, you selfish little bitch! Not a tear for our esteemed leaders? And you such a favourite of theirs. Well, well. Of course you are free, as long as I have your allegiance?'

'Of course! I hated the Council, they were greedy and corrupt.'

'Hah, you say that like it's a bad thing. Seriously though? You thought that little of them? I heard a little rumour they asked you to join them.' Abigail slips an arm around my shoulder, turning me back towards the hall.

'They did ask. I refused. I didn't trust them.' I walk besides her obligingly, betraying no sign that I am convinced she is escorting me to my death.

'Really? Well now, just goes to show you need to be careful of gossip. I was led to believe you knew all sorts of secrets and would join them in time?'

I don't need to fake my look of shock. 'No, they asked me to stay and be trained, I spent about half an hour considering it, but decided that much as I did not want to return to the Farm, there had to be another option that didn't land me in that nest of vipers. So I turned them down.'

'Oh dear, oh dear me,' Abigail chortles, snatching the refilled wine bottle her bodyguard is holding out to her. 'All that effort to read your memories. Yee gods, what a waste of time.' She tilts her bottle at

Sebastian, who has also reached the top of the staircase, arms being jerked here and there as his charges scramble and scurry in every direction.

I laugh, and Abigail pierces me with a furious gaze. 'Oh, I'm sorry, I shouldn't laugh. It's just, you only had to ask. I would have told you everything I knew, but it really wasn't much.'

'Well, yes. I can see that. Never mind. The rest of the plan worked beautifully.' She beams at me as she strides through the doorway of the hall. 'Ah, just look at this. Magnificent. Utterly magnificent.' She spins leisurely around, arms held wide, head tipped to appreciate the full scale of the desecration.

'You don't really get to appreciate the full effect while you're actually creating it,' she muses. 'It is nice to get a chance to return and spend some time truly absorbing it. Especially with a fresh pair of eyes.' By now we have stopped in front of the Councillors' table. I glance quickly over my shoulder, Guillaume stands quietly behind us, hands clasped before him, head slightly bowed, in an attitude of calm respect. Behind him her mob have fanned out and are also taking in the destruction they've wrought with smug satisfaction.

Abigail contemplates the tableau before her critically for a moment, gives a small nod of pleasure, and then hops her tiny derriere onto the table, sitting between rivulets of blood, legs swinging happily over the edge. 'You don't think it's too much, do you?'

'How on earth did you manage this? I thought they were invincible?' I smile and dodge her question. She contemplates me for a moment, while she takes a swig of her drink, then she seems to make a decision, pats the table besides her, so I sit next to her. She passes me the bottle, and I take a tiny sip holding the bottle to my mouth longer, so I appear to take a great glug. She smiles in approval.

'Well, they certainly felt that. They were too confident. Too bloated with arrogance to believe anyone could beat them. To believe anyone would even try.' She giggles and leans forwards conspiratorially. 'I've been working on this for years, seeking allies, watching for weak points. I had an idea of what I could do, and then I stumbled across Amunet and Ahmes. Oh, sorry about that by the way. What he did to you. That wasn't meant to happen. Little shit slipped his leash. His guard paid for it, believe me. Are you okay?' She gazes at me, turquoise eyes huge with supposed concern, but brittle curiosity lurks ruining the effect.

'I'm fine. That wasn't the first time someone has tried to assault me, but it was the first time I've had the strength to fight them off and ensure he'll never hurt anyone again. And that felt good. That strength.'

'Well, good. Yes. And we didn't need him; bit of a loose cannon, as it were. In all honesty, you probably did us a favour. Would have been interesting to know more about that transition, though. Very interesting.' Her blue gaze turns inward for several disturbing seconds and I quail at what she could be contemplating. 'Anyway, he's gone, you're okay, and Amunet will get over it.'

'Ah, yes.' I'm at a loss for what else I could add.

'So, where was I? Oh yes, so I met Amunet, and it took a little while to remind her of her birthright, and persuade her to return to the vampire community, and take her rightful place as our leader, but she came round to my way of thinking soon enough. Once we had her at the helm, followers rushed to her cause. We were able to cherry pick the very best Gifts to join our attack force, and Sebastian started creating his little darlings. They are wonderful. He's a Destroyer you see, and when Amunet described how feeding off a Destroyer had started Ahmes' madness, he came up with the idea. He selects them carefully, got to have the right personality type, to begin with. Homeless teenagers, and kids in the care system are best. Broken, and less likely to be missed. Then he only feeds them his blood, and look what we get. They are spectacular to watch, honestly, so utterly annihilating. For god's sake, don't get too close. They don't care who they kill. They have no loyalty at all.' She flings her head back and laughs. 'And so easy to replace.'

'Very impressive, but how did you even get them in here?'

'Well, that's where you came in. I really was quite stumped about how we would ever get through the doors, and then I heard about you. Just as I was wondering whether to cultivate you as an ally, or seize you by force your silly little Pride started hunting on my patch. I couldn't believe my luck. An enraged email to the Council got me permission to go and sort the situation out, so we could come and visit you. I wasn't sure how much of a pet you were you see. I had spies in the Council work teams, but no one very high up. They could only bring me whispers, nothing concrete.

'Attempts to access your memories of the inside of the schloss proved futile, and it became apparent you were far too morally upstanding to be interested in forging an allegiance, or so it appeared anyway. Then one of my computer dweebs found the photos of Layla in that nightclub, and the perfect solution just fell into my lap. I made a few phone calls, got a bit of trouble stirred up in several Prides, so Council delegations had to be sent out to deal with them, while staff was thin on the ground, I had Amunet make her first approach, demanding a meeting, so a large retinue of high up and trusted delegates had to be sent to spy on her, and meet her and generally get themselves into a right tizz over exactly who she was and what she wanted. Stupid fools, she told them straight up. They just wouldn't believe her. Funny how truth has been my best ally in this whole enterprise.' Abigail grins at me again, eyebrows raised.

'Into this melee, I send the photos of Layla, a little souped up I confess, but I needed to know that the Councillors will respond, not just leave it on the backburner until everything else is sorted out. I phoned them, demanding to be there when they interviewed you all, after all it was my patch she did it on. Me she put in danger.' She raises the bottle at me and takes a big swig, passes it to me, but is blessedly back into the full flow of her story again immediately, so doesn't notice that my own drink is faked again. 'As soon as it was obvious that Layla and David have done a runner, yet another team are dispatched to hunt for them. Nice touch, thank you for that. Then all I have to do is turn up here, invited, and take advantage of how distracted they were. Once Seb and I were in didn't take long. We were brought up here, to meet with our sanctimonious friends before you arrived, so he could spray them with his blood as we approached them, blinding them with his poison.' She claps her hands in glee. 'So bloody jolly. I was able to bar the door while he and I did our stuff in here, while our little friends down in the bowels of the building were able to sneak out of their rat runs and open the doors. By which time our allies were arriving, and they were able to get straight to the slaughter. Oh, it was spectacular. Truly spectacular. I wish you could have seen it. We are down to the useful ones now, just deciding who we can keep, because, you know, useful skills, and who will have to go, but only after we've tortured their secrets out of them. You know, vampires are much more fun to torture than humans. So much more resilient.'

'Clever,' I concede, nodding. 'Very clever.' I wait a beat. 'So, we can go then?' I slip off the table and take Guillaume's hand again, turn to her hopefully, determined to appear unafraid.

'If you like, dear, if you're sure you don't want to stay and play. There's going to be a lot of posts vacant you know. And I really don't think you should try to be a Pride Leader anymore, do you?'

'No, you're right, I'm terrible at it.' I laugh uproariously at my own lack of leadership skills, while, slowly, slowly edging backwards towards the door. Abigail slides off the table and saunters after us. 'Now that Guillaume and I have, you know, sorted things out, I plan a nice quiet future at the Farm with him.' I hope I imagine the slight tremor that runs up his arm as I describe our future together. We are opposite Seb now, at the doorway, and I hope desperately he will let us pass.

'Hmm, quite the little slut, aren't we, hopping from bed to bed like this? Does he know about Brian, Sebastian and Matthieu?' she asks, smiling cruelly. For a horrible moment, I think she's going to ask me where Mattie is. Trying to keep track of what I'm supposed to know, as if I hadn't explored his memories is starting to overwhelm me.

'Oh yes, don't worry. I'm not his first Pretty One, he knows I can't help myself.' I wink lasciviously at her. I edge around Seb, and continue our slow creep through the door, skirting carefully around the freakish, slathering creatures Sebastian is holding.

'Oh! How marvellous. What fun. Off you go then, my dears. I'll know where you are when I need you.' The command is implicit, as, I believe, is the threat. We are at the stairs now, and it takes every nerve I possess to go down them slowly.

'And Layla? She'll be safe too?' I ask as nonchalantly as I'm able. Abigail arks one elegant eyebrow at me as she considers.

'Hmm, I suppose so. As long as he's in charge of her.' She waves her bottle of blood towards Guillaume, who nods confirmation. 'Yes, go on then. As long as she's an ally too. As long as she can evade the team who were after her. Although I'm sure they've found a way to call them back with all this going on.' She gestures around her. I nod, still beaming inanely, sure at any moment she will laugh at our foolishness, and grab us and kill us. We stroll slowly across the lobby and pause at the threshold to wave cheerily to the ensemble of monsters by the staircase.

The parking area is thronged with more blood-drenched vampires, wiping their weapons, sinister in their silence. They all stop what they are doing to watch us, faces expressionless. As we pass the cattle truck, a snuffling sets up from around the locked air vents, and I realise the creatures inside with Sebastian are just a small portion of the mass pestilence they have at their disposal. We make our way slowly to the car, smiling and nodding at the other vampires. I pause and pull Guillaume in for a kiss before he climbs into the driver's seat and I get in on the passenger side. Flicker feels the tension in the air, and cowers on the back seat, whining softly. Guillaume toots his horn twice cheerily as he pulls away, and drives down the lane.

'Fuuuuuuuck!' I breathe softly as I watch the house slowly fade into the distance in the rear-view mirror, scanning the road to check we aren't being followed, heart pounding with fear. 'Right, go,' I say as we turn a final bend, and the property finally completely disappears.

Guillaume puts his foot down, and drives like a demon, tearing around bends, wildly taking one turn off, then another. Until we are flying across a barren moorland land and we can see for miles around us, and can finally be totally sure that no one is following us. He slows down.

'We can't stay at the Farm,' he says. 'We have to hide.'

'Yes, we just need to grab Georgette, they'll come after her because she's a healer, and then go and hide with Layla and David,' I reply.

'But you don't know where they are, and you told them to smash up their phones.'

'Did that work?' I ask, grinning. 'Do you really not know from my blood that I've got another phone stashed in your boot with her new number on it?' Guillaume looks startled, and then shakes his head smiling.

'I should have known you'd find a way. Okay. We'll get to the Farm, get Annie and Georgette, grab one of the camper vans, and you can ring them and see where they are and we'll go and hide out with them. Let everything settle. Let that bitch forget you even exist.' He squeezes

215

my fingers, and we drive in companionable silence for a while, with just the Land Rover's rumbling engine, and Flicker's panting as the sound track to our escape.

Then I let out a big sigh.

'I have to go back.' Guillaume shakes his head. I nod sadly. 'We can't let those monsters hold all that power. Hiding isn't going to work. You saw in my memories how Amunet and Ahmes hunted down all the vampires they created. They'll never just let us disappear, and they will destroy the world as they look. Vampires, humans, no one will be safe. You have to rouse a resistance, and I need to be on the inside, feeding you information, letting you know their weaknesses.' His shoulders slump in resignation, and he stops the Land Rover, hits the steering wheel with the heel of his hand.

'Shit,' he swears succinctly.

'The phone is in the boot, use it to get Layla back, get her and David to hide Georgette and Annie. You need to contact every vampire you know and try to find allies. Without letting Abigail know you're a threat. I'll share everything I can with you. It's going to be hard to overthrow them, but this will be the only chance we have. While they are still settling in, before they sort out the power battles between them, and find out how to use all of the equipment in that place.' I lean over and kiss him once, sweetly on the lips, trying to draw enough strength from it to sustain me for what must come. I daren't look at him.

One glance is all it would take to abandon this madness and decide to drive to safety instead, and let this awful coup play out as it will. Instead, I lean between the back seats, pat Flicker and grab my bag containing Layla's human disguise and my knives. Not much of an arsenal, but it's all I've got. I slide out of the vehicle, and wave once, before setting off at a steady lope in the direction we came.

Author Bio

Chloe Hammond is an Aquarius, very Aquarius. Born in Liverpool in 1975, she grew up in West Wales, but now lives in Barry in South Wales, with her husband and rescue cats and dogs. She always wanted to write, but life got in the way. A few years ago she was diagnosed with extreme anxiety and depression, which caused nightmares and sleepless nights. In her typically contrary way she used this to her advantage. The nightmares flavoured her writing, and the sleeplessness nights were when she found time to write. Then in 2017 her best friend died, and she reeled off into grief. Writing saved her again, and although she is missing her greatest support and number one cheerleader, she knows Dina would have demanded she carry on.

She has a lovely sea view from her writing desk, which she gazes at to still her mind so her characters can burst forth and have their say. This is her second novel, and Rae and Layla are demanding book three in the trilogy is written as soon as possible, they have adventures to live.

Hi,

I really hope you enjoyed my novel. I put my heart and soul into writing it. I'd love to know what you thought of it, and Darkly Dreaming. Reading your reviews on Amazon and your Blogs make me very happy. They keep me going when doubts set in. They also help my Amazon rating, and for every 25 reviews I get, Amazon helps that much more with promotions and marketing.

Reviews don't need to be long or complicated, a star rating and a word or two about how my writing made you feel is plenty. I love to hear about anything you particularly enjoyed, or didn't like too.

Keeping in touch with my readers is important to me, and you can find me on the social media addresses below. Pop over and say hello, you'll be making me smile. You can sign up to my newsletter on my website, and this way you'll know when Darkly Dazzling, Book 3 of The Darkly Vampire Trilogy, and any other writing I'm involved in, is being released.

Thank you for joining my on my writing adventure,

Chloe Hammond

Links:

Website:-
www.chloehammondauthor.com

Email address:-
books2@chloehammondauthor.com

Facebook:-
www.facebook.com/chloehammondauthor
www.facebook.com/pages/Darkly-Dreaming/750124258345038

Tumblr:-
https://www.tumblr.com/blog/chloehammondauthor

Twitter:-
www.twitter.com/chloehammond111

Blog:
www.chloehammondauthor.com

Linkedin:-
www.linkedin.com/pub/chloe-hammond/91/8b6/b50

Printed in Great Britain
by Amazon

79666731R00130